Paul Hoover's
SAIGON, ILLINOIS

"Paul Hoover has a real talent for seeing and reporting the unexpected and often bizarre hidden lives of his characters. His vision is deep and wide, never settling for surfaces. His voice is unpretentious, wise and true. This is an important book, full of what we all need to know—how to find hope and keep it."

—Kaye Gibbons, author of *Ellen Foster*

"You'll laugh and cry and wonder—guaranteed! *Saigon, Illinois* launches the fiction career of a really fine writer."

—Larry Heinemann

PAUL HOOVER

SAIGON

. . . . . .

ILLINOIS

VINTAGE
CONTEMPORARIES

VINTAGE BOOKS
A DIVISION OF RANDOM HOUSE
NEW YORK

A Vintage Original, September 1988

Copyright © 1988 by Paul Hoover

Author photo copyright © 1988 by Lynn Sloan-Theodore

Library of Congress Cataloging-in-Publication Data

Hoover, Paul, 1946–

Saigon, Illinois.

(Vintage contemporaries)

I. Title.

PS3558.O6335S2   1988   813'.54   88-40039
ISBN 0-394-75849-8 (pbk.)

Chapter 13 was originally published, in a slightly different
form, in *The New Yorker*.

Designed by Barbara M. Bachman

Manufactured in the United States of America

10 9 8 7 6 5 4 3 2 1

IN MEMORY OF OPAL CATHERINE HOOVER
AND FOR
MAXINE, KOREN, JULIAN, AND PHILIP

ACKNOWLEDGMENTS

I AM INDEBTED TO
PAT MULCAHY FOR HER ENCOURAGEMENT
AND ASTUTE EDITING; LIKEWISE TO
VERONICA GENG OF *THE NEW YORKER*.
I WOULD ALSO LIKE TO THANK
MAXINE CHERNOFF FOR
EARLY READINGS OF THE NOVEL.

1

■ ■ ■ ■ ■ ■

You can call me Holder. It's one of your basic names, like
Gold, Paper, and Anxious. Most of us belong to the Church
of Peace, which is German Protestant—midwestern and rural.
It's a lot like the Mennonites and Amish. Wherever you see
a quaint horse and buggy on a rural highway, you know
there's a Church of Peace, and maybe some Holders, in the
area. Most of us have given up the horse and buggy for red
sports cars and pickup trucks, but you get the idea. We also
refuse, absolutely, to kill anyone with a gun, or with anything
else except good intentions. This is irritating to some of the
neighbors, and during World War II there were some broken
friendships about it. Ernest Blanding, the housing contractor,
hated his good friend from high school, John Yoder, because
Yoder had stayed out of the army as a conscientious objector,
working in a nursing home, while Blanding had served in a
submarine and seen action. They used to go bowling together

and date the same girls, but now Blanding wouldn't even let his kids talk to the Yoder kids.

I wound up in the hospital, too, only not in a small town like the people of that generation. I went to Chicago, the nearest big city, since the draft board allowed you to find your own position, and who wanted to stay in Malta, Indiana, anyway, with its silos, memories, and boredom?

The draft board, Local 13 in Malta, was famous already. There had been an article about it in *Life* describing a young father being dragged away from his wife's hospital room while she was giving birth to their first child. He was sent off to Vietnam, and a month later he was killed. The Malta *Prairie-Sun* put the news of his death back on page eight, next to ads for cars. Everybody knew about Local 13. It was bad enough to get a letter from Selective Service. If the letter came from Local 13, your friends' voices would resonate with doom.

It was the summer of 1968, and I'd just graduated from college. I was working for Ernest Blanding, saving money for grad school in English, when a letter came from the draft board. Now that my student deferment was at an end, the president and my fellow citizens had chosen me to defend the country. I responded with an application for status as a conscientious objector, along with a letter requesting immediate induction into "alternative service."

Two weeks later, I got a reply from the draft board. They would not accept my application on face value. I was to appear at a hearing to prove my sincerity as a pacifist.

On the day of the hearing, I combed my hair, put on a suit and tie, and drove downtown. The clerk of the local board, Mrs. Factor, who looked like a sadistic librarian, ushered me into a conference room in back where two older men were already seated, folders open in front of them. They introduced themselves as Edwin Mulroony and Cappy Knight. I sat in a chair facing the long table. I recognized them. Mulroony owned the hardware store, and Cappy Knight the infamous Black Cat nightclub at the edge of town, where underaged drinkers were served. You could also spend time with a prostitute upstairs, if you had the right kind of money. Mrs. Factor joined them, making the third panelist.

Mulroony was apparently the chairman. Leaning over the table, face sagging like a bag of cheese, he asked the question everyone asked conscientious objectors: "What would you do if you found a man raping your sister?" Cappy Knight's face gleamed like an anvil as he waited for my answer. Mrs. Factor pursed her lips in expectation.

"Well," I said, "to begin with, I don't have a sister. I'm an only child, and my parents were very old when they had me. Secondly, most rapes are not carried out in public. So I take your question as pure speculation.

"I assume, of course, that my presence itself would be enough to send the rapist running away. This would amount to a kind of emotional jujitsu. In clear view of the rapist, I would symbolize the displeasure of society, and guilt would overcome him. Moreover, he would have no idea his victim was my sister, so the flight response would probably not be superseded by a stand-and-fight reaction. Because I'd remained calm, even the most salacious rapist would flee the scene."

I made gestures in the air, as if catching fireflies. The board looked at me with profound distaste. They had expected quotes from the Bible, Dr. Spock, and Tolstoy. But I could tell they liked the quasi-military metaphor, even if it was oriental. Most of all, they liked the pragmatism with which I perceived the situation. Morality was a matter of convenience for them, too, in running the hardware store or bar and grille. Besides that, I was a twit. These COs were always twits, using words like *salacious*.

"Tell me, Mr. Holder," said Mr. Mulroony, aggressively tapping his pencil on the table, "what would you do if you were confronted in an alley by a man with a knife, and there was no means of escape? Wouldn't you fight to protect your own life?" It was apparently also one of his favorite questions. He settled back in his chair and gave a knowing wink to the others.

"Mr. Mulroony," I said, "to tell you the truth, I wish harm to no living thing. It makes me sick to see an animal run over on the highway. My grandfather nearly fell from the roof of his barn when he hit his thumb with a hammer. This runs in the family. My uncle Ralph walks down the street in a zigzag, trying to avoid the ants. I don't like cherry pie because of the color. If the attacker killed me, that would be God's will. I wouldn't fight back, because that might bring harm to him. The fact is, the more passive you are, the more you are feared. Passiveness not only exudes confidence; it can also be frighteningly aggressive."

Mulroony liked the part about God. His eyebrows shot onto the top of his bald head. The others were happy with it, too. They were also Christian fatalists. It was all in God's hands, but they assumed God sided with them, like in John Wayne movies. This meant I was protected from the man with the knife—I knew about God's will and submitted to it. The bad guy lived only by his wits, so he knew nothing about surrender. That's why, in the end, he couldn't hurt me. Fatalism would protect me, and they knew it. Mrs. Factor seemed both instructed and amused.

"On a more practical basis, however," I continued, "I might be aggressively tender."

Mulroony gasped like he'd swallowed an egg. Cappy Knight looked up from the backs of his hands as if he'd just discovered their use, and Mrs. Factor's face could only be described by an ornithologist.

"Did you say 'tender'?" Cappy Knight said the word the way others say "sanitary napkin." He broke it into two awkward syllables that seemed never to have belonged together.

"Yes. As Jung once said, 'Sentimentality is a form of brutality.' I would approach the man with an excess of kindness, which, given the hateful conditions of his life up to that point,

would confuse and disarm him. I would approach the of-
fender with my arms extended, as if to embrace him."

I stood in front of the chair with arms extended, like a
divinity student about to bless some macaroni.

"I would counter his violence with a caress. At first he
would be suspicious, watching for concealed weapons. But
when he realized I only wanted to embrace him, he would
run away, fearful of such kindness."

Mulroony was bright red, either from anger or embarrassment. Cappy Knight seemed to be memorizing my face,
in case I ever came into the bar. Mrs. Factor smiled like a
lizard.

Mulroony's voice came from a dark cave, from about two
thousand years ago.

"Mr. Holder, are you, or have you ever been . . . a, a,
a . . . homosexual?"

"No, sir. Absolutely not!" I said, knowing that "yes" would
have kept me out of the army forever. Seated again in my
chair, I felt like I'd been caught in the act of reading Proust.
Had I fluttered my hands while talking? Crossed my legs at
the knee and checked my fingernails?

There was a rustle of papers as the three leaned to confer.
Then Mulroony rose to his feet and asked me to leave the
room. A week later I received a letter indicating that I was
to work for two years in public service, in a civilian capacity.
There was no doubt about my pacifism and no end to the
board's bewilderment. They suspected I was queer, but better
than that I was odd.

2

■ ■ ■ ■ ■ ■

Metropolitan Hospital is located on Chicago's Gold Coast, a few blocks from Lake Michigan. It has 900 beds, 18 floors, and seen from above, looks like the letter *H*. Associated with a major university, it's a teaching institution for both nurses and doctors—just the sort of place where hospital melodramas are set. There would be legions of tough nurses with big hearts, eager but overworked interns, arrogant resident physicians, conniving administrators, and frightened, often victimized patients. My first interview was with Mr. Bolger, an officer in Personnel. He was impeccably preppy, wearing a blue blazer, school tie, and shiny penny loafers. This was also, more or less, how I dressed at the time; we sat there, older and younger versions of an ageless archetype. When we first shook hands, I thought we might melt into each other, like water into water. But his talk was all Texas, and he could crease your clothes with his gaze.

"Says here you need a CO job. We're always glad to have your kind," he said with comfortable ambiguity. "At least with you COs we know you'll stay around for a couple years. Believe it or not, COs also tend to make good employees."

"That's nice."

"But let me tell you something," he said, leaning over the desk. "This is a nonunion hospital. The first word we hear of your organizing the staff, or of any political activity whatever, and we report it to the draft board. Understand?"

I nodded yes, but my eyes were narrow.

"We had this kid in the laundry room—thin white kid from Indiana, just like you, who started organizing the black employees. This we could not take."

"So you fired him?"

"Only been here a few weeks, and already he's organizing. Unbelievable!"

I assured him that he didn't have to worry about me. When he smiled, I found myself staring at his teeth, which leaned against each other like a shelf of books.

"It gets hot down there, you know."

"Excuse me?"

"In the laundry. It gets to about a hundred and twenty degrees on a summer day, and there's no air conditioning or windows for ventilation, just these fans that move the hot air around so you think you're going to choke. Over in the corner, under the laundry chute, there's a pile of sheets higher than your head with shit and blood and pus all over them. The smell is just unbelievable!"

Did he want me to work in the laundry, or was this his way of issuing a friendly warning? If I didn't behave, would I find myself assigned to the shit chute? He gave me a confiding look and patted the back of my hand, which rested on the edge of his desk. It was obvious there was a reason for the organizing of employees. It was also clear that most of the workers there were black. If they had put the other CO in the laundry, would they put me there too? On the other hand, I had the right to refuse an assignment. It was up to me to find any means of employment at a certified institution, just like any citizen. The job didn't have to be demeaning, but they tried to make it so, out of patriotism. Why should the boys in Vietnam have to suffer and COs get off with easy tasks? In spite of my own beliefs, this made perfect sense. I was prepared for whatever miserable task they offered, but first I wanted to see what was available.

Bolger sent me on three interviews, none in the laundry. The first was in the Gastro-Intestinal Center, in the Radiology Department. Ahmad, a small black man in a stained lab coat, took me into a dark room containing X-ray equipment. He explained that my job would be to stay in this room eight hours a day, with an hour off for lunch and breaks, sticking tubes down people's throats. The tubes, some of which were big enough to choke a catfish, were used to introduce a ra-dioactive dye into the stomach, which was then repeatedly X-rayed as I manipulated the tube for different effects. The main problem, he said, was that people gagged a lot and threw up on the table. Most of them were very sick in the first place, usually with cancer. I had a vision of jaundiced, skeletal patients, like survivors of Auschwitz, struggling in my grasp. In order to keep them quiet, said Ahmad, you had to strap them down. He pointed to four large leather straps that hung from one end of the table. I leaned over the table as he instructed me in their use, eyeing the gleaming grom-mets and hefty buckles. He stroked one of the straps with the finger and thumb of one hand.

"This is my idea," he said. "I used to work up in Psych, and ain't nobody gonna get out of 'em." There was a small flash of light near his chest, then a bright V in the air. A religious medal had fallen from his shirt as he leaned over and now it dangled in the air on its silver chain. On it was a writhing Jesus Christ, with eyes closed in an attitude of suffering. Ahmad quickly tucked it back into his shirt. His reaction left the impression the room was used for more than professional purposes. As we left the room, he looked back fondly at the table, now shiny in the hall light, the way some people eye a new car. He was completely in love with the object. Late at night, after everyone but the janitor had gone home, he probably returned to the room, strapped himself or a friend onto the table, and did those things only mirror and chrome understand.

I decided against the GI Center, as it was called. Bolger pretended he was miffed, but in the corner of his eyes there was amusement.

Next was the research wing, located on the fourth floor behind two metal doors, completely separate from the patient-care areas of the hospital. Its smell explained why. Halfway down the hall I entered an olfactory fire storm of alcohol, rubber, urine, rotting meat, dust, fur, and something like tapioca on a hot day. This experience was multiplied upon entering the research area itself. Agonized howling of many large dogs. Cages clanking and rattling. Inside one room several lemurs sat quietly in a cage, wearing helmets to which a halo of screws was attached. In another, a frog was crucified on a metal frame, all four limbs stretched to the limit. Each leg had an electrode attached, as if to measure the amount of muscle quiver. Surely somebody named Igor would step into the hallway, holding a candle.

Instead, it was Dr. Perez, a Filipino researcher with a round angelic face and a continental suaveness you see only in old movies. I had no idea how he'd gotten there; he'd simply appeared, as if he'd stepped through a wall. His handshake was smooth as smoke. Wordlessly we entered a laboratory to the left. An entire wall was filled with bloodhounds in cages, the great sad hounds of Basil Rathbone movies. The noise was monstrous and rare, but Dr. Perez silenced them with a wave of his hand.

"What do you use them for?" I asked.

"Oh, these," he said with a disdainful wave of the hand. "These are not mine. Dr. Sarnisi uses them for his heart research."

"You mean . . . ?"

"The heart of the bloodhound is the same size as that of

man," he said. With a magisterial gesture he indicated the shelves around us. I saw for the first time that they contained pale dog hearts in solution.

I failed to mention that I'm tall and thin. When I'm not wearing a shirt, you can see the ribs rising and falling with each breath. My face is long and thin, like a dog's. I could feel my heart blowing around in my chest like a piece of tissue paper. The room began to stagger, and someone in it gave a low howl of disbelief.

It was me, but the doctor didn't seem to notice. He slipped into his office around the corner and offered me a chair. He sat on the edge of the desk, one hand in the other, like a basketball coach preparing to have a serious talk with one of his players. There was only one attempt at decoration, a large pastel drawing of a mouse, the kind people buy for their kids at Lincoln Park Zoo. It wasn't as cute as it should have been. Standing on its hind legs with sharp claws sticking out, looking as if it had just eaten something, it glared at me knowingly over Perez's shoulder.

"I see you admire my picture."

"Oh, yes. Very nice."

"Mice are wonderful animals," he said dreamily.

"I imagine so," I said.

"We find them very useful in our experimental projects. They're small and easy to manage, and moreover they are cheap."

"What is it, exactly, I'd be doing here?"

"I have a grant of three million dollars from the National Science Foundation for the study of semipermeable membranes. We take a specimen of tissue and place it in various solutions, like water, alcohol, and so on, to see how fast—and in what volume—the liquid is absorbed. Your job is mainly to kill the mice, about ten of them each morning. You then remove a section of intestine and make a small balloon from the tissue that surrounds it, much as one makes sausage. These you will place in the solutions, and after a controlled period of time you record the data gathered."

"I have to kill ten mice."

"That is correct."

"So that's about two hundred mice a month, not counting those with thirty-one days. In two years, I'll have killed maybe five thousand mice."

"That is sufficient for our studies."

"And five thousand mice into three million dollars is about . . ."

"It is six hundred dollars per animal," he said with pride. "That is what the grant allows for." He leaned forward, as if awaiting my decision—to be, or not, the Eichmann of mice. The mouse on the wall seemed to move, as if wind had blown through its fur. Ursa Major, light-years away, moved slightly on its axis. Cars streamed down Lake Shore Drive, taking their occupants off to jobs, shopping sprees, and love affairs. Fish in the lake were rising, gasping for air. The city worked like a woman in labor. What did I do? I told Dr. Perez I'd be back in touch, shook his hand, went straight to a bar, drank six beers and three shots of bourbon, danced with the waitress, kissed the bartender on top of his head, and went home to bed. When I woke up, there was a woman in bed with me. Thank God, I thought, for this.

Her name was Vicki Cepak. We'd known each other since college, but as far as I could remember, this was the first time we'd slept together. Then I remembered another time, dozens of times, but I couldn't remember last night. She was watching the Cubs game on the ancient black-and-white television. Randy Hundley, the Cubs catcher, wobbled in a dream toward the bunt Lou Brock of St. Louis had just laid down. He got out of his crouch the way your father gets out of his chair after a big dinner. Hundley overthrew first base and Brock cruised into third. Vicki smoked a cigarette and leaned against the wall at the head of the bed.

"About time you woke up," she said.

"What time is it?"

"Third inning." If you lived in Chicago, you knew what she meant. On summer afternoons, you didn't tell time by the clock. The game started at one thirty, so it had to be around two thirty.

"How did the interview go?"

"I can either stick tubes down people's throats or make balloons of mice intestines."

"Charming," she said, like Lauren Bacall. So that's who she was today. Yesterday it was Ethel Mertz. She could be cute and flirty or cranky and wise, but she was always trying to be somebody else—that's how you knew it was Vicki. Today, she was whiskey-voiced and sexy, letting her red wavy hair hang over her shoulders, but mostly she was a girl from Wisconsin who'd learned to smoke last year. I thought maybe we liked each other for all the faults we shared, but I couldn't say if it was love. One thing was for sure. Her period was ten days late, and she'd come down from Richland Center to get a pregnancy test. She'd gone to the clinic yesterday to give a urine sample, and they said to call back in about two days.

I took a drag on her cigarette and developed an erection. It wasn't something you could hang your hat on, but it was sure there. One thing about living in the sixties was, you didn't have to worry about how much noise you made. We did it head-on, sideways, and upside down. We did it loud, soft, and moderato. Right at the end, Vicki got very soprano, like a small locomotive straining uphill, finding its plateau, and coasting down the other side with happy shrieks. We were sweating a lot by now. My head was butting the wall where Rose the Poet had painted a muddy Christ figure. Applause could be heard from the kitchen, just outside the bedroom door.

Right now, Vicki looked like she was fifteen years old. She had small soft features and thin bones. When she was happy, she was pretty, and when she was angry, she looked kind of mousy. Lately, she had been incredibly happy, a Pre-Raphaelite madonna with half-closed eyes.

"Hey, what's the score in there?" It was Rose the Poet, one of the roommates, and he didn't mean the game.

"Tied!" shouted Vicki, already going back to sleep.

I gave her a kiss, put on some jeans, and went into the kitchen to greet David Rosenstone, whom we called Rose the Poet, sitting in front of a bowl of brown rice. He ate it often, with a sixteen-ounce Coca-Cola. The rice was supposed to clean the system and make you a better person. Everything he did had some philosophical purpose, but the more rice he ate, the weirder he became. Or maybe it wasn't the rice, but all the drugs he'd taken. He'd recently resigned his job writing the *Playboy* Advisor column and was living on his profit sharing, which would give him about a year of free time. One day he just got tired of writing articles on the joys of mutual masturbation, rose from his desk, and never returned. The first day of his "retirement," he took some speed, wrote thirty poems in two hours, all containing the words *pink* and *electric* in capital letters, and had a nervous breakdown. Often, in the middle of the night, we'd find him testing the door to see if it was locked. He would stand in front of it for hours, opening and closing it, a look of doubt on his face. He also liked to walk around in the nude, and sometimes he answered the door that way. Once this caught the landlady by surprise, and she plunged back down the dark stairwell, mumbling an apology, as if *she* had committed the indiscretion. There was so much residual lysergic acid in Rose's system you could start a car with it if you could get him hooked up to the jumper cables. At least that's what the Selective Service psychologist said when he declared Rose emotionally unfit for the army.

"You look well rested," he said, staring into the rice he'd warmed up from yesterday. The congealed leftovers were still in a pot by the stove, next to some remaining shallots and a bottle of Tamari.

"Looks good," I said, "but maybe I'll eat some wallpaper instead."

"Was that the game on in there?"

"Yeah. Cubs and St. Louis. You want to check it out?"

"All right!" he said, with more enthusiasm than expected.

He wasn't much of a sports fan, but we'd gone to Wrigley Field a couple of times out of what Rose called "sheer sensibility." He also spoke eloquently of the "pastoral aestheticism" of the game, but I suspected he'd read the phrase somewhere. He said he didn't believe in competition, though he was an intrepid competitor, giving the impression on the tennis court of an explosion in a bell-bottom factory. Neither of us played very well. The real players in their perfect whites stared at us with contempt. We always played in jeans and T-shirts. Once Rose even went onto the court in street shoes, which drove a middle-aged man on the next court into a rage.

We decided to go to the game. I kissed Vicki, who wanted to sleep, and threw on some clothes. We were halfway out the door when the phone rang. It was Bolger. He had another interview for me and I'd better be there first thing in the morning. If it all went all right, he said, I could be a unit manager on the evening shift, for twice the money the other positions offered. There was something in his voice between a growl and a purr, which I took to mean, "I like you, kid, but don't fuck around."

I said I'd be there, and off we went in my car. Rose broke out his grass, and we got so slowed down and high that everything rose up in front of us like a billboard or monument. A bag lady crossed the street in front of us and showed us happy teeth. I couldn't tell whether the car was moving or standing still.

Looking in the rearview mirror, I realized we couldn't have appeared any more different from each other. He had long black hair parted in the middle and wore farmer jeans and basketball shoes. I had on beige stay-pressed chinos, a blue oxford cloth shirt, and brown penny loafers. My blond hair was neatly combed.

About three years later we arrived at Wrigley Field. I parked the car illegally in front of the Sports Corner bar at Addison and Sheffield, then we bought general admission tickets and headed up the zigzag ramp leading to the upper deck. Half-

way up, we stopped and looked back at the street, where a
fat cop, his foot on the front fender, was giving my car a
ticket. There were already fifteen or so forming a warped
bouquet on top of the dashboard. He looked at them in irritation. We laughed and climbed the last ramp, which sus-
pends you over the general admission seats.

On the upper deck we were almost overwhelmed by the
pointillist fervor, the bloom and buzz, of the crowd. They
chatted, dozed, ordered beer, and rose suddenly to cheer the
double tying the game: it was like watching a human flag
wave in the breeze. We watched with pleasure as cheering
rolled out of the park and down Waveland Avenue to the
lake, then over the park like a great balloon, swelling up
Sheffield, past old couples on lawn chairs, and entering Grace-
land Cemetery, where Louis Sullivan, Potter Palmer, and
other famous Chicagoans lie beneath beautiful stones.

The color of the grass was amazing, as if painted, and on
it players moved like threads of neon. For no apparent reason,
a beer vendor handed us two beers and said they were on the
house. For the rest of the game we strolled the concrete
walkway separating the box seats from the general admission,
watching the game, taking in the crowd, and goofing around
with the Andy Frain ushers, who looked like they'd just
escaped from a marching band. Rose loved the white gloves
they wore, which reminded him of Mickey Mouse, and we
listened to the swish of fabric as a beautiful young usher
walked by, a stern look on her face. Then someone hit a fly
ball that hung in the air so long it was evening before it
landed. We stood with our jaws open, staring at the sky and
getting older.

That night Vicki and I sat on the couch, and Rose sat on
the floor next to the television set with a quart of beer. As
usual, the news was all about Vietnam. In the field, a camera
jaggedly took pictures of some mud and weeds, machine-
gun fire rattling softly in the background. The cameraman
had gotten caught in a cross fire and fallen in a ditch. The
legs of soldiers flickered by on the road above, and you could

see a couple of abandoned trucks in the distance. If the GIs couldn't see the enemy to shoot them, how could cameras catch their quick shadows? Then Walter Cronkite reported that fifty-three U.S. soldiers had died in the war that day. It seemed like a lot.

One of them was Terry Grubbs of Tin Cup, Indiana, who'd lived in the same dorm as me at Rhineland College and become one of my best friends. I couldn't believe it. They had prepared a special story about the small town he was from, and how everyone had known him. There were pictures of him from different times of life—Terry in the fifth grade with a silly-looking crew cut, Terry on the basketball team. They interviewed one of his high school teachers, who wore a flowered dress and looked very mean, like she was trying not to cry. Then there was a film clip of metal caskets being unloaded at an air force base in Delaware while an honor guard stood by. It was the same film they had shown yesterday and the day before, taken from a file. Terry had stepped on a mine, the reporter said, and the body inside the metal casket was terribly broken. Vicki had known Terry, too, and she cried and held me tight.

Terry had lived just down the hall from me in college. He was a phys. ed. major and president of the roller skating club, which had about four members. He also used to play Mantovani and Johnny Mathis records when everyone else was interested in rock and roll. He even thought he could sing like Mathis, but his voice was terrible. From the beginning of the war, he talked about wanting to fight in it, but he worried about being too tall. He was 6'6" and 250 pounds, and he feared they wouldn't take him when he enlisted after graduation. He got his local congressman to send a letter to the draft board on his behalf, indicating his value to the army. He did push-ups and sit-ups and ran in place. He cursed the television when there were scenes of draft resistance. I thought he was one of the stupidest people on earth about politics, but we were still friends.

Suddenly I was on my feet, punching a hole in the wall by the TV set. Rose scrambled for cover, plaster dust in his hair, and Vicki held her hands over her mouth. There was blood and plaster dust on my knuckles. I walked to the door, went downstairs into the street, threw up in some bushes, and headed toward the park.

Terry had always owned a gun, even when we were in college. One day he called me into his room, locked the door, and took down a dictionary from the shelf. Inside, where he had cut out the pages, there was a very real, cold, and heavy pistol.

"It's for protection," he whispered, looking furtively at the door. He was big enough to throw me out the window, and he needed a gun for protection? The college was located in a little town in the middle of cornfields. There weren't too many criminals around.

"It's just in case," he said. "Dad gave it to me for my birthday. He said I would probably need it up at the college, what with all the draft dodgers and all." He looked at me with no special significance. His paranoia had a certain sweetness, and in some ways he was a true innocent. It was his father who'd made him think these things. He took to such opinions the way other kids make model airplanes.

His father, Russell, was a furious crypto-fascist who lived for illicit arms, survivalism, and antisemitic tracts on cheap paper. He ran an insurance agency for a living but didn't do too well, so he sold Knapp shoes door to door, meaning farm to farm, for extra money. There was always a copy of *Soldier of Fortune* or *Plain Truth* in his truck, bleached by the sun. The world was coming to an end anyway, and Russell Grubbs wanted to be there when it happened. He wasn't about to lose the final battle—he'd already lost all the others. The real desolation angels weren't motorcycle outlaws and suburban beatniks; they were ordinary grocery clerks, mechanics, bank presidents, and housewives who believed in the inevitability, therefore the beauty, of the first nuclear dawn. They were the phoenixes that would rise from the ashes of small-town America, and they knew it; that's what gave them such frightening confidence in their daily hatreds.

Terry said his dad attended survival training camp every summer. He and his buddies would enter a wilderness somewhere in Idaho, where they would shoot at each other with live ammunition all morning and share a can of Spam for lunch. During one of these exercises his dad dropped from a tree onto a deer and killed it with his pocketknife. Then he drank the blood from a neck vein because he'd read Genghis Khan used to do that. The Khan, next to Hitler, was his biggest hero. His father was a harmless-looking guy, the kind you might see at Sears, pricing a set of wrenches.

In spite of our differences, I spent a lot of time with Terry, especially in the summer. We were thrown together by a lack of other choices. I'd just moved to the area and didn't know many people, and Terry was a loner naturally. We'd drive around looking for girls. Once in a while we'd get lucky. In Kokomo, Indiana, we picked up two girls at a place called Sam and Flo's Horn and Hoof (they served only red meat) and drove to one of their houses. While Terry went inside with his date to watch TV, my date and I took the chaise lounge on the porch. We kissed for a while. I felt her bony chest. Afterward, when the light was better, I saw that she was wildly cross-eyed. Terry kidded me about Penny the Planaria for a long time after that.

Heading down Armitage toward the park, I put my hands in my pockets, as if by making them disappear I might make myself invisible, too. I wanted to get as far away from television as possible; but at the corner of Armitage and Hudson there was a fire in an apartment building, and the television crews were just arriving. Four or five fire trucks were already there: flames blew like curtains from the third-floor window. A crowd of neighborhood people had gathered, excitedly talking and pointing, while their kids played among the hoses covering the street. The rest of the building was on fire, too, including the restaurant on the first floor. It appeared that the restaurant owner had torched the place because of a lack of business and somehow overdone it. The fireman looked sensational silhouetted against the flames.

I crossed Clark Street and passed a Park District building where old people in lapidary science classes polish stones until they disappear in their hands. Stockton Drive: the public rest rooms where Rose said guys meet to give each other blowjobs. In fact, two men in tight jeans stood outside, smoking cigarettes and checking out the slow-moving cars. At the lagoon, green scum and potato-chip wrappers floated along the edge among the metal boats nobody ever rented, the weeds being too thick for navigation. I could smell the oxygen coming off the water, and stood there for a while watching a sliver of moon in the evening sky. To the left was the Farm in the Zoo, where antiseptic pigs and chickens slept on immaculate straw—no mud, shit, and rusting farm machinery in evidence. Its most popular attraction was the Clydesdale horses, huge and frightening, like something you'd ride into war. A small red barn with perfect white trim could be seen through the trees. It was the kind of barn rich people build on their estates to store their extra Ping-Pong tables.

Off I went in a different direction, toward the dead end of the zoo nobody ever visited, down a long narrow walkway next to a chain link fence, on the other side of which was a large wooden bowl with bright grain spilled around it. The grass was worn down to mud where the animal had been anxiously pacing in the same pattern. There, in fact, was the animal, an ostrich with patches of feathers missing, as if it had taken bites of itself. It stepped from behind some trees and came straight at me, stabbing its head straight at my face. This was not hunger; it was hatred. Stride for stride, it followed me the length of the fence, making low choking sounds, pink eyes gleaming. I looked back and saw the ostrich still glaring at me, dipping its wedge-shaped head. No, I thought to myself, this grotesque animal has nothing to do with Terry's death; but I walked back to the apartment differently, as if pursued.

Rose the Poet was testing the front door in his underwear when I got home. He seemed unconcerned with what had happened earlier that evening. He said hello with a grunt and wave of the hand and returned to his consuming task like someone studying a movement in chess.

Vicki was reading *The Floating Opera* in bed when I climbed in beside her. It was still early in the evening, but when she was visiting we stayed in the bedroom because of the room-mates.

"Are you all right?" she wanted to know. I breathed in the affirmative and stared at the ceiling. You could hear the building settle, the way old wood does on summer evenings. It sounded like someone was climbing the stairs.

"I'm sorry," she said, putting her head on my shoulder. "Maybe it wasn't him. Maybe it was another Terry."

"It was him, all right. There are only eight houses in Tin Cup, Indiana, and only one Terry Grubbs."

"It isn't fair!" she said, kicking the book off the bed.

"If I know Terry, he was probably relieved it happened," I said. "I mean, if you die at least something important has happened to you."

She leaned on her elbow. "That sounds kind of cold, you know. Who knows what will happen with any of us?"

"The way I see it, Terry's mission in life was to die as soon as possible. He'd drive his car like crazy and take all sorts of chances. Once he threw himself out of his dorm window on a dare and broke both arms. He even asked some guys to tie him to the railroad tracks one night, but the train didn't come through as scheduled, and he only caught a cold."

A car moved down Halsted Street, throwing a wedge of light across the ceiling. We lay there for a while, deciding if we really liked each other. I got out of bed and stood beside it, agitated.

"What's the matter with you?"

"I've got to call Terry's parents," I said, knowing it was a dumb thing to do even as I said it. "I've got to do some-thing—I was his friend."

Standing in the dark of the hall, I called information and listened as the exchanges clicked in, working their way into central Indiana. The operator had a southern accent, which surprised me. Maybe I had one, too, and didn't know it. I dialed the number. There was a long pause and it began to ring: lonesome rasps like you hear only on country phones. After six rings, Mr. Grubbs picked up. He didn't say hello, so I didn't either. He just breathed into the phone with a masculine patience that meant, "Yes, my son has died, you contemptible weakling. What are you going to do about it?" It also meant he would never forgive Terry for beating him to the punch. He was supposed to be the bloody hero, going down in a firefight with the state police. Now survival was all that was left, and the fun had gone out of it. He had probably been sitting there most of the day with a pistol in his hand, wearing his commando gear and eating from rations cans. Now we breathed at each other over the phone, a kind of conversation.

In this way, we mourned Terry together.

3

．　．　．　．　．

Bolger was elated. I was perfect for the unit management program. He thought Mr. Janush, the supervisor, would like me, too. I'd have to cut my hair, of course, and a suit and tie were required, but it was the beginning of a great new career in middle management if I "played my cards right." Bolger gave me the thumbs-up sign. He, too, had started out as a unit manager.

Using his directions, I took the nearest elevator to Seven South, where in room 721, Gary Janush—tall, handsome, and Polish—shook my hand and offered me a chair. There was something about him that I liked already. He had the sad but efficient manner of a professional father. Someone would break his heart in life someday, but I knew it wasn't going to be me.

On his littered desk was an executive toy consisting of four ball bearings attached to strings in a V. If you knocked one into the group, one flew out the other end. The business metaphor was clear: the day is a series of crisp clicks; one's efforts can be fully realized. I thought of a title for it: *The Executive Dreams of Newtonian Physics.* In a photo cube on the desk a little girl in a blue dress stood by a Christmas tree, and a cheerful woman with a good figure posed in the kitchen with her hands on her hips, pretending she didn't want the photograph taken. In the backyard a boy of about six held his father's rifle. Next to him, on a slab of concrete near the garage, there was a dead deer with dark blood seeping from its mouth in his direction. The boy smiled proudly at the camera.

The interview went well. I remembered a tip a high school guidance counselor had given me about asking plenty of questions. It shows you're interested in the job. Actually, I *was* interested. Janush said I would supervise the station clerks, make sure the laundry and food showed up on time, and take care of practical problems such as housekeeping and maintenance on three floors of the hospital, meaning six nursing stations. There were as many as 40 patients on each unit, so I would be responsible for the nonnursing care of about 240 people.

Janush liked me from the start. He gave me a fatherly wink and patted me on the shoulder. I would not only do; I was to report to work as soon as the papers were cleared. This would take about a week. The personnel department had to notify the draft board, so I wasn't to worry about that. I would be free to leave the job two years from the starting date. Meanwhile, there was to be a physical exam here in the hospital. I had to be cleared by Health Services, just like any other employee.

He also assured me that he didn't share my political views. He was a U.S. Army reservist and really loved the summer camps. His sly look suggested card games, dates with the local women, and lots of boyish good fun. He said he believed in what Patrick Henry said about "doing your own thing." It was a free country because of the "necessary limits" every decent society places on itself. There were plenty of other countries that didn't have our freedoms, which is why his father had left Poland in the first place. That I was working in the hospital instead of serving in the army was a credit to the democracy in which we lived, and he was damned proud of that.

For a moment I thought he was going to cry, but he pulled himself together and walked me to the door. He would be in touch, he said, and shook my hand. Then he returned to his tiny office and waved good-bye, looking for all the world like an Olympic javelin thrower, circa 1930.

I decided to walk back another way, down the hall to the nursing station, since there had to be another set of elevators. There were four or five rooms on each side of the hall, each with its wide door open. Most of the rooms had four beds. It must have been Orthopedics because nearly everyone had a cast of some kind. A guy with his leg in traction and a can of beer in his hand toasted me as I walked by gawking. Everywhere I looked there was plaster. Toward the end of the hall sat a patient dressed in a gown and wearing paper slippers. There was nothing wrong with him that I could see. As I passed, he got up and went into a room, holding the back of his hospital gown with one hand. You could see most of his backside, in varying shades of pink, through the parted-curtains effect. The last door on the right was closed, and behind it one of the saws used for removing casts growled and whined.

Behind the nursing station two nurses moved like storks. They wore different caps, which, I found out later, meant they'd gone to different schools. One was the standard kind, a modified flying nun design, but the other was crepey and fancy, like a coffee filter turned upside down. A nurse burst out of the station and passed me carrying a small silver tray with pills in little paper cups and three lethal-looking hypodermic needles pointed in the same direction. I couldn't help watching her walk down the hall, hips swaying neatly.

In the back of the station, three black nursing aides in

salmon-colored dresses were talking and laughing. The color was just right on them, moist and warm. One of them pointed in my direction, and more laughter followed. Blushing, I stepped clumsily toward the elevators. There, in a corridor, several wheelchairs were jammed together in random storage, one of them containing an old man with wispy white hair and spots on the backs of his hands. His arms were tied with straps to the arms of the chair, and he trembled softly as if listening to music. I punched the down button and looked into a large room on the opposite side of the elevator bank to see if anyone was there. It was lit with fluorescent bulbs and filled with three-tiered stainless-steel carts. In a corner, taking trays of food from a dumbwaiter, was a black man with a surgical cap on his head. I gave him a little wave to get his attention, pointed at the old man in the hall, and mouthed the words "This yours?"

In crisp, clear tones he said, "Are you fuckin' crazy?"

A tall doctor with a red face walked up in a hurry and hit the up button. Pacing back and forth, he talked to himself in an agitated way, and scratched the backs of his hands, which were bright red. He looked incredibly neurotic, but his long gray smock with "Dr. Rocks" stitched on the breast pocket meant that he was an attending physician, a real big shot. The blotches on his face were either from drinking or a skin disease, and his chin stuck out like a stone. The overall impression was of imperial command. With a surprisingly athletic move, his foot nearly level with his chest, he kicked the center of the three elevators.

"When are you going to get these things running?" he shouted.

"Excuse me?" I said. His face was close to mine, the great chin jutting out. All I could think was, can his name really be Dr. Rocks? The black guy from Food Service stuck his head out of the door to see what was going on, but when he saw Rocks, he ducked back into the room again. Apparently the doctor had a reputation already.

"When are you administrative people going to get these

elevators working? I'm taking this to the executive committee, God damn it!"

"Sorry," I said, "but I don't work here." And of course I
didn't, at least not yet. The down elevator finally arrived,
and I stepped onto it gratefully. The operator, a young Latino
guy in a blue cotton jacket marked "Transportation," stepped
away from his control panel and wheeled the old man onto
the elevator. The doors closed on the red-faced Dr. Rocks
and we descended to the first floor, where I stepped out, and
the elevator operator shoved the old man into the hall and
closed the doors again.

Here next to the emergency room, there was a good deal
more traffic, but still nobody claimed the patient. People
walked by quickly or dreamily, depending on their desti-
nations. Some were probably headed for a cup of coffee;
others had just received the results of their tests, and now
had to tell the rest of the family. I stood for a while beside
the old man, as if we were somehow connected. An old
woman passing by nodded, as if to say, That's a nice boy.
Finally I figured some sort of official procedure was at work,
so I left him where he was. I exited through the electric double
doors where on a busy night they wheeled in the gunshot
victims, DOAs, and women who had given birth in cabs.

The living arrangements on Halsted Street were tolerable,
given our lack of money. It wasn't just Rose and I living
there, however: things were complicated by the presence of
Randy and Penelope. Randy was a bit of a pain, I thought.
He was 5'4" with thick blond hair and looked like a pudgy
nine-year-old kid. He worked for a company called Academic
Industries, which published illustrated versions of classic novels, mainly for adults who were learning to read. Penelope
was the daughter of an Australian banker, or so she claimed,
but if she had a lot of money, she didn't let anyone know.
Slightly bent at the waist, she walked with a limp, as if she
had a pain in her side, but this was never explained.

We'd gotten together through an ad in the paper placed by a guy named Edgar, who had this huge apartment all to himself but was leaving for Mexico. There were four bed-rooms, a dining room, living room, large kitchen, and a study near the living room where there was lots of light. It was cheap, too, since it was in a marginal neighborhood. It was a four-flat, very tall. The landlady, for some reason, chose to live in the basement. This kept her out of our hair. She was a professor of English in the city college system and got the building in a divorce settlement. Every now and then the sewers backed up and her things would float out the door—art books, hand-sewn rugs, Bic pens, and notes for her lec-tures. She'd lay everything out to dry on the sidewalk and take it back in a couple of days later. The thing I noticed about Mrs. Carter was how little garbage she produced. Once a week, this tiny white bag of antiseptic trash, so small you could put it into your purse, would appear in the garbage can that all the apartments shared.

On the first floor were Gus and Larry, the basketball play-ers, seven or eight feet tall. You could drive a truck down their faces and have to stop for coffee before you got to the hairline. They had played for Temple University, and Larry had a brief fling in the pros before he got cut. Both of them fancied themselves ladies' men. They looked a little ridiculous when they tried to flirt, leaning against the wall at a party, trying to get their faces close enough for contact. But they were successful, always accompanied by a sensational-look-ing woman. We lived upstairs from the giants, and above us was someone named Williams whom no one knew. We could hear his feet going up on the stairs, slowly and patiently, as if he'd had a hard day at work. There was never a sound from above, and while the basketball boys were always hav-ing parties, shouting "ya-hoo" and "ee-ha," Williams never had company. I began to suspect he suspended himself from the ceiling or walked around in foam-rubber clothes, like Gumby.

Edgar was something else. Earlier that year, on a trip by

train to attend a socialist institute in Mexico, he'd fallen in love with a thirteen-year-old girl in a private-school uniform. An affair begun holding hands in a sight-seeing car quickly resulted in her getting pregnant. Her parents sent her to London to have the abortion, and she was instructed never to see him again on threat of his imprisonment (Edgar was twenty-five). But their destiny was set. The girl planned to run away from her home in New York City and meet him near an Aztec temple. We imagined them making love in the moonlight on an ancient blood-soaked altar, romantic and ridiculous. Both of them were from wealthy families. What would happen when the money ran out and Marielle, the Lolita of Schuyler School for Young Women, had to wash her clothes in the river?

The apartment was ours until Edgar returned with Marielle. Meanwhile, we had to take care of John Reed, Edgar's dog, whose habits were not good. He liked to urinate on the furniture, what we had of it, and he always did so with a confident look that meant "I'm Edgar's." He had bald patches in his thin brown fur—the sort of skeletal creature that hangs around a medieval village, waiting for scraps of fat. Whenever he entered the room, the mood would change to subtle horror, and Penelope, in spite of her antivivisectionist opinions, would shudder with loathing. "Please," she would implore, thin hands over her face like a caul, "get that horrible beast out of here!" But John Reed, as if to make her suffer further, would place his head in her lap and look up at her with enflamed eyes.

As the days passed, Penelope learned to tolerate John Reed, just as we learned to live with each other. Sometimes this wasn't so easy, especially with Randy. He would sit on the couch, smoking a cigarette and talking incessantly about his favorite topics, the misery of being in love and the history of the comic book. We learned more than we ever wanted to know about his juvenile enthusiasms and disappointments, for in many ways he was still a child. His eyes gleamed when he talked about Rubber Man, "Spidey," and other heroes of metamorphosis. There was a "Hegelian dichotomy," he insisted, in the character of Superman. The Hulk, green and muscle-bound, was "clearly a hero of the nuclear age—grotesque, mutant, and essentially primitive—in indirect proportion to the technological complexity that made the Apocalpyse a certainty." Of all the heroes, Randy liked the Hulk the most. He, too, wanted a muscular id in hillbilly pants, a monster of moral imagination, to settle his scores when he got angry. Randy had the fury and essential selfishness of children, who are the sternest puritans and also the consummate victims.

On the morning following my interview with Janush, the consummate victim burned a hole in the couch with his cigarette. As he talked, smoke rose from between his thighs—the acrid, dangerous smoke of burning foam rubber. As Spiderman crawled the wall of Randy's most recent theory, the theorist was oblivious.

I pointed at the source of my discomfort. It was, after all, my couch, a Swedish modern cheapie Mark Samples had sold me for ten dollars before leaving for San Francisco to discover himself through Scientology, Tibetan Buddhism, murder mysteries, and a better diet.

"Fire!" I screamed. I was up and waving now, jabbing a finger at his crotch. Randy leapt to his feet and stared at the growing hole edged with fire. It was as if a rip in the universe had opened but somehow failed to claim him; already the event was taking on cosmic importance. I slapped out the fire with my hands.

"Son of a bitch! It's ruined. My new couch is ruined."

He looked at me with prolific unconcern. "Something like this once happened to Submariner," he said. "He put out the fire by converting to water." He took a drag on his still-lit cigarette.

Penelope entered the room, fanning the air dramatically. "Good heavens," she said.

"Sorry about the couch," said Randy.

"Oh, that's all right," I said.

Penelope walked around the couch with small mincing steps, sniffing the air like a prize poodle. She was tall and thin, but always seemed small somehow. Her bent walk gave her the universal air of apology. "It smells like burnt almonds," she said. "Once, on the plains of the Serengeti, we placed almonds in the campfire. They're quite delicious."

Vicki had entered the room and was standing behind Penelope. As Penelope talked, Vicki mocked her, making yak-yak with one hand. Before coming to Chicago, Penelope had spent some time in Africa, and she never let you forget it. When she talked, she would stand a little too close to you, hands crossed on her chest like a saint or corpse, and tilt her head.

"Having a campfire, girls?" said Vicki. Joan Crawford? Hermione Gingold? The tone was clear, but the reference was not.

"Randy was immolating himself for the sake of the war," said Penelope. She made a major monument of the word *immolating*. A shudder passed like a rumor through the group.

"I'm laughing," said Randy, pretending to yawn. Then he went over to the television and tuned it to channel 32. We pissed him off, and he was going to watch an old Chillie Willie cartoon to put us out of his mind. He lit a new cigarette and watched Chillie slide across a patch of ice into an outraged walrus. Half of him laughed, and half studied the screen with dark intellectual ambition. Meanwhile, we watched him watching. Chillie did this and Chillie did that, and nobody cared more than he did. Rose the Poet shambled into the room wearing nothing at all, a kaiser roll in one hand and Kahlil Gibran in the other. Nobody paid him any attention, and he sat on the couch, eating and reading.

To get away from the roommates, that night Vicki and I went to a movie, something strange by the French director Godard. There was no story to speak of, and characters simply stood around in a barnyard, talking straight at the camera about political issues that were obscure to us. But the movie was interesting, in a sense, because it was so boring, and the audience was attentive. There were even points where the audience laughed heartily. Vicki and I looked at each other, wondering what the joke was.

During the movie, Vicki whispered that the lab had called earlier that day. She was pregnant for sure. She could have a second test, but they were rarely wrong.

I was stunned. It was not me watching the pretentious movie; it was someone else's body I was visiting for a few years, on a trial basis. This was the body that embraced Vicki and kissed her, not on the mouth, but softly next to it. I rattled around inside it, and the movie began to make sense for the first time. One of the characters stood in the middle of a field while the camera moved around him in a full circle, and then another one. He talked about politics as usual, and a fly landed on his forehead. We left just as one of the characters was slitting a pig's throat with a long-bladed knife. Blood slid heavily from the wound and soaked the muddy ground. The camera jerked around as if the cameraman had lost his footing. We heard the pig's desperate cries as we hurried up the aisle. We could still hear them on the other side of the doors as we headed for the street.

4

∎ ∎ ∎ ∎ ∎ ∎

When I arrived at the hospital at nine in the morning for my physical, the place was bustling with activity. This was the time when all the surgeries are scheduled and most of the tests are conducted. The hallways were littered with patients on carts or in wheelchairs, waiting their turns for the X ray or operation that possibly would save their lives. I entered through the front door this time, where an Egyptian-looking doorman helped people in and out of cabs, a service only to be found at a place like Metropolitan. At City Hospital, located in a bad neighborhood, there was no doorman. There you were lucky if you could get the broken doors to open on your own, and if someone reached out, it was probably to steal your wallet. The doorman gave me a big smile full of gold teeth and opened the door. He looked very happy in his work, and the gold stitching on his brown coat said "Mama." It was a good name for him. He looked like he might pick you up in his arms and rock you right to sleep.

The lobby looked like the nave of a Gothic cathedral. A red tapestry with an abstract design hung from the high ceiling, and the walls were Indiana limestone. The place seemed to breathe dignity and money. To the right, unobtrusively set in an alcove with oak trim, was the cashier's office, and to the left was the Ladies' Auxiliary Gift Shop, filled with get-well cards, stuffed animals, and magazines. It was always crowded, with a huge line at check-out, because all the clerks were volunteers and didn't know what they were doing. But they were awfully nice, and everybody forgave their incompetence. The gift shop smelled of cough drops, perfume, and old ladies with silver hair.

I took the elevator to the basement, where Health Services was located, next to Nuclear Medicine. The cancer patients had their tumors reduced there with gamma rays, down the hall from a long winding tunnel leading to the medical school.

Health Services consisted of two small rooms, one for the doctor and one for an aged male volunteer wearing a white smock over a Brooks Brothers suit. He might have been a distinguished lawyer thirty years ago.

"May I help you?" he asked, peering at me over his reading glasses.

"My name is James Holder," I said. "I was told to report here for my employee physical."

The desk was clean except for a clipboard containing a single sheet of paper. He consulted it with shaking hands, holding the board close to his face.

"It's Holder," I said, "spelled H-o-l-d-e-r."

"Not related to Ernest Holder, are you? Fine fellow, Ernest." You could tell Ernest had been dead for years.

"Not that I know of," I said.

"A fine man for golf, Ernest. Wicked with the mashie niblick." He chopped down with his right hand, and the long white fingers shook. They were so white they almost looked blue.

"I play golf," I said unnecessarily.

"Well, that's fine, young man, just fine!" He was glad I'd offered the information. It made all the difference to him.

I shifted my weight, trying to peek into the doctor's office. A white light filled the room, a quality of light you only see in hospitals or doctors' offices.

"Here it is, young man. Holder. That you?"

"That's right," I said. "Holder, just plain Holder."

A short blond doctor appeared in the doorway. She was about fifty years old, and appeared to be very serious. She looked me up and down and without another word waved me into the office.

"You are Mr. Holder, I suppose," she said with a German accent.

"That's right."

"I am Dr. Waldheim. I am told you seek a position in management here." She seemed to doubt this was possible. There was a pause, because I didn't answer. It seemed perfectly clear who I was and why I was there.

"I am waiting for your answer," she said crisply. She crossed her arms and impatiently tapped one foot on the floor.

"Yes," I said meekly. "I've applied to be a unit manager, in the Service Department."

"And you feel that you can be of service to our patients?" She said "our" as if they were her patients only. In fact, she had no real patients. She was only a medical service physician on a base salary, hired to prevent goldbricking by nursing aides and orderlies.

"Well, yes," I said, "I do believe I can be of help. I've always been a helpful person." I looked around the room for pieces of paper to put in the wastebasket. What proof did she want, anyway?

She reached onto a shelf, grabbed a small plastic cup, and handed it to me. "Take off your clothes," she said coldly, "and put on one of those gowns. Then fill this cup with urine. You can use that room." She pointed to a bathroom set into the wall and watched as I entered. She was in the same position when I came out again, clothes heaped in one hand, the cup of warm urine in the other.

Dr. Waldheim took the urine and told me to put my clothes on the chair and sit on the examination table, which was covered with a long sheet of paper. She held the urine up to the light and looked through it. Then she dipped some litmus paper into it. She seemed satisfied with these results, because she didn't say anything.

The examination was thorough. I was probed, poked, and stared at. I coughed, sweated, and let her look in my ears and mouth. When she grabbed my front teeth with two fingers and wiggled them back and forth, my whole head shook.

"Hey!" I yelled.

"The teeth are loose. They are not real." Excited, she made a mark on the chart. Her manner changed from suspicion to gleeful discovery.

"One is false," I said. "The other one is mine."

"You have had much trouble with your teeth. The teeth are very bad."

It was true, but so what? My mouth contained about five pounds of silver, and hardly a tooth was spared. I never yawned on dates, because they might see the dark clots of silver.

When she asked me to stand and drop the gown, I did so, but with embarrassment. Suddenly I had a horrible fear of getting an erection, and the more I thought about it, the more it became a possibility. My balls were shriveled from cold or fear, and the penis began to twitch. I cleared my throat and tried to think ugly thoughts: spiders crawling up and down my legs. It worked. Cold sweat ran out of my armpits, down both sides, and onto my hips.

She walked around me as if I were a statue. She asked me to bend my knees and stand sideways, then backward. I touched the tip of my nose with an index finger and held my ear with the other hand. Then, holding this position, I hopped up and down on alternate legs. I bent over while she looked for hemorrhoids with a flashlight. When she inserted her middle finger into my rectum, pressing hard on the prostate, I groaned. I coughed obediently while she stuck a long finger, like a sharpened broomstick, under each testicle. Dr. Waldheim looked up my nose, under the fingernails, and behind my ears. She counted the hairs on my chest and under each armpit. She smelled my breath for something funny. Blood was drawn, X rays were ordered, and questions were asked. Did I smoke and how much? Was I an alcoholic, a pederast, smuggler, scholiast, or seminarian? Was I vegetable, mineral, or composed of various cosmic gases? What was the nature of my dreams, and what did I do with the property of others after I'd stolen it?

As an afterthought, she looked at my wrists. There was a scar on the left one, which she spanked and stroked with the tips of her fingers.

"What is this?" she asked with a menacing smile.

"That is called a scar," I said. The old man in the other room was humming a song, just loud enough to be heard.

"How did you get it?"

"I've had it since I was a year old and fell on the sidewalk with a jar of pennies. They had to rush me to the doctor to have it sewed up. It looks funny because the doctor was in a hurry to stop the bleeding and didn't do a very good job."

She leaned so close I could feel her breath on my face. "You can tell me the truth, you know," she said. "It's nothing to embarrass you."

"What are you talking about?"

"This," she said, jabbing a finger at the small twisted scar, "is clear evidence of a suicide attempt. I insist that you tell me about it."

She was a bounty hunter, paid to catch employees with drug habits, frailties, old suicide attempts. Her teeth had small crack lines that had turned brown. She looked like a vase put together again.

"I told you the truth," I insisted. "The scars are twenty-two years old."

"Tell me about your mental depression," she said. "Tell me how you put the blade to the skin and twisted it. Tell me about your cowardice, your refusal to face life. You know nothing about life!" She had made a tight little fist as if squeezing a fly to death. In her anger, her sallow face almost took on color.

"You're crazy!" I said.

My clothes were in the corner. I pushed past her, stark naked, and bundled them into my arms. Should I rush into the hall and search for a bathroom? Fly past the volunteer in a pink panic? Already I could see Mulroony's gloating face as he sent me off to Vietnam, marking the orders with a flick of his wrist.

I tried to be calm. I sat in a chair and put on my shoes and socks. Then I stood up and put on my pants, hopping around the room. They were too tight because of the shoes on my feet. Nervously I fastened each button on the shirt, and wrestled on the sport coat. There was only one thing wrong. I'd forgotten to put on underwear. Alone on the chair, they were proof of the doctor's assertions. I picked them up and held them in my right hand.

All along, Dr. Waldheim had said things like, "What do you think you're doing?" and "Where do you think you're going?" But now she said, "My report will go to Mr. Bolger as soon as possible."

"And?" I said.

"I shall disrecommend," she said crisply and coldly.

By this time the noise had reached the other room. The ancient volunteer opened the door a crack and peeked in. I waved and he waved back.

"You vill never, never work in this hospital," said the doctor.

"I do not give a damn," I replied, storming out of the room. In my anger, I felt about six feet wide in the basement hallway.

That night, at home in bed with Vicki, I started to worry about it all. Here she was pregnant—which is why our backs were turned to each other—and I'd screwed everything up. I spent the night tossing and turning, but in the morning Bolger called and then Janush. I had the job, no problem. They'd gotten the report from Waldheim, all right. She had walked it up to Personnel herself and stormed around the office. That's what she always did. They'd gotten used to her, and the blood tests and X rays were mainly what they needed anyway. They figured the rest out on their own. Janush offered congratulations and hinted that he and Waldheim used to date each other. I imagined them doing the bunny hop in a German restaurant.

But I had another theory about Waldheim. Her real name was Rosa Teal, and she'd escaped from the psych ward the night before. She'd hidden in a laundry basket and emerged wearing a white lab coat with "Dr. Waldheim" stitched on the vest pocket. It was a simple matter, with such credentials, to become the doctor she had always dreamed of being. Now she was Elsa Waldheim, a simple girl from the mountains, but one with a mission.

5

■ ■ ■ ■ ■ ■

The next day I arrived at Janush's office for orientation, walking down the hall in the direction of the crease in my pants, which today was straight ahead. Janush wasn't in, but Yvonne, the secretary, was.

"Hi!" I said.

"Carumph," she replied, pointing to her mouth. I saw she had half a piece of chocolate in the other hand, hidden behind the desk.

"Candy," she finally managed. "You want some?"

"No, thanks," I said, "they make me break out."

"How about some Sanka? I got Sanka."

"No, really. I'm fine."

"Gary will be here in a minute. You just have a seat."

I sat in a chair near Janush's desk, and in sauntered a guy wearing a gold sport coat, black pants, black shirt, black tie, and black shoes. He had bright red hair combed straight forward, but the front was butch-waxed up to a point, like a gangster Woody Woodpecker. He had a pencil-thin red moustache in the middle of a pale white face. Even though he was about my age, he seemed of an earlier generation.

"Hey, how're you doing?" he said, as if we were old acquaintances.

"Fine."

"Ee-glosh," said Yvonne.

"Name's Ed Grabowski," he said, extending his hand.

"Jim Holder." His hand was surprisingly warm. He took the seat next to me.

"This is orientation, right?"

I told him it was. Yvonne nodded yeah.

"I look forward to this here," he said. "This management thing is just my line of work."

I said that was good.

"Fits right in with my plans, being around the bodies and all."

Bodies?

"Yeah, Nancy's old man owns Princetti's, the funeral parlor on Cicero and a hundred and fifth. You know the place?"

I didn't, but Yvonne was listening with interest.

"Got a hell of a good business. Three, maybe four funerals a week. It's not bad money, you know." He unbuttoned his coat, thrust his arms through his sleeves, and leaned back in his chair. "The old man lets me do some embalming when they get busy. I get a hundred bucks for the drain and flush," he said with pride.

Yvonne looked down with disgust at her half-eaten chocolate.

"The old man's gonna set me up in my own business someday. This here's kind of a sideline while I study undertaking. You know Merrymount Academy on Western and Ninety-seventh?"

Yvonne said she did. That was her neighborhood.

"Well, that's the one," he said.

We were quiet for a moment, then he leaned close and whispered, "Tell you what, though. . . ."

Yes?

"You can make some good contacts here with the doctors. Who do you think tells them where to find a funeral director?"

"The doctor?"

"Damn right," he said.

Janush, dressed in a blue suit, entered with a tall black-haired woman in her late twenties, whom he introduced as Barbara Stevens. He put his hand around her waist. She gave him an irritated glance, but he didn't notice.

We followed Janush down the hall to a conference room filled with men and women, in roughly even numbers, wearing tan lab coats and plastic name tags. Most of them were fairly young. Everyone sat on folding chairs.

"First," he said, "let's welcome three new members to the service team. They are—stand up, Ed, attaboy—Ed Grabowski, who comes to us from Merrymount Academy, where he's studying hospital management; Barbara Stevens, recently of City Hospital, where she worked as an assistant in Medical Records; and Jim Holder, who recently graduated from Rhineland College in Indiana. He's young, boys and girls, but he's willing. Now, let's get down to business. It's been reported that people aren't handling the syringe disposals right. There have been two major stickings resulting in gamma globulin shots this week. Remember, please, to ask the nurses to twist off the needles with the pliers provided and dump both syringe and needle into the box. They're putting in the needles attached, and the damned things are punching back out through the cardboard. Ellie McCarthy, the nurse on Fifteen North, got a used needle right through the palm of her hand.

"Second, make sure you get these carts out of the hall. They're piling up by the elevators, and there's no room to move. Arrange them up and down the hall where there's room, and no hoarding carts and wheelchairs! You people on the surgical floors have got to stop your raiding of the medical units."

A few of the older hands were giving each other the eye. You could tell who the hoarders were, just by their smart-assed looks.

"And you people on the evening shift," continued Janush, "Bobby Leonardi tells me there's been some going home early. No hitting the elevators until the stroke of midnight. Romona will speak to the issue."

From a corner of the room came a short fat woman with gray hair pulled so tightly, it must have given her a headache. Her red lipstick aggressively overran her lips, perhaps to make them look fuller; but the effect was somewhat grotesque, as if there were blood on her mouth. She held a clipboard in one hand and a skinny cigarette in the other. This was Romona Fisk, our supervisor on the evening shift. She was never without the cigarette or clipboard, even when dancing. Standing next to Janush, she took a drag and started to talk, but it didn't amount to much. You could tell she thought the meeting was a bore, and on the evening shift she'd run things her way.

Janush and she mumbled on for a while, and Grabowski reached over Barbara to hand me something. It was a photo of his wife, standing on the bedroom stairs in a blue negligee. The picture was pretty murky, but it looked like she had nothing on underneath. You could see the shadows of nipples under the frothy nightgown, which was the "shorty" style popular at the time. She'd recently had her hair done, and her teeth were extra-shiny because of the photographic flash; but it was an honest smile.

"Nancy," he said with pride.

Barbara leaned over to look.

"Very nice," I said for his sake, and for hers I added, "His wife, the former Nancy Princetti."

"No!" she said with evident sarcasm. "Not one of *the* Princettis. Really?"

"That's right. The ones and onlys."

"Let me see that." She took it out of my hand and held it up to the light. Romona was droning on about Food Service.

"Well," said Ed, "what do you think?"

"She's very pretty, Ed," I whispered. But I was thinking, Who shows his wife in a nightgown to people he just met?

"She's lovely," said Barbara, "but she looks like a five-dollar whore. Next time you take a photo, why don't you have her put some clothes on?" She said it in the sweetest, most disarming way, almost as if she were flirting.

Ed did a double take. This lady next to him seemed pretty nice, but she didn't act like the girls back home. Maybe she was kidding him, that's what it was. She was a kidder.

"And another thing, Ed," she continued, "blue is not the color, simply not the color. You tell Nancy to get something else." She patted the back of his hand and stuck her chin toward the lecture. Her authority was such, Ed felt instructed rather than insulted. He would probably go home that night with a pink nightgown for Nancy. They'd make love, and he'd pose her on the stairs for a new photograph. Barbara had changed Ed's life for the next three weeks or so.

But she wasn't so happy herself. She'd never had the children she wanted, and then her husband left. He fell in love with a woman named Sylvia, who happened to be their milkman. According to Barbara, Sylvia was ugly to the bone, but he fell in love with the uniform. They ran away to Albuquerque and lived in a trailer home, and nothing ever happened to them. That's why Jack liked Sylvia so much. She made nothing happen, and you can depend on that. Barbara, on the other hand, made everything happen, especially to herself. She said she got a "jackalope" postcard from them now and then, showing a cowboy riding an animal that was half jackrabbit and half antelope; but there was no news to speak of. Once Jack pasted a picture of his face over the cowboy's face and drew a speech balloon near the mouth that said, "Ha, ha!," to show how much fun he was having. He'd been a lawyer in Chicago, but all he did in Albuquerque was sit around the trailer home and cook up his special chili.

"Oh, poo," she said, "this is boring." And so it was. Janush was back on the floor, talking about a form the clerks should use for visual acuity tests. I looked around the room: people were half asleep. But I wasn't. I was having the time of my life.

The next evening I reported for work. The hours were four until midnight, and when I pulled up near the hospital, parking spaces were easy to get. Everyone else in the world was headed in the other direction, looking tense and driving crazy. They flowed north on Lake Shore Drive, thick as mud, while only a handful of cars headed south toward the Loop. It was like free-falling. The sensation was giddy and happy, but there was also the feeling of everything blowing past your ears at high speed.

Romona Fisk held forth from an office near the sixth-floor elevator. To my surprise, it had no windows, and the room was intensely hot. A small squat fan sat in the corner making white noise, a dull drone that went on like a headache. She had her elbows on the desk, a cigarette held in both clasped hands. The others in the room were Ed and Barbara. It was Romona's job to break us in.

"Hey!" said Ed, giving me the "bang, you're dead" sign with his thumb and index finger. Barbara said hello with her dimples. Romona opened the palm of one hand by way of greeting. Otherwise, she didn't move, since her main principle was the conservation of force. After all, this was the evening shift, and things went slower. Let the rest of the world bang into each other. It was those on the evening shift who sanely held it all together.

Her first task was to check in the clerks, but she did it without moving. They came by the office. If somebody was missing, she'd have the clerk on one unit cover the other one, too. They rightfully hated this practice, and sometimes we would take up the slack ourselves. There was a clerk missing on one of my stations, Six South, but the clerk on Six North said she would handle it, to my great relief.

Romona took us on the two-dollar tour of the hospital, pointing at things of interest with her lit cigarette. We went past Housekeeping, Maintenance, Transportation, Medical Records, Admitting, and even X Ray. We saw huge stainless-steel pots of mashed potatoes being churned in Food Service, and got special permission to visit the second floor, where Surgery was located. In a cold blue-tiled hallway, we stood peering through a window at a brain surgery in progress, in spite of the late hour. It was surprisingly informal. The surgeon seemed to be telling jokes, because he waved his instruments around a lot, and the nurses were laughing. At one point, he jumped down from his stool and did a little dance in the middle of the floor. Our view of the brain was obstructed. Ed was disappointed.

When the tour was over, Romona dropped us each off at our stations and introduced us to some of the staff. Then she went to her office, saying she'd see us in the cafeteria around six P.M.

My stations were all those on the fifth, sixth, and seventh floors, including Intensive Care, Pediatrics, Orthopedics, and two large general medical and surgical units, one of which was "Social Service." This meant the people on the unit were all poor, and the state or nobody at all was paying the bill. All the equipment on Social Service, or Six South, was cheap, borrowed, or old. The beds were old wooden ones from the 1930s, with stiff hand cranks. The other units had new electric beds that did everything but the breakfast dishes, but the rooms on Social Service looked like mill-town tenements. They were also very full, six beds to a standard room. Since the sixth floor was also the lowest floor with regular patients, there was some symbolism to where the poorer patients were placed. Wealthy patients were usually given rooms on the top floor of Metropolitan or on the executive diagnostic unit, Fifteen South, where people from the big corporations went for three days of testing each year, mainly for ulcers and heart disease. These rooms were all private and had elegant furnishings. The hallways were kept in semi-darkness after dinner, and the nurses seemed to walk on cushions, noiselessly. But on Six South, there were no easy graces. All was public and loud, with clattering carts, screaming nurses, and nursing aides who could rip off your jaw just for the recreation.

I walked from one unit to another, trying to look as though I had some role. Finally I headed back to my office, which was smaller than Romona's and even less well situated. Actually, it was a former storage room, about six by eight, with ceramic tile walls and no windows. I tapped my fingers on top of the desk for a while, looked through the drawers, which were mostly empty, and went back into the hall.

There stood Robert Sage. He looked like Frankenstein's monster after three years on a diet. Two purple scars, with marks where stitches had been, ran the length of his scalp, and the hair had not grown in. His color was yellow, and his eyes were dead, but he smoked a cigarette and strolled around in an old woollen robe. As he passed by like a creature from *Night of the Living Dead,* I saw a note on his back: "My name is Robert Sage. Please return me to Six South"

"Lobotomy," said Betty Marder, one of the nurses.

"They still do them?" I asked.

"No law against it. In fact," she said, "the state of Illinois ordered this one. He couldn't stop beating his wife, he set fire to the house, and the kids are wards of the state. You should see the chart. It's amazing."

She pointed to a rack of metal charts. The patient's name was taped to the front of each chart, and they were arranged by room number. The station clerk, whose name was Ruth, had a bunch of them piled in front of her, transcribing doctor's orders. The doctors indicated when this was needed by slipping a pink piece of cardboard into the chart.

"What's more," said the nurse, "they gave his wife one, too. She's up on Eight South, in about the same condition."

"Why up there? Why not give them a double room?"

"Insurance, what else? You just take a look at the chart," she said and walked briskly down the hall, an enema bag held high in her hand.

For the first time, I entered the nursing station, and Ruth, the black station clerk, gave me an evil look.

"Whatchu doing in here?" she said.

"I need the chart of Robert Sage," I replied. "Do you have it?"

"You're not gone be looking in these charts," she said, giving what I hoped was her sternest look.

"Oh, yes, I am," I said, picking up the nearest one. Thank God, at least it was the right one.

"Romona's gonna hear 'bout this," she said, wagging a finger.

"Yes," I said, "but you work for me, and Betty said I could look at the chart."

"Well, why didn't you say so?" she said. "If Betty says so, you can do it. Just make sure you put it back where you got it."

The new management program, which hired mostly college kids and other misfits, didn't sit well with the nurses, especially the supervisors, who saw their own roles threatened. Nurses ran hospitals, by God, nurses and doctors. Ruth thought that way, too: besides, she had been passed over for promotion when they started the program.

I took the chart to the back of the station and sat on a chair. The history and progress notes, on lined paper, told the story. After several years of odd behavior, including tattooing his penis with the picture of a whale and setting fire to the neighborhood cats, Sage had brought on the slow wrath of the state, which made the lobotomy decision. Drugs and shock treatments hadn't worked, and he had a green card, so the state would cover his expenses. Since his wife was also crazy (made crazy, perhaps, by him), they'd ordered one for her, too. But her financial situation was different. Through her father, Ellen Sage had insurance, which meant she could stay on the neurological unit. After the Sages recovered, the social worker planned to have them live together again, like Adam and Eve in the garden. The main problem was who would do the cooking.

"This is a hoot," I said.

"Mind your own business," said Ruth.

Betty Marder came by and shrugged.

"I thought lobotomies went out with dungeons," I told her.

"Believe me," she said, "he's happier now. Just look at the guy."

There he was again, leaning on his elbows at the tall nursing station desk.

"Cigarette," he said, pointing at his mouth.

"Not now," said Betty in a slightly loud voice, as if he couldn't hear. "You have cigarette later, before you go to bed."

"Heap big cigarette, ugh!" said Ruth, which got her a punch in the shoulder from Betty.

"I keep all his cigarettes here," she said, taking a set of keys from her pocket and opening a drawer at the back of the station. There were two or three boxes of very small vials, each with a different color-coding, and a pack of Pall Malls.

"Narcotics. This one here is morphine," she said, holding up one of the vials and flicking it with her finger. "It'll cure whatever ails you."

"And then some," said Ruth, as if she knew.

"Narcotics," repeated Robert Sage, pronouncing the word perfectly.

The nurse put the vial on the desk and locked the drawer again. Then she reached onto a shelf and pulled down a disposable syringe and needle, each in its own paper wrapping. After assembling the two, she snapped off the head of the vial, removed the plastic shield from the needle, and sucked the watery liquid into the syringe. All of us watched with fascination.

"Me," said the patient from 601, pointing.

"No, not me," said Betty, sticking out her chin. "You have a cigarette later."

"Later," he said.

"You give me now," said Ruth, holding out her arm and spanking the vein. "Make Ruth feel good."

"This is for Mr. Johnson, fool," said Betty. "Cancer give much pain."

There was a light on down the hall where somebody needed help, and the room number on the chart indicated it was William Johnson's. The Kardex, which listed each patient's drug and treatment regimen, said he could have morphine every four hours. More often might kill him, and only the disease itself was allowed to do that. A woman stood outside Mr. Johnson's room, looking down the hall at us. Her arms were folded, and she looked impatient.

"Pain," said Robert Sage, pointing at his head.

"No pain," said Betty Marder, already halfway down the hall, holding the syringe.

A failure of technology can result in acts of kindness. Years ago, the hospital had installed an intercom system so the nurses could talk to the patients directly and not have to walk to the room. Being the first of its kind, it didn't work well, so the nurses forgot about it. A long panel of lights and switches that looked pretty antique rested at the front of the station, between two sections of charts. Everyone ignored them, watching instead for lights above the doors of the rooms. This was nicer for the patient, since it meant more contact with the staff, but it also meant more steps for the nurses and aides. They had to walk to the room, find out what the patient wanted, return to the station to get it, and then go back to the room. On a given evening, a nurse would walk about twenty-five miles. But the sheer exertion of answering all the lights sometimes had the opposite effect: in the absence of the nurse, aides would sit at the station talking while the halls were lit up like Christmas trees. While Betty was taking care of Mr. Johnson, three lights were shining on the other corridor.

Robert Sage still stood congenially at the desk, a Mona Lisa smile on his face. He reached over, picked up a chart, and opened it, as if to read.

"Hey," I said, "you can't read that."

"He shore can't," said Ruth, "that's why we let him do it," and then, under her breath, she said, "Stupid honky."

"Honky!" Robert Sage said brightly.

"You damn right!" said Ruth, giving a square-toothed smile.

Ed and Barbara walked around the corner.

"How's it going, my man?" said Ed. "You ready to eat?"

"I hear the meat loaf is simply divine," said Barbara.

"Yum," I said and joined them.

We left Robert Sage to his own devices, flipping through the medical chart with the appearance of understanding.

"Who was that?" asked Barbara.

"Dr. Robert Sage," I said, "who sees through stone."

"Huh?" said Ed, hitting the down elevator.

"The wisest of the wise," I said, "and the happiest man in the world."

"Except for you, Ed," said Barbara, giving him a punch on the shoulder. He blushed, because he didn't know what else to do.

Romona joined us in the cafeteria. She was halfway through a story about her son, the real-estate failure, when the gravel voice of a woman came over the loudspeaker system: "Dr. Blue! Room 621, Six South. Dr. Blue, Room 621, Six South." It was repeated several times, but by the second, half of the medical staff in the cafeteria had jumped to their feet and were running from the room.

Romona was flushed and excited. "Come on!" she said. "This ought to be good. It's your unit, Jim."

We headed after the fleeing doctors and nurses. Some of them were standing by the second-floor elevator, impatiently staring up at the light; others were clambering up the staircase. Romona decided on the elevator but pointed toward the stairs for the rest of us. "Not for me," she said, pointing to her heart. "But the rest of you go that way."

"What's the deal?" said Ed, shrugging his shoulders.

"Somebody's having a heart attack," said Romona. "Hurry up, for Christ's sake! They might need supplies."

Ed and I headed up the stairs as fast as we could go, but Barbara was just behind us. The stairwell was filled with breathing and clatter, and we burst through the sixth-floor door dizzy with the exertion. People were streaming down the hall in white coats, interns with their pockets full of notes, residents in longer white coats, stethoscopes bouncing around their necks. We followed timidly, trying to act like we knew what we were doing. Romona wasn't there yet, so we stood around on the other side of the hall, trying to catch a peek of the action.

It had to be Mr. Johnson. His wife was standing alone at the deep end of the hall, holding her head with both hands. Barbara walked down to her, and, after a few words, they sat down like they'd known each other for years.

Romona came lumbering up, swinging her clipboard and half out of breath, even though she'd taken the elevator. "You're gonna love this," she said. "Come on." She led us into the room, where we could see what was going on. The medical personnel had filtered down to about five people called the "arrest team." Every evening one was assembled: the medical resident on call, in this case a Dr. Rickles; the intern assigned to that unit; the anesthesiologist on duty, a Dr. Ramanujan; an EKG technician; and an inhalation therapist, who hadn't shown up yet.

The resident stood at the head of the bed, shouting orders. Beside him, sticking a tube down Mr. Johnson's throat, was Dr. Ramanujan, but it wasn't going too well. She maneuvered and pushed, but the tube wouldn't cooperate. In frustration, she threw it to the floor and reached into the drawer of a large red portable unit, called the crash cart. Every floor was supposed to have one. It was my job, in fact, to stock the thing. On it was everything needed for an emergency like this: saline solutions, various drugs for the heart, IV tubing, a portable EKG machine for monitoring the heart, and a lethal-looking device with two round metal "paddles" called the defibrillator. This was used in case the heart stopped altogether; you placed these paddles on the chest and shot electricity through the body, to shock the heart into action.

The anesthesiologist had trouble finding a tube the right size. The new one didn't seem to work either; when she removed it from his mouth there was blood on it. If she kept this up much longer, she was going to dig the guy a new throat. The resident looked pissed.

"Give me that, God damn it," he said, and grabbed the tube out of her hand. "I'm going down through the nose." Tossing the old one aside, he took a thinner tube of red rubber, greased it with a packet of KY jelly, and pushed it down Mr. Johnson's nose with slow, twisting motions. Dr. Ramanujan stood against the wall, her arms folded calmly over her chest; you could tell she was humiliated. The resident had seriously broken protocol, and there would be confrontations later. Meanwhile, Mr. Johnson, his chin thrust toward the ceiling, eyes closed, turned bluer and bluer. That's why they called Dr. Blue over the loudspeaker—the patient turns blue, or cyanotic.

Dr. Rickles taped the tube to Mr. Johnson's face. Then he attached a large rubber bulb, the Ambu bag, to the end of the tube and started squeezing with both hands. The bulb gave off an ugly wheezing sound, like water going down a bathtub.

"Hey, you!" said Dr. Rickles, looking at me.

"Me?" I said, pointing at my chest.

"Commere and squeeze this thing," he commanded.

"Go!" said Romona, giving me a shove.

I tripped over some wiring and stumbled across the room, but soon I was squeezing the Ambu bag on the count of twelve per minute, as Rickles had instructed. The room was a blur of action. All the while, the intern, a sleepy-looking

guy not much older than me, had been pushing with the heels
of both hands, his arms stiff, his full weight thrown, on Mr.
Johnson's breastbone. You could see the chest sink under his
pressure. This was keeping the heart going, while I was doing
Mr. Johnson's breathing. Betty Marder was busy setting up
an IV. At the same time, the EKG technician strapped electrodes to the arms and legs and placed a brass cup on Mr.
Johnson's chest by means of a suction device. All these were
attached to wires that ran into the crash cart. By now the
whole area was littered with wiring, like the engine of a car.
Rickles gave his attention to the EKG machine perched on
top of the cart. Out of it ran a thin gray strip of paper with
mountainous black marks that indicated the rhythm of the
heart. It slid through his hands—where he read it like a stock
report—and dangled to the floor, adding to the other debris
of death. Rickles ordered drugs as the paper demanded. These
were injected by the nurse right into the IV tubing, through
a little rubber membrane.

The intern looked winded. By now he had both knees on
the bed and was sweating over his task. "Need . . .
some . . . help . . . here," he panted.

"Let's get the board in place," said Rickles, pulling two
pieces of equipment from the back of the cart. They looked
like Rube Goldberg had made them. One was a highly pol-
ished piece of wood, about three feet long and two feet wide,
with holes and metal collars on both ends. The other was a
piece of stainless steel bent into an elongated U to which a
plunger, made of red plastic the size of a fist, was attached.
At the count of three everyone, including Ramanujan, lifted
Mr. Johnson by the shoulders while Rickles slipped the board
beneath him, level with his chest. Then we let him fall back,
and I resumed his breathing. Rickles and the intern, working
on each side, snapped the metal piece into the board's metal
collars. The "fist" was now located a few inches over Mr.
Johnson's breastbone. After a few adjustments, like lowering
a piano stool, Rickles had it set right, and the intern, with
far less effort, started pumping on the handle. The red fist

pressed into his chest with powerful ease, then sprang up again.

The patient was apparently stabilizing; Rickles looked calmer. My hands began to ache, so I skipped a beat now and then to let the strength come back to them. Romona and Ed still watched intently, the best spectators a heart attack ever had.

A heavyset inhalation therapist burst through the doorway, mumbling apologies. He started in my direction, as if to take over.

Rickles was beside himself. "Get out of here, jerk," he roared, sticking his index finger under the poor guy's nose. "Get fucking out of here!" He pointed to the door like the evil baritone in an opera. As the therapist fled, humiliated, Romona gave him a withering look of disdain.

"Asshole!" hissed Rickles, as an afterthought. Then, after a pause, he said, "Shit!" I saw what he was referring to: the EKG was going crazy. The thin black stylus flew back and forth wildly, making marks on the paper like an angry two-year-old. You could hear the machine clicking desperately.

"Tachycardia," said Rickles. "Everybody step back."

When he twisted a dial on the defibrillator, a red light came on. Then he picked up the paddles; the intern, without being asked, squirted a white fluid on them that looked like runny toothpaste. This was to help conduct electricity. He placed the paddles on Mr. Johnson's chest, each side of the heart, at a distance from each other, and looked around the bed. "Back!" he screamed at me. "Nobody touch the bed." I backed away as far as I could, and he pushed two red buttons attached to the paddle handles. A needle on the machine swung all the way right, and Mr. Johnson's body seemed to leap a foot off the bed, first the head and then the feet, in a kind of ripple effect. Immediately, everyone took up his old position, as if nothing had happened.

Rickles looked at the EKG again, but nothing had changed. Tachycardia, I later learned, meant the heart was totally out of control, literally collapsing upon itself. When the heart was normal, its contractions created a "sinus rhythm" on the EKG characterized by a sharp "spike" or *V* followed by a slurred lower-case *r*. These would parade confidently when everything was going right, accompanied by a small beeping sound.

"Again," said Rickles, poised with the paddles. Everyone stepped back, and Mr. Johnson again took to the air by force of his own muscular contraction. Nothing had changed on the EKG. While we mechanically moved the blood and breath, the heart itself was giving up. Every tactic the doctor tried only created a new dilemma. Finally, the EKG stylus fluttered and stalled, and a straight black line appeared on the paper, the straightest line you'll ever see. The moment of death spilled out of the machine and piled up on the floor. The machine hummed with eerie satisfaction in the otherwise quiet room.

6

∎ ∎ ∎ ∎ ∎ ∎

"My God," I said to myself.

"Aw, shoot," Romona said softly, in her corner of the room.

"That's it, folks, let's bag it," said Rickles, tossing the paddles onto the crash cart and snapping off the EKG. "Samuels, you do the write-up, and I'll sign it later." The intern nodded and started to leave the room, but Rickles called after him, "Time of death, six forty-three. I'll talk to the wife."

Everyone but Betty Marder, the anesthesiologist, and I immediately left the room. Ed and Romona left, too, giving a sign that they'd meet me later.

Already the nurse was cleaning up the place, picking up used endotracheal tubes, pieces of paper and plastic, used syringes. It looked like a battlefield. The only casualty lay on the bed, his skin in various shades of red, blue, and gray, his open mouth revealing old yellow teeth. She took the IV

out of his arm, and a drop of blood appeared at the point of
entry, at the center of an enormous bruise. A murky catheter
stuck out of his penis. On the whole he looked like a battered
puppet. The anesthesiologist removed the Ambu bag, but
the tip of the endotracheal tube still protruded from Mr.
Johnson's face. This last task completed, she left quietly,
apparently still smoldering.

Betty Marder gave me a shrug and continued cleaning the
room.

"Is there anything I can do?" I asked.

"You can tell one of the aides to get her tail in here," she
said. "You'll also have to order the death pack and take care
of the belongings. I think there's a watch and wallet," she
continued, pointing at the bedside table. "It's your job to
release them to the family, plus take him downstairs."

"Downstairs?" I said.

"To the morgue. It's the manager's job—there's no transportation around in the evenings."

There was a wedding ring on Mr. Johnson's finger, but
Betty was having trouble getting it off. I handed her a packet
of KY jelly that was lying on the crash cart. She smeared
some on the finger, twisted, and in an instant the ring slipped
off. "This goes with the belongings," she said, handing it to
me. "There's a list inside the death pack."

"Wonderful." The ring was surprisingly warm to the touch.
I slipped it into the pocket of my tan lab coat and went into
the hall.

"You did just swell," said Romona, "a real classy job."

"Yeah," said Ed, envy in his voice.

"Don't worry, Ed," said Romona. "You'll get your chance
real soon. You got Neuro Intensive and ENT. There's a lot
of action up there."

"What's this about a death pack?" I said.

"Don't worry," she said. "I'll order it for you." She went
over to a drawer, took out a yellow form about the size of
a traveler's check, and stamped it with Mr. Johnson's charge
plate. Then she went to the back of the station where the

pneumatic tube system was breathing and hissing, picked up one of the clear plastic tubes with leather and rubber to cushion each end, inserted the form, opened a roaring valve, and sent the tube slithering through the pipes down to Central Supply.

"That man's been through hell," said Ruth, referring to Mr. Johnson. "Cancer of the spine." At the end of the hall, Barbara, Mrs. Johnson, and Dr. Rickles made a sad-looking trio.

"Better call the Reaper," Romona said to Ruth.

"Already done it," she said, "but that man can smell it on his own."

"Speak of the devil," said Romona.

Around the corner came a thin elderly man in a cheap brown suit. He, too, was carrying a clipboard, but he held it like a scroll.

"I understand you have an expiration," he said to Romona.

"That's right. William Johnson in 621."

"Has the family been notified?"

"See for yourself," she said, pointing down the hall.

"Very good. How about the belongings?"

"We're waiting for the pack right now," said Romona.

"And who are these young men? I don't believe I've had the pleasure."

"Norm Cane, Jim Holder and Ed Grabowski. Jim is in charge of the unit."

"Well, that's nice, young man," he said, offering a limp hand that smelled of cigarettes. "Just remember, death is an important event, and we must be judicious in dealing with the family." He put a finger over his lips when he said the word *family,* as if it was sacred. His name tag said "Normal Cane, Administration."

"I'll remember," I promised.

"Things to do," he said, waving his clipboard and turning in the direction of the doctor and Mrs. Johnson. His silver hair, mixed with dirty blond, was shiny under the ceiling lights. Robert Sage, who'd been walking up and down, gave him a little wave as they passed in the hall.

When he was out of range, Romona said, "Now you see why we call him the Reaper. He's the evening administrator, but there's nothing to do but release a body now and then. He spends all his time hanging around the corpse's family, pretending he's somebody important."

"What a bizarre character," I said.

"I kind of liked the guy," protested Ed.

A red light started flashing near the nursing station. Ruth got up and opened the silver doors of the dumbwaiter, and there was the death pack wrapped in plastic.

"You take it," she said, handing it to me. "These things give me the creeps."

"Actually, it's a scam," said Romona. "There's only a couple of sheets in there, some safety pins, an ID tag for the big toe. That and the valuables list. And we charge the insurance company seventy-five bucks."

I opened up the pack, and she was right. It was like opening a present and finding only empty boxes, one inside the other. There was only one thing she hadn't described, a large pad of some kind with gauze strings attached.

We took everything into the room, where Betty and the nurse's aide were giving Mr. Johnson a bath. They had him turned on his side, just like a living patient, but his limbs and mouth gave him away. On the whole, he looked much better. The catheter and endotracheal tube were gone, and his hair was combed. Much of the equipment was back on the cart, properly washed.

"What's this thing?" I said, holding up the mysterious gauzy object.

The nursing aide thought this was very funny.

"It's a diaper," said Betty Marder without a trace of humor.

"Come on," I said, "what is it really?"

"It's a diaper, honest to God. We put them on the expirations so they don't shit on themselves."

I didn't believe it.

"It's true," said Romona.

"It's the anal sphincter," said Ed with seeming expertise. "We get them like that all the time, like they was babies."

"Huh?" said the nurse.

"Never mind," I said. "Here's everything you need."

We watched while the body was dressed. The ritual was overpowering: the ablutions, diapering, binding, and wrapping. There were no preservative powders or eucalyptus leaves, of course, only a couple of worn-out sheets with "Chicago Laundry Company" stamped in ink on a corner.

Romona, Ed, and I watched them put on the diaper, and it did look like a baby's. Then they tied the ankles and wrists together with gauze, in order to make the handling of the corpse more manageable. The wrists crossed over the chest, palms down, like old statues of saints. One ankle rested on top of the other. The ID tag, which had been stamped with his name and patient number, was tied to a big toe. Finally, they wrapped him in his cut-rate shroud, which was laid out under the corpse like a diamond. When all the ends were wrapped tightly and secured with safety pins, Mr. Johnson looked like a handmade cigarette. Using safety pins, they attached two more name tags to the outside of the shroud. Now the job was done.

"Aren't you forgetting something?" said Romona.

"What?" said the nurse.

"What if the wife wants to see him? He's all covered up."

"No problem," she said, neatly unwrapping only the head, so the face peered out of its bunting, serene and distant.

"How's that?" she said, stepping back to inspect her work.

"Beautiful," said Ed.

"Let's get the things together," Romona said, "then we'll see the wife." There was an atmosphere of preparation and care, as if a party were being planned. She opened his locker, which was set into the wall, and pulled out the clothes. They were old sturdy things: black tie shoes that would never wear out, a white dress shirt that was a little frayed at the collar, and a blue suit styled in a forgotten fashion. The jacket was surprisingly heavy, as if there was sand in the lining, and the seat of the pants was shiny. We lay the clothes on a neighboring bed.

"How do we know if this stuff is his?" I said.

"It's his, all right," said the aide. "Don't you worry about that." She reached into the bedside table and pulled out a watch and wallet.

"Let me see that," said Romona. She started to go through the limp old wallet, which smelled of sweat and age. There was a five-dollar bill and three ones, and a faded photograph, now very much wrinkled, of Mr. Johnson and an attractive brunette. It must have been the forties, since he was wearing an army uniform. It wasn't clear to me if the woman was Mrs. Johnson, but it might have been. She was standing up very straight and smiling into the camera brightly. There was an orchid pinned to her dress that opened toward her face.

"Sad, isn't it?" said Romona, holding it for me to see. Ed, meanwhile, was efficiently listing everything on the bed. One blue suit, one white shirt, two black shoes, eight dollars in cash, two packs of Camels, a toothpick, a pair of white socks. Everything had to be listed, even the lint in his pockets. The hospital wanted proof in case the family claimed something was missing.

"That's about it," said Ed.

We put everything in a large brown paper bag and attached another name tag to it. Romona attached one copy of the valuables list to the top of the bag. "All done," she said.

Outside was a patient who'd been ousted from the room in the commotion. "Can I come in now?" he said. "My wife's supposed to call." He looked to be in his fifties, and was wearing a bathrobe from home with little blue anchors on it.

"Not yet," Romona said. "It'll be about an hour."

"I guess he died, didn't he?" said the roommate.

"I really can't say," Romona said, closing the door behind us.

"Too bad," said the man. "He was a nice fellow. White Sox fan, like me."

There wasn't much we could say to that.

"You come back in about an hour," Romona repeated.

"Fine, fine," He turned back toward the lounge, where another patient was waiting for him, looking up expectantly. They shook their heads back and forth, as if to say, "Now, isn't that something."

Barbara, Norm Cane, and the wife approached. Ed handed the bag to me. He and Romona stepped to the side.

"I understand you have something for me," the wife said tensely.

"Yes, ma'am," I said, holding up the bag. "There's a list of belongings we'd like you to sign."

She eyed the bag as if it contained a trick of some kind.

I started to read from the list. "There's one blue suit, two black shoes, two packs of Camels . . ."

"Never mind all that. Where do I sign?" She seemed enormously tired, and signed the form jerkily, as if she might not finish. I studied her face to see if she was the one in the photo; but if she was, age and worry had disguised her.

"I'll take these things for you," Barbara said, picking up the bag. They started toward the patient lounge, but Cane said, "Wait a minute. We have to make sure of the money. How much was there, young man?"

"Eight dollars," I said.

"Does that sound about right, Mrs. Johnson?"

"I really don't know," she said. "Bill never carried much money."

"How about a watch? Was there a watch?"

I said there was, and Cane checked the list to make sure.

"There's always a watch," he said. "How about a wedding ring?"

You couldn't have knocked me over with a sledgehammer. A great force had fixed me to the floor. Barbara looked at me funny, as if my face had done something acrobatic.

"There was a ring," I said. "I have it here somewhere."

Nervous fingers a mile from my shoulder reached into my pocket and pulled out a perfect circle of gold. I held it up for Cane to see, then handed it to Barbara. I was afraid if I gave it to Mrs. Johnson she might start crying again. "I'm sorry," I said, "but in the rush of things I forgot to include it."

"This looks very bad, young man," said Cane.

"Oh, shut up, Norm," said Romona.

Mrs. Johnson thanked us and dropped the ring into her purse. She seemed more relaxed than before. It was as if, by having the belongings, she had attained some understanding.

"Would you like to visit the room?" said Romona.

"Do I have to?" said Mrs. Johnson, looking at Barbara.

"It's up to you," she said.

With Barbara holding her arm, she headed toward the room. Romona joined them, refusing to miss the visitation she herself had suggested. Betty Marder and the nurse's aide would still be there, standing discreetly to the side.

"It's a touching moment," said Cane in a voice like organ music.

"Yeah," agreed Ed.

"I guess we'll need a cart," I said, "to take him to the morgue."

I walked to the service side of the elevators and found a gray cart with a two-inch pad on top. Two straps hung down at the sides, like the seat belts in cars. I wheeled it around by the front of the station.

"You have to take off the pad," said the Reaper, "in case there's any drainage."

Ed and I removed the pad and stuffed it into a small supply room next to the station. Then we pushed the bare cart over by the wall where it wouldn't look too obtrusive when Mrs. Johnson came out. Pretty soon she appeared, crying worse than before, and Barbara looked a little angry, as if the visit was a bad idea. Romona followed them, beaming with satisfaction. They went straight into the lounge. Romona came back and joined us.

"The tough part," she said, "is getting the body out of the

room and into the elevator without anybody seeing what's happened, but first we've got to get him on the cart."

Cane went to the rear of the unit, where Samuels and Rickles were working on the chart, but they completely ignored him, so he sat down by the station clerk, who shifted away.

Wheeling the cart ahead of us, we headed for the room. Mr. Johnson's face was now covered, and he looked like a mummy. We shoved the cart right next to the bed, which the aide had raised so it was slightly higher than the vehicle. It's hard enough to lift a body; you want gravity on your side, not working against you. The technology was all worked out. The nurses had also placed a doubled sheet under the body. Each of us was to grab a corner, and on the count of three we were to lift and swing the body over onto the cart. I stood on the far side with Betty; Ed and the aide took the cart side. The only problem was, the body was distant from us, and we couldn't get leverage. The first heave failed, and Mr. Johnson landed on his side, half on and half off the bed.

"Shit!" said Betty. "We've got to get on the bed."

To Ed's great amusement, the nurse and I climbed onto the bed and stood on our knees in order to get a better hold on the sheet. The next attempt was easy. The body floated over the cart and landed as smooth as fog. The aide strapped the body down, in case we took a corner too sharp, then covered it with another sheet.

Betty and I climbed back down from the bed, blushing. When we were on the bed, a fierce sex static had passed between us, and we looked at each other differently now.

"You two looked good up there," said Ed with a stupid grin.

"Get lost!" said Betty.

Romona gave me a knowing wink. "OK," she said. "Time to call the elevator." Picking up the patient phone, she dialed three numbers and talked directly to the elevator operator.

"Bud?" she said. "Romona. Got a live one for you. Sixth floor."

Betty and the aide went back to their work. Romona and I waited with the body, just inside the door, while Ed closed all the doors on the hall, as well as the doors to the patient lounge. The idea was to prevent anyone from seeing the body. Then, on Romona's instructions, Ed stationed himself in the hall where he could see the service elevator. It only took a minute, and he waved to us furtively, like a convict inviting his buddy to dash across a prison yard. Romona and I, one on each side of the cart, sped out of the room and down the hall, glancing in each direction. Robert Sage stood at the door of his room as we sailed past, but nobody minded him, and he looked straight through us. The operator, seated on a stool, was a very old man whose right hand trembled. "Where to?" was his mumbled, apparently standard joke. Romona rolled her eyes, the doors slid shut, and we descended in one long motion into the cool basement.

It didn't matter who saw us there, since only employees were allowed in the area. Anyone who worked near the morgue had to expect a body to cruise around the corner every now and then. A maintenance man walked by, dressed in workman's green and wearing a belt full of tools. He gave Romona a friendly wave and continued on his way. Robert Holiday, a well-dressed young black man who supervised the maids in Housekeeping, stepped out of his office and smiled.

"Hi, Bob," said Romona. "How're you doing?"

"Oh, pretty good," he said. "How about you?"

"They're dying like flies up there," she said with mock drama.

"Well, you tell them to stop that, Mrs. Fisk."

"Got a bed needs making up," she said. "Room 621."

"His?" he said, nodding at the body. "You need the Bomb?"

"No," she said. "It was only cancer. Just wash the bed like usual."

We went around the corner to the morgue. Romona inserted her key, and pushed open the door. It didn't look like much, but Ed was excited. He entered eagerly and gawked at the walls. There were only two small rooms, not what you'd expect from a large hospital. The one we were in was painted gray and kept very chilly. On one side was a row of doors with the same kind of locks you see on trucks. There were twelve of them all together, four rows of three, but the top ones were pretty high, at the level of my shoulders. Only two of them had cards on the door, meaning they were oc- cupied, and all those were on the middle row. They often used the bottom ones, Romona said, for left-over specimens, but I didn't ask what she meant. She pointed at a vacant one in the middle row, and I snapped open the door. It was empty, all right. Cold sick air came out of it and struck us in the face.

"Pee-yoo!" said Romona. "Let's get this over quick."

I pulled on the freezing metal handle, and the slab came sliding out. It was about six inches deep, and in one corner there was congealed blood and plasma. We pulled the cart next to the slab, as we had with the bed, but this time the slab was higher. We were going to have to lift, and conditions were awkward. On the count of three, we heaved on the sheet, but we'd forgotten to lock the wheels of the cart. It slithered away as the body brushed against it. Now we were holding the full weight of the body. Ed made a second des- perate effort, which caused Mr. Johnson to roll up my arms, right into my face. I was virtually holding him by myself. Seeing the emergency, Romona threw her weight under the body, lifting it over the edge of the slab. The head and shoul- ders struck with a thud, and the legs dangled. There were going to be bruises on the body that would surprise even the undertaker.

Ed thought it was very funny. "You should have seen your face," he snorted, doubled over in a laugh.

Romona couldn't conceal her smile. "It's tough the first time," she said. "You'll get used to it."

We put the legs onto the slab, and I tried unsuccessfully to push it back into the wall. Apparently the weight of the body had bound the metal track. On Romona's advice, I lifted and pushed at the same time, and the slab sailed in smoothly. Ed suavely flipped the door shut and put yet another ID tag inside a slot on the front of the door.

"Want a cigarette?" Romona asked, lighting up a Lucky Strike.

"No thanks," I said. "How long are we going to stay here anyway?"

"What's the rush?" she said. Blue smoke from the cigarette rose slowly through the cold air.

"Hey, look at this!" Ed said. He'd wandered into the neighboring room, and we followed. The walls were lined with shelves containing various organs. It looked like they were mostly brains, and they were tilted in many directions, like people at a ball game. There were other fleshy objects, but you couldn't tell what they were, probably kidneys and livers. He walked from jar to jar, reading the labels with intense fascination.

A damp coldness came out of the cement floor and walls, but it was nothing compared to the chill created by the stainless-steel table at the center of the room. Designed like a trough, it had a drain at its center, and at the head, laid out neatly, were several instruments, the most dramatic of which was a compact power saw. Romona said the pathologist's assistant, known as the Diener, used this to cut the body open from the crotch to the chin. Then he would lop off the top of the head. After they spread out the ribs a little, the doctor would search inside the body, detailing what he found on a tape recorder. This explained the microphone attached to the side of the table by a gooseneck extension. It made the table look strangely like a pulpit, and what a church it was. The choir was always in attendance, including a row of fetuses with large beautiful heads, one of whom had its back turned like a recalcitrant deacon. While the doctors would vary from day to day, the Diener and congregation were always the same. Romona said the Diener was a tall black guy with sunken cheeks whom everyone knew as James. Nobody knew if that was his first name or his last, and nobody asked.

Whenever he entered the cafeteria, wearing his long white coat, the place got very quiet.

Ed asked if he could see an autopsy someday. Romona said sure, she'd seen lots of them. The worst part, she said, was the smell of bone when they cut through the skull.

That was it for me. The smell of formaldehyde, the sense of being watched by the bottled fetuses, and all this talk: it was too much. I grabbed the cart, threw open the outer door, and left. Romona and Ed caught up with me in front of the elevator, still gossiping about the morgue. My breathing was fast and shallow, as if there wasn't enough room in my lungs, and my throat was so tight it was hard to swallow. This was the first time I'd ever felt this way, but over the next couple of years it would come back of its own account, for no apparent reason.

Bud, the elevator operator, mumbled angrily as we got on. It had something to do with red ripe tomatoes. I noticed one of his arms was lame, as if he'd had a stroke.

Back on the sixth floor, we put the pad back on the cart. Then we remembered we'd missed our dinner. The three of us joined Barbara in the cafeteria, where the assistant head of Food Service, Ulysses Thomas, a former football player who looked like a muscular Buddha, arranged for us to get new trays of food without extra charge. We ate in silence at first, then Romona started to tell her hospital stories. There was one about the rich woman on Nine North who had kept a stack of five-dollar bills on her bedside table to tip the orderlies and nursing aides. The strategy proved so effective that aides were lined up in the hallway outside her room; they came from all over the hospital, hoping to get a chance to serve her. If someone took her to X Ray, she gave them five dollars going down and another five coming back. Romona said the rest of the hospital nearly shut down for lack of help. Alma Pinson and Malvinia Graven, the powerful nursing supervisors, flew onto the unit in a rage, but the aides were too quick for them. They disappeared like spirits into patients' rooms, and the supervisors failed to get the goods

on a single employee. When Pinson and
the woman's room, she offered them each fiv
her off the bedpan.

We stayed in the cafeteria for almost two hou
realized we were less Romona's employees than h
audience. She didn't care if we got back to work, and
were glad to stay. In no time at all, our first day on the jo
was over.

Graven went into
e dollars to take

rs, and I
r new
we

7

■   ■   ■   ■   ■   ■

It was Saturday morning, and everyone was around the apartment. In his room Rose the Poet worked on a poem about the world's fattest man. He'd been at it for a day and a half without any sleep, keeping himself up with coffee and speed. He'd gotten the idea from a show on television about a man in Scotland who weighed eight hundred pounds. I told him I didn't think anyone in Scotland really weighed that much. They always looked so bony and hardy. He said you could believe most of what you saw, especially on TV. The work was two hundred pages long and still growing, composed in what he called "clandestine dithyrambs." I took this to mean free verse, but I never got a full explanation.

Vicki had gone back to Wisconsin for the week, and we'd kept in touch by phone. I thought we were too young to get married, but she wasn't so sure. Whenever we talked about what to do, I could see a Methodist church deep in her face.

We had to do something soon, one way or another. She was getting more pregnant, not less, and while it created a bond between us that hadn't existed before, it also placed an obstacle.

The day after she learned the results of the test, we went down by the lake, walking all the way through the park, past the entrance to Lincoln Park Zoo, where the ratty bears slept in their cages and the lions were too tired to come outside on a hot summer day. We passed the statue of Shakespeare, hidden in a bunch of bushes across from the Conservatory—all you could see was the top of his bald head sticking above some trees. In the Conservatory itself the city grew exotic plants, many of which you could find in your grandmother's living room: rubber trees, snake plants, and patches of baby tears. We turned right on Fullerton and went by a group of picnickers barbecuing spareribs. Their kids ran around in circles just to be running, but the adults were already wilted at eleven in the morning, that's how hot it was. One fat woman sat on a blanket with her legs spread, staring blankly at the ground. She didn't move as long as we were there, and when I turned at the end of the block, she was still in that position. They'd chosen a spot right next to the parkway, which was filled with cars and noise; on the other side was the sidewalk. There should have been a sign in the ground that said The American Family, Modern Era. If they thought this site was bucolic and peaceful, what kind of neighborhood were they from? Other families were picnicking in the parking lot itself.

At the end of the zoo was the rookery, with a small lagoon surrounded by flat rocks and trees, and some ducks clacking. It wasn't much, but a few young couples were scattered around the place, trying to fall in love. Vicki pointed at a couple holding hands and kissing with just the tips of their lips, as if they were birds. They looked like the sort of people who would dress in matching T-shirts that said "I Love Bob" and "I Love Nancy."

We walked through the spooky underpass at Lake Shore

Drive, which was cool but smelly. You could hear the cars roaring overhead. It seemed each tire left a thin trail of rubber, like a snail. Everything was connected by heat, sweat, and endurance. The day was so brightly overexposed, it gave you an ache between the eyes.

The worn triangle of grass at Fullerton Beach was beginning to fill with sunbathers. Few bothered with the water, which in Chicago, even in late summer, could be pretty cold. Stripping down to our bathing suits, we sat on a concrete ledge, watching the hectic families try to keep their kids from drowning. There was a clear separation of social groups. We were the singles, aloof and cool, with perfect bodies. They were chaotic, elemental, and real—to be avoided at all cost. A pack of kids, sand and mud all over their bodies, ran into the lake, shrieking with delight. The mothers sank back into their gothic romances.

Vicki put her lips up to mine, pretending we were Bob and Nancy.

"Kiss, kiss," she quacked, then stuck her tongue in my mouth. She smelled salty and earthy.

"I love you, Holder," she whispered.

"I love you, too."

"Say it like you mean it."

"I love you, too," I said.

A motorboat went by just beyond the buoys dividing the swimming area from miles of lake beyond, bouncing on the waves with a spanking, tinnish sound. Two hotshots inside waved their cans of beer.

"What are we going to do?" Vicki asked.

"I don't really know," I said, squinting out at the water.

"You do, too," she said. "You want an abortion."

I denied it, but we both knew what would happen, and that night, back in the apartment, sweating, I called the number Vicki had gotten from a friend who'd gone through an abortion last year. Everything had worked out well.

The phone rang, and as instructed, I asked for Dr. Wells. The answering service said someone would call right back.

Abortions were illegal, except, we'd heard, in London and Kansas City. London and Kansas City? It didn't make any sense. But you could also get one in Chicago, if you called Dr. Wells.

Half an hour later, the telephone rang.

I picked it up nervously.

"You want Dr. Wells?" said a tough male voice. It sounded like he had a cigar in his mouth and was calling from a pay phone.

"Yes, someone gave me your number. She said you provided . . . a certain service."

"Yeah, that's right. What kinda service you lookin' for?"

"Uh, well . . ." I couldn't bring myself to say it. What if the moment I said *abortion* the vice squad broke down the door?

"My friend is pregnant," I said, voice trailing into the wire.

"You telling me you want an abortion?"

"Yes," I managed. "Yes, that's right."

"Don't worry, kid," he said, "it happens all the time. You knocked her up, you can unknock her, right? You got seven hundred?"

"Seven hundred dollars?"

"Yeah."

"I think I can get it," I said. Seven hundred was everything I had: I could feel the blood draining out of my face.

"Here's how it works. You drive her to the Evergreen Shopping Center, nine o'clock Tuesday morning, section Nine-F of the parking lot. You got that?"

"Yes."

"There'll be a blue van parked there, no windows. She gets out of the car and you drive away, right? You don't come along, just her. She climbs inside the back of the van and closes it, and she sits there in the dark. It's scary, right, but she's OK. Somebody comes along and locks the back door, but that's no sweat, 'cause that's me. Then this somebody drives her to see Dr. Wells, but before she gets out of the van she has to put on a blindfold. Then this somebody walks her into a place and she lies down on a table. It's nice and clean in there, and it's OK. The doctor comes in. He does his little job, and a little later it's back in the van."

"I want to come along," I said.

"No way."

"How do I know she's going to be safe?"

"She's got me, pal. You got any problem with that?"

"I'm sure you're fine," I said, "but how about the doctor? How do I know he's going to do it right?"

"You a doctor or something?" His voice became suspicious and feral. "If you're a doctor, you can do it yourself," he said, and the phone went dead on the other end.

"What was that all about?" said Vicki.

"You wouldn't believe it."

"I've got another number," she said, digging in her purse, "but it's in Milwaukee."

A week later, I picked up Vicki in Richland Center. She was living with her parents, and she told them we were going shopping. Mr. Cepak was in the living room, sitting back in his Barcalounger and reading the paper. He greeted me vaguely and I sat down on the couch.

"How do you like Chicago?" he asked.

"Oh, fine," I said.

"Big town," he said.

"Yeah," I said. "It sure is."

Mrs. Cepak came into the room wearing her weekend clothes. I realized it was the first time I'd seen her out of uniform. She was a nurse for the local school system, and even at night she'd have on the tight-fitting dress and spongy white shoes.

"How come you're going all the way to Milwaukee?" she said. "If you wanna go shopping, there's lots of stores right here."

"Got the Lewisville Mall," said Mr. Cepak.

"I've got to return a sweater," I lied.

"Seems a long way to drive to return a sweater," she said.

"Well, I'm thrifty that way. No sense letting it go to waste."

Mercifully, Vicki came down the stairs. "Hi, everybody," she said. This was her June Allyson voice, but it wasn't working too well. There was a tremor of anxiety in the way she talked, and dark circles under her eyes.

"Are you all right, hon?" asked Mrs. Cepak.

She said she was, but needed an aspirin. She took three Bayers and kissed her mother, and we drove all morning east to Milwaukee. The man on the phone, who sounded vaguely British, had said three hundred dollars, and all you had to do was walk in the door. I could come along, and nobody had to wear blindfolds. Along the way, we listened to the radio and talked about people we knew. She sat in the middle of the front seat, hands in her lap, looking straight ahead.

It was about noon when we got there, and we grabbed a bite to eat at the edge of town. It was a fancy hamburger place called the Tee-Pee, and the center part of the restaurant was a stucco teepee, naturally. Above the cashier's head, a chandelier hung down from the vaulted ceiling.

"Suburban Brown Derby," I said.

"You're pretty big-city, aren't you?" she said, giving me a look.

"Just relax," I said.

The waitress took our order, and when she brought it back, she said we looked real cute. "You two remind me of somebody on TV," she said. "You know the weatherman on channel seven?"

We didn't.

"He's got hair like that," she said, pointing at my head.

"Disappearing," said Vicki.

We arrived at the address, which was in a black neighborhood, and got out of the car. It looked like a doctor's office, all right, but just barely. There was no name on the door, which was locked, and nobody responded when I knocked. Standing on tiptoe, Vicki peeked through the window.

"It looks pretty dirty," she observed.

You could see the waiting room from the window. All the furniture was piled in the corner, including the lamps. The room was dark and dusty-looking, as if it hadn't been used in years.

"It doesn't look good," I said.

"Maybe we should forget it, Holder." She was wearing an orange dress of modest cut, like something you'd wear to church. In the middle of the ugly sidewalk, she looked incredibly fragile.

"There's a phone booth on the next corner," I said. "Let's call the number and see if he's there."

Sure enough, he was. He picked up on the second ring, and his voice was friendly and open, just like before.

"How may I help you?" he said. The question had about seven tonal levels, rising and plunging like music.

"This is Mr. Holder. I called you last week?"

"Oh, yes, Mr. Holder. We're expecting you any moment."

"We tried the front door but nobody answered."

"You have the right place, all right. Come back again, and you'll find it open." He exuded warmth and common sense, and I imagined him wearing an old tweed jacket, slippers, and a pipe. He would be sitting in a comfortable office with a spaniel at his feet, and as we entered from the devastated waiting room, he would rise to greet us with athletic grace.

We went back, and the door opened easily. As we stepped into the waiting room, a woman in her thirties, wearing sharply creased pants and a man's sport coat, walked out of the inner office, a purse hanging from her shoulder. I thought for a moment she was there to greet us, but she passed us with a curt nod of the head and went into the street.

The doctor stepped to the inner doorway and motioned to us to enter. He was a tall black man of medium build, wearing tan slacks and warm-weather loafers, the kind only black men, old aristocrats, and gay men wear. The silk shirt was loosely cut and of European design.

"How do you do, Mr. Holder?" he said, shaking my hand. "And this is?"

"I'm Vicki Cepak," she said, offering her hand.

"We don't have to use last names," he said with a bow. "It's so official. But I'm delighted to meet you."

He led us down the wide hall, in the middle of which was an old wooden desk with papers on top. There was plenty of light, an old-fashioned office chair, and photos and framed certificates hanging from the wall. One was a medical certificate from the Antipodes School of Medicine in the name of Randolph Mitchell. It was printed over a drawing, in gold, of a spreading coconut palm, which seemed to be the school's official emblem. Another frame contained a black-and-white photograph of some men standing in a tropical location. All were wearing white shirts and smiling broadly. It looked like a graduation photo. The one I took to be Dr. Mitchell beamed his optimism into the camera.

"You're Dr. Mitchell?"

"That is correct."

"Where's the Antipodes?" I wondered.

"It's anywhere you wish," he said, "provided your point of view is the other side of the world."

I didn't know what he meant, but it seemed a social comment. I imagined party lanterns stretching from tree to tree at night. I could feel them shake as a hurricane struck the island, and guests fled into the house or quickly departed in cars. I could hear musical laughter disappear across a lawn, in a place surrounded entirely by blue water.

A white woman with black hair appeared at a door behind us. She was not wearing a uniform, but her blouse and skirt were very neat, and she exuded confidence.

"Please come with me," she said to Vicki. Vicki gave me a look of assurance, and the two of them disappeared through a brown door in a paneled wall.

A small black-and-white TV played soundlessly on the other side of the desk. The picture was very blurry. It looked

like one of those roundup sports shows. One second there
was a bicycle race, and the next someone was doing a triple
gainer.

"I have the money here," I said, pulling out my wallet and
counting out three hundred dollars in twenty-dollar bills.

"That is fine," said Dr. Mitchell, not bothering to count
it a second time. He stuffed the wad into his pocket casually.

"How long will it take?"

"About twenty minutes. The nurse is preparing Vicki now."

"I'm worried," I said. "What if something goes wrong?"

"It is a simple procedure," he said suavely, with confidence. His long fingers elegantly gestured disregard for trouble, and he headed for the door. "You know how it works,
of course."

"Not really."

"Dilation and curettage, or D and C. We introduce an
object into the uterus that causes it to open, then a surgical
instrument is used to scrape the walls of the uterus. The fetus
is detached and is automatically expelled by the patient's own
contractions. It is somewhat like birth itself, in that way
only."

He seemed apologetic about the last detail, but it was clear
he did this with all the patients, so they knew what to expect.
If he weren't an abortionist, I thought, he'd make a pretty
good doctor.

"Please wait here," he said. "I will return shortly."

As he opened the door, I could see Vicki in the corner of
a very large room, lying down on what appeared to be a
gynecological examination table. There was a drape over her
knees, and her shoulders were bare.

The doctor was gone, as if he had never existed. I was in
an abandoned building some shyster had taken over for this
afternoon only. There had been no nurse, and Vicki herself
was an illusion. This desk was an apparition. I could probably
pass my hand through it, touching only the thick, dusty air.

But at least the television was on. That was a pretty good
sign of the world's reality. I sat down and watched a pole

vaulter miss one attempt and then another. On the third try, he placed the pole but lost his nerve and ran straight through the pit. It was humiliating for him, and the camera showed the serious faces of the crowd. Then I was drawn into the photograph of the young doctors, the sea behind them, palm trees moving in the wind. It was very pleasant. I was lost in thought.

The door opened again. "Mr. Holder, please," he said, rubbing his long fingers together. "You may come in now." Vicki was still on the table, and the nurse gave me a terse little smile. She was straightening up from the operation. There wasn't any evidence of what had happened. A couple of stainless-steel bowls sat next to a sink, and there was a cabinet near it; but they were the only things in the room.

"She can get dressed now," said the nurse, and joined the doctor in the outer hall. Vicki and I were alone, and she was drowsy.

"It hurt," she said, pointing to her stomach.

"Are you all right?"

"He didn't put enough pain-killer in, and had to do it twice—the whole thing twice. I think he gave me too much."

"How are you feeling now?"

"OK. Sleepy."

I helped her get to a sitting position, and the drape fell to her waist. She was entirely nude, but her clothes were neatly piled on a chair.

"I don't feel so good, Holder."

"You'll be all right," hoping desperately I was right.

Slowly, with my help, she got dressed, and I walked her into the hall. She was starting to recover her equilibrium, almost a step at a time. We were very close at that moment, but both of us knew it was over. We'd go back to her house, I'd mumble something to her parents, and I'd drive away. She would hate me and hate me, and an ocean of difference would open between us.

On the way back to Richland Center, in brilliant sunshine, we said very little. She sat where she had before, holding the bottle of Tylenol with codeine the nurse had given her. Halfway there, we passed a small flower stand, and I pulled over. The guy had carnations and roses, that's all. I bought two dozen red roses, each bunch tied with a piece of string, and walked back to the car.

"For God's sake, Holder," said Vicki with a tired smile.

We headed down the road, one dozen in her right hand, trailing down onto the floor, and the other on the seat between us. Halfway to her parents' house, without a word, she tossed one dozen out the window and they scattered on the highway behind us. The huge truck following us ran over them, and the driver's eyes were big in the window as he tried to figure out what was going on.

Vicki didn't say anything, and she didn't turn to look. A little farther down the road, she threw out the second dozen. I looked in the rearview mirror; the truck was no longer there. The roses bounced onto the empty highway.

8

■   ■   ■   ■   ■   ■

One night Randy came home beaten up and went to bed without telling anyone. But when he tried to get some breakfast in the morning, Rose the Poet saw the condition he was in and sent out a shout that drew us all.

"What a marvelous set of bruises," said Penelope. She'd seen all the violence in American movies, but this Chicago event made Capone seem real. She tried to touch his small, blue face, but he turned away in anger.

"Don't touch me," he said, pouting, and stuck his face in the refrigerator.

"What happened, man?" said Rose. "You fall off your trike or something?"

"Eat shit," said Randy, taking a Swanson's roast-beef dinner out of the freezer.

"Oo, him mad at me," said Rose in his Tweety Bird voice. "Dat not good."

"Let me guess," I said, "you got mugged on the el."

"Nah," he said through a much-changed face. Whatever had happened to him, they'd really done a job. His head wasn't lopsided yet, but it was welted and lumpy. It looked like sandpaper had been rubbed on his skin.

"Hey," said Rose. "Is that my roast-beef dinner? You can't eat that."

"All right, all right," said Randy, and rubbed the frost from the front of the package. Sure enough, in black Magic Marker, the word *Rose* appeared. We believed in sharing up to a certain point, but when it came to food, we were fanatic. If you bought a quart of milk, you wrote your name on it, likewise with TV dinners, which were the principal part of our diet. At any given moment, there might be three to four quarts of milk in the refrigerator, and everyone had his favorite dinners, except for Penelope, of course. She ate real food, but nothing that looked worth eating. Her favorite was liver and onions, but she'd only steam the liver for three or four minutes, and it was almost raw. Rose and I would run gagging to the local Steak 'n' Egger, eat hash browns and toast, and wait for the smell of liver to clear from the apartment.

"Please," Randy begged, "I'm all out right now."

"Shame on you," said Penelope, shaking her finger. "Television dinners for breakfast!"

"Tell you what," said Rose. "You tell me about last night, and you can have it."

"Didn't you go out with Anna last night?" I said. "To the samurai movies or something?"

"Uh, well . . . ," said Randy.

"Oh, my goodness!" said Penelope, holding her face in amazement.

"You got beat up by your own date!" exclaimed Rose in triumph.

It was true. For the last few weeks, he'd been dating a woman named Anna, who was a terror. She was twice his size and walked like a biker. Her masculine presence was made even stronger by the dress she always wore. On another woman it might have been a summer shift, full of air and room. But in the sleeveless dress with roses all over it, she looked like a sofa or Ted Kluzewski, the old White Sox first baseman. Her huge arms were often placed on her hips akimbo, which made her look butch and stern, but the face was mild. You expected it to look older, given the rest of her appearance.

Anna did own a motorcycle, only it was a little Honda put-put, one cut above a Mo-Ped. When they had a date, it was Anna who picked up Randy. She'd sit on the street in front, revving the engine, and he would run down the stairs. Randy always sat behind Anna, arms around her thick waist like a baby holding its mother. It was Randy who wore the only helmet, and off they would go, in a trail of blue exhaust, to get some Japanese food and see Toshiro Mifune cut men in half with his sword.

Anna loved battle. That's why the samurai movies were so appealing. The kill scenes came in swarms, an ecstasy of surgical swordsmanship. There was one about a left-handed swordsman who'd become a free-lance killer because he'd broken the warrior code of honor. Having dishonored himself with his shogun, he was doomed to roam the countryside without patronage or protection, picking up whatever work he could. Randy said you could tell from early in the first reel that this was one bad dude. He comes upon a pilgrim praying at a roadside shrine, and without explanation, cuts off his head. The camera cuts to the head rolling in the dust, and its lips are still moving. Then it pans up to the left-handed warrior, and his lips are moving, too, in compulsive horror. He knows he's further damned himself, but he can't help it. After all, he's left-handed. At the end of the movie, the character is so degraded, he squats in the mud outside the house where his little daughter is staying, eating a frog that's hopped toward him in the rain.

"Wonderful!" said Anna after that particular movie. "You must see it."

Anna's favorite, Randy said, was the Blind Bat Swords-woman. It was a metaphor for the heroic condition of women everywhere.

"That's right," said Anna, seated on the couch where Randy had burned a hole. "She's the spirit of vengeance and knowl-edge."

"And intuition," said Randy eagerly.

"Who's telling this, anyway?" she said, slapping him in the face with a fierce look.

"You are, Anna," he replied.

"The Blind Bat Swordswoman is the wife of a shogun who's being held for ransom. The ransomer offers to release the husband if she will sleep with him, and he's also holding their two children. It is hers alone to save the family, because their lands have been lost and all the warriors and servants dispersed. It is a medieval time of outlaws and itinerant kill-ers, and she goes out on the road, dressed in blue and purple silks, her only protection the small sharp sword she keeps inside a bamboo cane. Along the way, she is blinded by a band of rapists, but this does not deter her. A white horse comes down the road and nuzzles her bleeding face. In the next scene, we see her riding it, looking peaceful and serene. She's blind now, but still in search of her family, and she seems to have special powers."

"She's very strong," said Randy with admiration.

"Soon we discover just how powerful she is," continued Anna, making two fists that melted back into hands. "When the next band of outlaws sets upon her, she pulls her sword and kills them all, in spite of her blindness. She can hear and feel them coming at her, and she cuts them to shreds in a killing dance."

"A killing dance?" I said.

"Whirling and turning," said Randy.

"It's beautiful," said Anna.

"And she saves her husband and kids?" I said.

"No," Randy said. "It's a series."

"If she saved them," said Anna, "there would be no quest."

She looked through the window at the street below, where her motorcycle was chained to a tree. "Without a quest, there is no life," she declared heroically, slapping the coffee table with the full flat of her hand.

This morning, after Rose and Penelope left, Randy told me what had happened. They'd gotten into a tiff over a movie interpretation, and she'd knocked him down, sat on his stomach, and slapped him black and blue.

"The worst part was," he said, "we were in bed. We'd just made love, but it hadn't worked out very well, and I think she was pissed about that."

"It's nothing to punch somebody over."

"I guess not," he said, gingerly touching a welt on his cheek. "It's just that she makes such strong demands."

"Oh?"

"You see," he said, looking embarrassed, "Anna likes to play these games. We can't just make love; there always has to be a plot of some kind."

"Sounds kinky. Don't tell me—the Blind Bat Swordswoman?"

"Promise you won't tell?"

"No problem."

"Anna likes me to pretend I'm violent. It really turns her on. She wants me to throw her back on the bed, rip off her clothes, and slap her around."

I was trying to imagine this, but failing.

"So it really wasn't the movie," I said. "She was showing you how she wanted it done."

"She got kind of carried away," he said. "She really got into it."

"Are you going to see her again?"

"This afternoon," he said sheepishly.

I figured we all were crazy, so there was no point now in giving advice. Rose came upstairs with the mail, and in it was a letter from Terry Grubbs, dated three months ago, with the return address of South Vietnam.

The letter had been forwarded from my parents' home

address, and the envelope looked like it had been around. Inside, the handwriting was what I'd remembered from Rhineland College, a tiny script belonging only to geniuses or morbid obsessive types to whom detail is everything. He'd been "in country," he wrote, for only a couple weeks when they sent his company out on some heavy missions. He'd been given the job of walking point, so if they got ambushed he'd be the first to get shot, except perhaps the lieutenant, and that would come from behind. On the second day, they took some fire, but they got off easy because only one guy got hit. The problem was, you couldn't see anything until it was too late, and then you were fucked. One night, while sitting ambush, he'd killed three gooks with claymores, which must have been some kind of bomb from the way he described them. He couldn't see them coming, but knew they were there by the smell of woodsmoke on their skin. He pushed the plunger three times, and in the morning they were lying together like dolls with arms and legs missing. Now he knew his father was right. Taxation was purely a waste, since the ordinary taxpayer can't choose who he wants killed or how. Lots of ammunition was being wasted every day, money down the drain. The American people had no idea how right this war could be, nor how poorly it was being run. The grunts were doing all the work, and all the credit went to the lifers, who, by the way, got five of his company killed because they couldn't read a map. They'd ordered one of their own tanks to fire on them. Basic had been good, however. He'd met a captain at Camp Lejeune who'd taken a liking to him and invited him home for dinner. After steaks and beer they'd played war games in the living room, hiding behind the chairs and sofas, and the captain had won. Then he said with tears in his eyes how Terry was going to be his man in Nam. The captain wanted to be assigned there real bad, but had a hunch he wasn't going to make it. Whenever they took fire, he felt bad that the captain wasn't with him. In a firefight the other day, a guy got his leg blown off, and before he knew what he was doing, he picked it up and hopped over to the medic, who freaked out there and then. The medics got blown away all the time, but they were a bunch of stupid COs anyway. When he got out of Nam, he was going to move someplace like Idaho scrub-brush country where even his goddamn mother couldn't find him. The other day, a bunch of them had sat on an embankment downwind from a fire in a field of marijuana, and it was such good shit they could smell their own blood in the air. He felt these horns and spikes coming out of his back, like a dinosaur or something. He was ancient, he was leather. He was just plain fucking pissed.

About a week after I got Terry's letter the evening news showed a suspected Viet Cong being shot by a South Vietnamese officer on the streets of Saigon. He had a fragile skull like you see on children, and the officer quickly put a small gun to the temple and fired. The pistol looked so much like a toy, it was surprising how fast he fell, his thin arms tied behind him. He went down like laundry, and everyone watching wondered how it came to be that you could see such things on television. It used to be Sid Caesar making a face at Imogene Coca or Charley Weaver reading a letter from the people back home, and now you couldn't even watch the evening news without turning to stone on the sofa.

9

■ ■ ■ ■ ■ ■

Emory Ashworth was a black nursing assistant on Orthopedics and the spinal cord unit. During the day he was studying to be a florist at Dominion College, a diploma mill. He weighed about three hundred pounds and was "queer as a three-dollar bill" in the words of Normal Cane. Everyone liked him a lot, especially the patients. He wanted to sleep with me.

One night I was sitting in the stationery closet on the sixth floor, counting how many drug requisitions we had, when the door closed and the light went off. I didn't see who it was, but it was something large and warm, and it spoke in a seductive voice.

"Let me make you happy," it said.

"Open the door, Emory."

"Oh, don't be such a bore."

"Open the door, please. . . ."

"Or you'll scream? Oh, my dear!"

He opened the door, and I stepped out, virginity intact.

"I could have given you such pleasure," he said, patting his hair with a pudgy hand, but we both knew he was camping it up. His offers were only half serious and partly made as entertainment for the other employees. A number of them were laughing and pointing as we stepped from the closet. By way of seduction, he'd given me a rug for my bedroom, but I was too innocent, or too greedy, to understand the tactic. A couple of weeks later, he rang the bell unannounced and asked to see the rug. When I showed it to him, his eyes yearned for the bed, but that was all that happened.

One of Emory's favorite stunts was to put a sheet around him so he looked just like a nun. Then he'd sit in a wheelchair and have another assistant push him from room to room, where he posed as Sister Bernadetta, hearing the patients' fears and confessions and holding their hands. As the sister, Emory also had a bawdy sense of humor, but nobody seemed to mind. Nor did they notice he was the orderly who had brought a snack tray or removed a bedpan a few minutes later. When they told him about "that wonderful Sister Bernadetta," he'd say what a comfort the sister had always been to him.

It was Christmas Eve when Emory came out of 675 holding a very large pistol with thumb and forefinger, the way you'd hold a wet towel. He had it by the handle, so the barrel pointed down at his foot, swinging as he walked.

"Holder, honey, would you look at this?"

Another nursing assistant came out of the room behind him and said they'd found it in Jack Triplett's locker while they were straightening up. It had fallen out of an open gym bag and landed on the floor.

It was a real gun, all right. Emory put it on the desk, and we all leaned over and stared at it.

"What's Jack Triplett doing with it?" I said. "He's a quad."

"Why don't you ask him?" said one of the nurses.

"OK, I will," I said, "but first we've got to get rid of the gun."

"How about the narcotics drawer?" said the nurse, getting out her key.

It was fine with me. I picked it up by the handle and placed it next to the vials of morphine. The nurse closed the drawer and locked it, and I told the station clerk to call Security. They were such clowns, they'd probably kill themselves with it on the way downstairs, but it seemed the right procedure.

I headed toward the room with Emory behind me. Jack Triplett was in bed one, the first on the right, in a four-bed ward. Everyone in the room was a paraplegic or a quadraplegic. Jack was a partial quad, meaning he had no use at all of his legs and only vague movement of the arms. While the paraplegics had the run of the hall in their wheelchairs, doing wheelies, having races, and even going out to the movies with special permission, the quads could only lie around on carts, usually on their stomachs. Jack liked to swing his arms around when a nurse was pushing his cart and pretend he was pinching her ass. Most of them would let him have a quick feel, and a couple others did more than that. Emory said Yolanda, the LPN, would draw the curtains every Tuesday after dinner, flip Jack over on his Stryker frame, and give him a hand job, using the same lotion the nurses used for back rubs. I said I thought quads couldn't get a hard-on. He said it was just the other way around. Sometimes they couldn't get rid of one. It would wave around like a flagpole, even though they couldn't feel it. They couldn't come either, he said with a sigh, but stroking it down with lotion was a lovely gesture anyway, like sending a birthday card. It wasn't just Yolanda who was giving such favors, from the pleased look on Emory's face.

Jack was facedown on the Stryker frame when we entered the room, the tray with his half-eaten dinner beneath him. He had curly black hair and a tattoo on one arm. Once he'd been a big man. Now his arms and legs were thin from disuse, so only his torso showed the strength he had once had.

"Jack," I said in a friendly way, "there's a little bit of a problem."

"Wha's that?" he said to the floor.

"There's a gun in your locker."

"Oh yeah," he said casually. "What about it?"

"Well, you can't have guns in the hospital."

"You can get 'bout anything else," he laughed.

"Only you can, Jack," said Emory.

"Hey, faggot," said Jack, "turn me over on this thing."

"Only if you're nice," Emory teased, but immediately he loosened a couple wing bolts on the frame and turned the frame so Jack was facing up. Locking the bolts again, he untied the seatbelt-like straps around the chest and legs, and removed a long canvas-and-aluminum piece that Jack had been lying on. Now the frame looked more like a regular bed, although a very narrow one. The catheter bag was still half filled with brown urine, but now it was on the other side of the bed. A large dressing on his hip was stained yellow. Like most of the spinal cord patients, Jack had trouble with bedsores. He didn't get very good care at home, and a bedsore had deepened, like a cavity in a tooth. Since the pain couldn't be felt, the sore grew and grew. It's finally infection that kills such patients, if not kidney disease from urinary problems. A nurse said they were taking pieces of bone from Jack's hip when they changed the dressings.

"Tha's better," he said, in a drawl that was both southern and alcoholic. "My pecker was gettin' sore."

"We can correct that in other ways," said Emory.

"About the gun," I said.

"It's a gift from my old man. He brought it the other day," he said, lifting his right arm like a wing.

"But why?"

"For protection, why the hell do you think?" He blinked at me as if I were crazy. Didn't I know what a gun was for?

"Why do you need protection here?"

"Ol' Louie over theah cussed me out the other day, the son of a bitch. He said he was gonna fix my ass good." He nodded toward the opposite corner, where a thin black guy named Louie Bottoms, completely broken and helpless-looking, was staring at the ceiling.

Jack couldn't pick up a toothpick, much less a pistol. To keep them from atrophying completely, the nurses had braced both his hands with Ace bandages and specially shaped pieces of plastic. This kept them from curling into birdlike claws from sheer disuse, something that occurred when the tendons overpowered the opposing muscles.

"How are you going to use a gun?" said Emory with such tactlessness it became tact again. "You can't even feed yourself."

"I wasn't gonna use it, unless he fucked with me. Then I'd figure a way somehow." He began to laugh, which caused him to cough; then he turned red in the face.

Emory waved good-bye and went back into the hall. He had better things to do.

"Tell Holder how you got here in the first place," said the patient from bed two, a paraplegic who rolled over in his wheelchair with surprising finesse. This was Honest John, and he was in and out of the unit for simple diabetes. Otherwise, he looked in perfect health. He was extremely handsome, with the slightly sharp features of a Polish aristocrat, and from the waist up he was very well built, because he worked with weights.

"Aw, hell, not that again," said Jack.

"Gunshots," said Honest John. "Go ahead, Jack, tell the man."

"Ain't nothin' to tell. I was fuckin' around with this woman and her husband got wise. So one day he laid waitin' in some bushes, tha's all."

"Jack is at the top of the apartment stairs, knocking on her door, and her old man steps in at the bottom. He shoots all six bullets, bam, bam, bam, just like that, and Jack falls down the stairs and lands at his feet." Honest John gestured the entire scene, holding the gun with both hands, like cops on TV shows.

"And then the motherfucker kicks me," said Jack indignantly, "just for good luck."

"Pretty good, huh?" said Honest John, relishing the story yet another time.

"He was a lousy fuckin' shot, though," said Jack. "Only one of them shots hit home."

"One's enough, my man," said Honest John, and the entire room seemed to murmur assent.

There was a silence. Then Jack said, "I laid there, thinkin' this ain't so bad. If I'm dead, I can still look around, and it don't hurt too bad. Never did hurt, by God."

"It's like a pinprick is all," said Honest John, "a little bitty pinprick."

"It's when you try to move," said Jack, "and the phone call don't go through."

"I got mine in a diving accident," said Honest John, "one night in a quarry. A bunch of us was drunk and somebody said we should jump off this cliff about fifty feet in the air, into the water. There was water all right, just not enough of it. Landed my ass right on a big damned rock that was under the surface."

"Ol' Louie got his in a car," said Jack. "Hey, Louie, how're ya doin'?"

There was no answer. Louie stared at the ceiling as if we weren't there.

"That Louie is on another plane of consciousness," said Honest John. "He is so far into being fucked up, he can't see out again."

There was a fourth guy in the room, but he was turned onto his stomach and didn't say anything. You couldn't tell if he was asleep or listening to all of this.

"That's Wilson," said Honest John. "He doesn't like us much."

"Fuck off," said Wilson in a loud clear voice.

"Hee, hee, hee!" giggled Honest John. He was the only one in the room who could move around, and it gave him a certain authority, somewhere between ambassador and talk-show host. He had all the confidence of a weight lifter, but his legs were remarkably thin under the blanket that covered them.

"If you want the gun, Jack," I said, "you can get it when you leave, downstairs in the cashier's office." The security officer would place it there, inside a yellow "patient's valu-ables" envelope, because that was the rule.

"Sure, man," he said, completely unconcerned. I saw Yo-landa, the LPN, standing at the door with a jar of lotion, washcloth, soap, and towel. She was pretty in a horsey way, with a long face to match her long legs. For a moment, jealousy made a sweet ache that started in my chest and ran out to the hands.

"Time for your skin treatment," she said.

"Is this Tuesday?" I said, looking at my watch.

Honest John knew when it was time to leave, and so did I. We went into the hall. Honest John smiled and did a wheelie that was nothing less than spectacular. He reared up in an instant and did a full 360 before dropping lightly down.

"All right!" I said, slapping his open palm.

"Be cool," he said and blasted smoothly down the hall toward the nursing station. He was going down there to flirt with the nurses, as he usually did in the evening. His diabetes was bad, however, what the doctors call "brittle." In time it was going to mean a lot of trouble for him. A cut on his foot would turn gangrenous and he'd have to have it am-putated, but for now he was as lively and good-looking as he would ever be.

Around the corner, passing Honest John with imperial dignity, came Emory dressed as Sister Bernadetta. Nicky, the nursing assistant, pushed him in the wheelchair. They headed toward 675, where Jack Triplett was having the time of his life, as usual.

I dropped by Romona's office, where the unit managers often hung out, and found Barbara and Romona smoking cigarettes. Barbara had obviously been crying, and her hand shook as she lifted the cigarette to her mouth.

"Oh, Holder," she said, as if she might start crying again.

"What's the matter?" I asked Romona.

"You know how Janush always wants the hallways clean?" she said. "Well, Barbara was straightening up the carts on Nine South when she saw a used Chux under one of them. She thought she'd do the nurses a favor by tossing it out, but when she picked it up, there was a baby inside."

"Oh," I said with dread, not wanting to hear the rest. Chux were blue disposable pads the nurses put under the patients, in case they soiled the bed.

"It may have been stillborn," Romona said, "and then again . . ." Her voice trailed off, and she rolled a look at Barbara.

Barbara studied the lengthening ash of her cigarette, which was bound to fall any second. "It was a little dead baby, with dead hands and dead fingers," she said. "Somebody must have given birth to it here in the hospital and left it to die."

"Oh, I don't think so," said Romona, concerned about her morbid tone. "I think maybe it was stillborn, Barbara, either here or at home, and the poor mother didn't know what to do with it. She probably thought the hospital was the right place to take it. If it was alive, it would have cried, and somebody would have found it."

We thought about that for a while. The smallness of the room was never more apparent. Though it was mid-winter, the room was stuffy, and a small circular fan throbbed in the corner. It didn't put out much air, however, and only added to the oppressive feeling in the room. Sometimes when the office was crowded, Ed would sit on its sturdy, flat top and pretend the vibrations were "getting him off," as he put it. I gave an involuntary shiver and looked at my watch. It was still two hours until break time, ten o'clock. We had nothing to do but sit here together, thinking of other topics for discussion. Romona sighed and studied her nails. She'd brought a romance novel with her but felt it wasn't the time to drag it out of her purse. Barbara stared fiercely at the wall, wondering why, of all people, she had to find the body. I sat wondering about the same injustice.

10

■   ■   ■   ■   ■   ■

It was about the time of the Christmas show that Barbara and I started dating. She was older than I was, but that didn't matter. She said from the beginning that she had no intention of getting married again, but she did want a baby before she got too old, and she needed a man to carry out the project. She assured me that wasn't her only reason for dating; but sometimes when we were having dinner with Ed and Romona in the cafeteria, I could sense her sizing me up, as if judging the quality of my gene pool. It was easy to imagine what sort of kids we might have had, since both of us were tall and thin. They'd be lanky kids with long teeth who were awkward on the dance floor.

We started going out with the others first, to a lively piano bar on State Street called Janie's. Romona was the one who discovered it, and it was very much of her era. There was a long bar along one wall and a piano in the corner with a bar built around it, in the curving shape of the instrument. Our group of five or six would always arrive around twelve thirty and sit at the piano, requesting songs from the Damon Runyonesque characters who took turns playing and singing. Usually it was a short skinny Irishman named Roark who looked like Hoagy Carmichael. He was always drunk, but that was the idea at Janie's. Nobody ordered beer, unless a shot came with it. Roark would lean into a song with his left cheek next to the keys, and you couldn't tell if he was hypnotized by its beauty or had fallen asleep. Suddenly he would lurch into the next phrase of a great talk song like "Scotch and Soda" or "My Funny Valentine," and Romona would toast him with tears in her eyes.

Barbara and I always sat together, feeling part of the group and not. It was like we were visiting another culture, a society that hadn't changed since World War II. They were a sturdy generation—almost unkillable, it seemed—and ours was fragile in comparison. How many of us had the strength to become the colorful characters lining the bar, wearing outdated clothes and living fearlessly in the present?

"Hey, Tony!" Romona yelled to a roly-poly bald guy behind the bar. "Sing 'Danny Boy.' "

"No, no!" He waved her off with a pudgy hand.

"C'mon, Tony," rasped Roark from the piano bench. "Sing it for Romona." His voice was almost a whisper, but Tony, a dark-skinned Italian in a white shirt who tended the long bar, responded to it. He nodded to Roark, braced both stout arms on the bar, and waited for the piano to give him a note. Roark played a single note, and Tony took off with the corniest, most operatic *a cappella* version of the old classic you ever heard. The noisy bar went silent as his song filled the room. Even a flashy salesman and his sexy girl friend looked up from making out in a corner, their faces bright in the shadows. The scene was so wholesome and seedy at the same time, I expected thick snow to start falling past the single small window.

Tony finished the song and went back to washing bar glasses, and Roark did a pretty good "Smoke Gets in Your Eyes" while his dangling cigarette got smoke in his watery eyes. Then Romona surprised us by doing a successful "Misty." She talked her way through it but had good presence and timing, and we were all proud of her.

"You didn't tell us about your hidden talents," said Barbara, while Roark took a break, which meant drinking as many ryes as he could with money from his tips.

"I used to be an entertainer," she confessed, "back when there were lots of clubs. Used to travel with an all-girl group called Eloise and the Flames. We played lots of big rooms, too, in Detroit, Cleveland, Albany."

"Oh, really?" I said, half believing.

"We really drew the crowds," she said. "It was a combination big-band and dance act, with some novelty numbers thrown in. I was a dancer in the chorus and did a roller-board act."

"What's a roller board?" said Barbara.

"You ever watch Ed Sullivan? It's where you put a short board on a cylinder, then stand on the board, rolling back and forth. Sometimes I'd sing while balancing, and sometimes I'd juggle things."

We thought that was amazing.

"Who was Eloise?" Barbara wondered.

"Oh, she was really something," Romona said with admiration. "She led the band, of course, and played the trombone. A very beautiful girl. In the opening number she'd come out dressed as a moth, and we'd all dance around her in our flame costumes—it was beautiful."

Roark came over to us, loose in the joints, and gave Barbara a moist kiss on the mouth, which surprised her. She started away from him as if death itself had taken the liberty.

"That's a pretty girl," he muttered, swaying back and forth.

Romona apologized and hurriedly walked him away from us. The couple making out in the corner looked up again for a second, a dazed look on their faces. Her face was very white and round, with full red lips, and his was dark and angular, with heavy eyelids.

Barbara wanted to leave, so we said good-bye to Romona and the others and I walked her north on State. It was about two in the morning. Along the way we saw a guy in long blue overalls take a butchered lamb out of the trunk of his car and carry it over his shoulder into a building. It looked like a lamb, anyway. I'd seen them hanging in the window of a Greek butcher on Taylor Street. It made Barbara shudder, and we walked arm in arm the rest of the way. By the time we got to her door on Goethe Street, it had begun to snow, and she asked me in. Five minutes later we were in her bed, completely wrapped up in each other. We made love like we were starving, pushing ourselves fiercely inside each other. She tasted sweet all over. I tasted her mouth, her neck, the back of her knees, and her sweet spot until she shook like a kid with a fever. It was exciting how athletic we were, because Barbara seemed anything but athletic with her clothes on. She even walked carefully, the steps measured and arranged, like a horse in a canter. Now she was somebody else, throwing her pelvis rudely into my mouth and pulling on my hair. She pulled me into her, petting and stroking, and when I came, it was down to the last nerve ending. We collapsed on the pillows and talked for a while. Then she got up on her knees in bed and showed me how one breast was larger than the other, but I couldn't see any difference. Barbara looked great like that, so I got on my knees, too, and we faced each other like skinny wrestlers, touching each other sweetly here and there. We made love one more time, and once she called me Jack, her husband's name. I said I didn't mind, because while we were doing it, I kept thinking of Vicki.

It had been a busy evening at the hospital. Romona was down in X Ray, gossiping with Don Leland, one of the technicians, when a body flew by the window. That is, it bounced on the third-floor roof outside the window. Romona and Don rushed over, and sure enough, there was a middle-aged man in a hospital gown. Don opened the window and stepped onto the tar-and-gravel roof, but the man wasn't dead. He looked up at Don with clear eyes and said, "Hello," as if they'd met at a bus stop. It turned out that he had attempted suicide by jumping from his room on the eighth floor, but because he'd failed to look down, he landed square on his knees on a roof level with the sixth floor. The impact put two large indentations in the roofing, but he wasn't hurt. He stood up, shook himself off, and walked over to the edge. It was a sunny winter day, so he decided to jump again, but this time he landed by the X-Ray waiting area, and to his disappointment, he still wasn't dead. That's what he told Don and the doctors who carried him back through the window, put him onto a cart, X-rayed his spine, and declared him in perfect health. When asked why he tried to kill himself, he said it was because he never succeeded at anything. Besides, hospitals filled him with dread. He wound up on the psych ward, where he became the unit's Ping-Pong champion.

That night, all hell broke loose on Twelve South, which was ENT. They called a Dr. Blue for room 1201, right next to the nursing station, and when Barbara, Romona, and I got there, Ed was going crazy. It was his unit, and nothing was stocked right. They needed all sorts of things that could only be found in obscure locations, like the emergency room and surgery. He was in a lot of trouble, and he knew it. I never saw him looking so scared. As well as we could, we tried to cover for him.

None of us realized, until we got to the room, that it wasn't the usual cardiac arrest. It was what they call on ENT a "carotid blow," meaning the carotid artery, which runs up the neck, had literally blown like an oil well. This sometimes happened after radical neck surgery, usually done for smoking-related cancer, because the neck muscles that keep the artery in place are no longer there. They try to pack the wound with dressings so this won't happen, and drugs are administered to lower the patient's blood pressure, but the carotid, being so near the heart, has to withstand tremendous force, and its walls can simply give out.

This had happened to Mr. McKechnie. When Ed got to the room, right behind the nurse, McKechnie was sitting up in bed, desperately waving his arms. Blood was shooting from his neck, splashing all over the room, and his eyes were wide in fear. The nurse, a recent nursing-school graduate, pressed on the neck with a dressing, but already the room was slick with arterial blood.

The doctors were working furiously on the patient when I got there, and the resident was angry. A scope they used for such emergencies had a dead battery, and the nearest one was on the first floor. Ed called to have them send it up by way of the pneumatic tube, but that wasn't going to work. The person who worked the tubes in Central Supply would often nod out and tubes would pile up for as much as half an hour. I yelled to the station clerk to have them hold it in the Emergency Room and headed for the stairwell. The elevator would be too slow, so I sailed down all twelve flights, leaping and swinging out on the railings. At the bottom of the stairs, holding the scope like a baton in a relay race, was the Emergency Room nurse. I grabbed it without a word and headed back, taking three stairs at a time. By the seventh floor, I was starting to give out, and by the twelfth I thought I was dead. Ed grabbed the scope as I fell to the floor by the nursing station, but after a minute or so, he returned, still holding the scope. Mr. McKechnie had died.

Patricia, the nurse on Twelve South, sometimes went out with us after work. I never saw her look so stricken. It was her first blow, and she broke down. Miss Cheever, one of the nursing supervisors, held her hand and talked with her. The nurse on the other unit came over and helped out for a while, but when she had stopped crying, Patricia still had to mop up the blood and dress the body for the morgue. Now she understood why all the nurses on ENT are required to keep a second uniform on the unit, in case the first one "becomes soiled." The blood had sprayed all over her, even up into her hair.

The four of us were waiting to take the body downstairs when Dr. Rocks came onto the unit. McKechnie was his case, and he'd been called by the resident to meet with the family. It looked like he'd just come from a dinner party, because he was wearing a tux under his coat, and his face was even more flushed than usual. He'd operated on McKechnie just that morning, but it wasn't his fault necessarily. Radical neck surgery has a large failure rate. Romona said only 5 percent survived three years after the surgery, and those were terribly disfigured. As a result, ENT surgeons were a very depressed group. Their suicide rate was high, even worse than dentists.

"Dentists?" I said.

"Yeah, how would you like to stare into people's mouths all day and have little children scared of you?"

"I see what you mean."

"There was a case at City when I was there," said Barbara. "An ENT man came to study a chart, and began looking out a window at the rear of the station. It was spring, and there was a park outside. After twenty minutes, he hadn't moved a muscle, so we checked on him. He'd turned catatonic. Dr. Ellsworth was his name. They carried him away in a stretcher. I heard he's still in a mental hospital somewhere."

"There was a baseball player like that," Ed offered. "He went bananas right in the middle of a windup."

"Baloney," said Romona.

"It's true," I said. "It was in the newspapers."

"I don't care," she insisted. "Baseball players don't go nuts."

"They do now," I said, and Ed nodded his head in agreement.

"Next you're gonna say firemen like to start fires."

"As a matter of fact . . . ," Barbara began, but Romona cut her off.

"A bunch of hogwash!" she said. "It's all the fault of what's-his-name, the shrink with the cigar."

"Freud?" said Barbara.

"That's him," she said, poking the air with her cigarette hand. "Freud the fraud."

"You're probably right," Barbara said. "I certainly wasted enough on psychoanalysis."

Romona was shocked. A nice girl like Barbara seeing a shrink? It was hard to understand.

"Just remember," I said, "Freud means 'joy' in German."

"Aw, go on," said Ed.

Dr. Rocks came out of the room, looking tired but no less arrogant, and met the family in the visitors' lounge. Ed said they took the valuables home a couple of days ago, including even the toothbrush, and two of McKechnie's relatives had fought over his wristwatch. Pretty soon, Rocks reappeared with the family. They wanted to go back into the room.

"Could be trouble," said Romona. "You heard about Rocks, of course. He's the least respected surgeon on the staff. For one thing, he's some kind of a nut. He won't perform surgery when the moon is full, because he says there are tides in the blood. It makes the pressure too high or something."

"Could be he's right," Ed said. "You should've seen it in there."

"And he's a terror in the operating room. They say he bounces instruments off the wall and screams at the nurses. The nursing school won't let their students go into OR when Rocks is there. What's more, the interns and residents refuse to call him 'doctor,' that's how little respect they have."

"What do they call him then?" I asked.

"Mr. Rocks," said Romona.

Rocks and the family came out of the room again, but instead of escorting them back to the lounge, he brought them straight over to us.

"Mrs. Fisk," he said. "This is the McKechnie family."

"How do you do?" said Romona with a nervous smile.

There were three in the family, a tall, stoop-shouldered

man in working clothes, a thin woman in a black dress who appeared to be Mr. McKechnie's wife, and a younger man with a vacant look who must have been in his twenties. They didn't smile when they were introduced.

"We have an unusual situation," said Rocks. "The family would like us to release the body to them. Is this in any way possible?"

"You mean they—you—want to take the body yourself?"

"That's right," said the woman in a country accent, "no funeral home."

Romona stiffened. "That's impossible," she said. "It's against the law."

"We don't care about the law," said the older man.

"Let me get this straight. You want to carry the body yourself, down on the elevator, and out of the hospital?"

The older man closed his eyes and nodded yes.

"You're going to take the deceased home in your car?" Romona's disbelief sent her voice into the upper registers.

Barbara, Ed, and I looked at each other. Would they stuff him in the trunk or prop him with a seat belt? And how would things go when a cop pulled them over for speeding?

Dr. Rocks displayed his impatience by glancing at his watch.

"I'll leave you to work out the details. I've an important engagement," he said, offering his hand to the widow.

"Thank you, doctor," she said.

"Let me know how it works out, Mrs. Fisk," he said, and walked to the back elevator. He was going back to his dinner party, where the bubbles in his champagne were still rising.

"What do you propose to do with the body once you've got it home?" Romona asked the wife.

"That's our business and none of yours," said the man.

"We're gonna bury him ourselves," the woman volunteered, "just like we always done in our family."

The young man nodded agreement to this. "We take care of our own," he said.

The Reaper arrived just in time. Ed, Barbara, and I stepped down the hall so they could hash things out. You could see the Reaper's head snap back when he learned their intentions, and pretty soon he was waving his clipboard at the family. Romona had to step between Cane and the other men. Would there be a tug-of-war in the hallway, the body stretched between us and the family?

"How weird," said Barbara.

"Cane is right," said Ed. "The law is the law."

Rose the Poet was talking about something like this just the other day. There was a hippie movement called Freedom for the Dead. They believed you had the right to do what you wanted with your body, since, after all, what was more yours than your corpse? The state and the church conspired to tax even the dead, said the leaders of the movement, by means of requirements like embalming and watertight concrete vaults. A free death meant a return to the old ways of dying; the family put you in a plain pine box and buried you in the backyard. One night when he was high, Rose phoned his parents and said he wanted to be buried the natural way; he hoped they felt that way too, when their time came to die. He couldn't understand why they hung up on him, since it was only midnight in Boston.

"Maybe the McKechnies are right," I said. "There are so many laws already."

"You're full of yellow tomatoes," said Ed.

Two security officers came to the floor, and Normal Cane and the family left with them. Romona came over and said Cane would have to call the Board of Health, since the family wouldn't sign the papers releasing the body to the funeral home. The Board of Health could take possession of the body after seventy-two hours. Meanwhile it would have to stay with us. All those years of life, I thought, and when you die you're an orphan.

When we entered the room to take the body to the morgue, the walls were still bloodstained, in spite of having been washed. Maintenance would have to repaint the room. I was also surprised to see a half-pack of Camels on the bedside table. McKechnie had died of cancer, and he had cigarettes in his room? Ed said he'd seen the guy smoking, but he didn't know it made any difference. When we put Mr. McKechnie onto the slab, a puddle of blood remained on the cart, and a Rorschach of blood was blossoming on the shroud. Before we left the morgue, I gave him a snappy salute, because I thought he deserved one.

The Christmas talent show was an institution, though it was only five years old. It was the brainchild of Jimmy Toedte, the feisty public relations head who was nearing retirement, and Romona, who always loved a show. To our disappointment, Romona herself didn't perform, but there were some pretty good acts. Barbara and I got chairs together just as the show began, and lights went down in the first-floor chapel, the unlikely but useful location every year.

Jimmy Toedte came out first and did a recitation that was in the Christmas spirit. It was the old O. Henry story about the woman who cut her beautiful hair to buy a gold watch chain for her husband, but meanwhile the husband had sold the watch to buy a barrette for her hair. Barbara and I rolled our eyes, but several people near us, including James the Diener and his girl friend from Food Service, were wiping the tears from theirs. Jimmy Toedte was an elfin man with ruddy cheeks, and as he told the story, he clasped his hands in front of him and rose up on tiptoe. The applause he got was sustained and sincere, and it was a good beginning.

The next act, introduced by Romona after her "Thank you, Jimmy," was the Marveltones, three black guys from the laundry room who sang doo-wop songs from the fifties. The singing was excellent, but the choreography was less than great. They snapped their fingers, did little turns, and changed positions, depending on who had the solo, but you could feel them thinking through each action, and they often turned in the wrong direction. The result was unexpected comedy. I was so charmed by their awkwardness that tears ran down my cheek, though only from one eye.

Then Arnold Egger, the head of Accounting, sang "What's New, Pussycat?" and it was exactly what you'd expect from an accountant singing a Tom Jones number. He rolled his hips and furrowed his brow. We could have died of laughter. It was like being a teenager again, trying not to laugh in church. Romona gave us a reproving look from where she was sitting.

After a few more numbers, including Mrs. Godlewski from Central Supply, who displayed her doll collection and spoke in doll voices, Emory Ashworth came out in a white satin costume and sang "The Candy Man" while holding a large candy cane. After the phrase "the candy man can," he'd lick the tip of the cane in a cutesy way, as if he were Shirley Temple. A number of black nursing assistants thought this was a howl, laughing and nudging each other. Then Santa Claus came out, who was really Henry, a maintenance man. He gave out little presents. Several employees had brought their children, and they shoved them toward the front. Henry played the role to the hilt; everyone thought it was funny when one of the kids slugged him in the stomach. The evening was warm and cheery, and it didn't matter who died that night. Death was simply part of our business. There was no point in sighing when the EKG went flat in our faces or the young husband died in Intensive Care. His wife and kids still had to sign for the belongings—the wallet with six dollars, the shirt he'd been wearing—and make the long drive home. During the following days, the widow would still have to decide if the shirt should be laundered and hung in the closet, and whether the money should be transferred to her purse, just for spending.

11

∎ ∎ ∎ ∎ ∎ ∎

Randy's face looked normal again after Anna's fit of rage, and Rose the Poet had finished his epic, "The Stuffing of America," which came to eight hundred pages. It included not a single revision—"My nose is my gesture," he said. Meanwhile, Penelope joined an anarchist group that met every Wednesday night to make banana bread and discuss the abolishment of prisons. Their belief was that people are born innately good; it is society that makes them do bad things like rob and kill. One evening we were discussing her involvement in this group when Edgar returned from Mexico.

He was taller and darker than I'd imagined. He had three or four days' growth of beard, and his hair was also fashionably unkempt. He seemed to be one of those people who looked good no matter what he did. His patched leather aviation jacket was just the right combination of down-and-out and L. L. Bean, and he could fit in with any company he kept. At his father's club in the Loop, he was the promising lad from Princeton, the college he had in fact attended. With us, he looked like the anarchist madman who tosses bombs into First National Banks. When Randy answered the door, I thought he was going to fall down and kiss Edgar's feet, that's the kind of charisma the guy had.

With him, standing in the shadows of the stairwell, was a black guy named Carlo he'd met at the Kropotkin Institute. Carlo was from Chicago, too, but from Cabrini-Green, the public housing project, not Winnetka. He was shorter than Edgar, but elegant nevertheless. He wore a long black coat with a Persian lamb collar, a purple beret, and black canvas shoes from China. His eyes were intensely muddy, but they did not communicate inattention. He seemed to catch everything that happened, even dust falling through sunlight.

We went into the front room. Randy made some green tea. Edgar wondered if they could stay with us for a while, until they found another apartment. We thought that was fine. They could set up sleeping bags on the living room floor. Penelope thought it was more than fine. She couldn't keep her eyes off Edgar. John Reed came out of the back room with Rose and recognized Edgar, slinking over to him more like a jackal than a dog. Edgar gave John Reed a patronizing pat on the head, but otherwise there was no affection. It made you wonder why he had the dog in the first place, unless its pathetic condition symbolized something for him.

Edgar said Marielle and he had gotten together all right, but she had changed. They spent a couple of weeks together, and it was one fight after another. She wanted to put curtains in the window, but curtains were bourgeois. He'd ripped them down and thrown them into the street. He couldn't imagine how Marielle had become so domestic at fifteen years of age. It was her adolescent raptures that had so attracted him in the first place. If he'd wanted a mother, he said, he'd have stayed home in Winnetka.

Carlo pulled out some makings and started rolling a joint.

It was the biggest one I'd ever seen, the size of a middle finger. He lit it up and passed it around, and within seconds we were so high we couldn't see the ground. Carlo saw how well it was working on us. He smiled broadly.

"This is some fine shit," he said, "pure Colombian." Rose was impressed. The stuff he smoked was usually pure window box or Indiana roadside.

"Marielle was a hausfrau," said Edgar through the smoke. "One afternoon, while she was taking a nap, I gathered all my things, called her parents, and cleared out. Her father was so well connected, I was only three blocks away when the police blew down the street. Five minutes later, they were going back in the other direction, and she was sitting in the backseat."

"Did you kiss her good-bye?" asked Penelope.

Carlo thought that was funny. He was slapping his knee and laughing. "Man, this bitch is something!" he said.

"I beg your pardon," said Penelope.

"Your head is up your ass," said Carlo. "My man Edgar ain't gonna kiss no bitch good-bye."

I thought for a moment Penelope would leave the room, but she only shook her head, as if to clear the smoke from it.

"Did you and Carlo meet in Mexico?" I asked.

"At the Institute," said Edgar. "As you know, I'm a student of Trotskyism. Kropotkin is the center for Trotsky studies in this hemisphere. Carlo and I met in a seminar on the new economics."

Rose asked what that was, and Carlo explained that it was the gradual replacement of "daylight economies" with black-market or "midnight" economies.

"Isn't it essentially the same money?" I asked.

"It may be the same monies physically," Edgar interjected, "but once it is ours it is shaded by us metaphysically. The political intention of the money is also darkened and corrected."

"Bad money becomes good?" I said.

"Now you got the idea," said Carlo.

"You'll be interested to know that Carlo just got out of federal prison," said Edgar.

"What for?" said Randy.

"Destroyin' draft records," said Carlo. "In Joliet."

"How fascinating," said Penelope.

Carlo and Edgar explained that they were part of the Union for a Free Union, known for short as the FU. While Edgar had not been implicated in the Joliet affair, he'd been a part of its planning. Carlo, a white college student named Tim, and two white women from Loyola University, one of whom was a professor of history, drove down to Joliet in Tim's car in the middle of the night. They checked the place out in advance and brought along a crowbar. Carlo pried open the back door, which proved incredibly easy, since in a place like Joliet they didn't expect this sort of thing. In no time at all, they poured glue into the typewriter, pulled all the current records from their files, and piled what they could into the car. Since the office was on a downtown street, where of course nobody went in the evening, they were able to carry the stuff right out the front door. They filled up the trunk and most of the backseat, leaving hardly any room for themselves. Then, for good measure, they poured ketchup over what remained and nailed a pair of shoes to the floor.

"Nailed shoes to the floor?"

"Yes," said Edgar, "shoes that belonged to Trotsky himself."

"How do you know they were Trotsky's?" I asked.

"Believe me," said Carlo, "we know."

"Well, they looked like Trotsky's," said Edgar.

I didn't have the heart to tell them no one in Joliet had any idea what Trotsky's shoes looked like, nor understood that they symbolized the immobility of capitalist society.

Edgar said that Carlo was a victim of society. That's why they'd asked him to come along. Carlo wasn't an original member of the group, which was mostly college students, but they felt illegitimate without some representative of the underclass. Elizabeth, who was majoring in sociology at Loyola, and Tim, who claimed "life experience" among the poor, went out on a mission to find someone who fully represented the horrors of modern society. That was how they found Carlo, a former member of the P Stone Nation, drug addict, burglar, unsuccessful pimp, alcoholic, you name it. They waited outside Cook County Prison for three days and interviewed each person that came out. On the third day, at two in the afternoon, they had their man. He had just been released on an armed robbery charge because the only witness, a Pakistani grocer, had been murdered.

"That's too bad," said Penelope.

"Yeah, that broke my heart," said Carlo.

Elizabeth and Tim brought Carlo back to the FU and began his revolutionary education. They gave him revolutionary books, bought him some revolutionary clothes, cooked lots of pasta fiesole, boeuf bourguignon, and other sturdy, no-nonsense foods, and let him sleep with all the women in the cadre. After two or three months of this diet, they'd taken some of the prison edge off Carlo. He no longer slept with a knife in his hand, and he didn't curse in his sleep. The main thing was, he could listen to groups like the Beatles and songs like "The Eve of Destruction" without collapsing in laughter. Carlo had become a true revolutionary, and he was going to lead them into Joliet.

Edgar had been in touch from Paris, where he was studying the structuralism of foreskins. He had a theory about the "maiming of male beauty" that had to do with Richard Nixon and LBJ, and not only did the University of Paris have the best library with regard to the penis, the city was beautiful that spring. The best approach, he wrote in code, was to properly advertise themselves. What use was the Joliet action unless there was proper publicity? While they couldn't notify the TV stations nor send out a press release, they could leave some memorable sign of what they represented. Edgar suggested the shoes, and Professor Kunkel thought ketchup would be vivid, since it represented blood without the shedding of it. Tim thought they should also smear the FU acronym all over the place, and it was absolutely necessary to leave certain tracts behind, certain sensible but very dark tracts. Edgar had written them, of course, but the author would be known only as Cyclops, the eye. Edgar thought the pseudonym had a "monadic intensity and mystery." The eye would radiate the truth of their action. In Professor Kunkel's apartment, above the offices of *Chicago Bowler* and the Progressive Workers of America on Webster Street, they printed the Cyclops tracts on a tabletop press, making sure to include the logo of the printer's union, even though none of them were members, so they wouldn't offend their brothers and sisters in the struggle. They wanted to include some of the PWA in their action, but Edgar wrote that half the membership of thirty-seven were FBI, and the other half had missing fingers of one kind or another, apparently from industrial accidents. Tim and Elizabeth thought this was a little too icky. How could those rickety old farts understand the needs of this generation?

The tracts were ready and plans were made. Tim went to a Standard Oil station and stole a copy of the needed map. This took some daring, since there was a junkyard dog between the cash register and the map rack, but Tim pulled it off. Not only was it important to conserve funds (the map cost twenty-five cents), but the group was also unwilling to give its money to Standard Oil. Sure enough, the map of northern Illinois had an inset for Joliet. There was the prison, there was St. Francis College, and there was Water Street, where the draft board was located. One afternoon, after synchronizing their watches, Tim, Elizabeth, and Professor Kunkel got into Tim's Dodge Dart with push-button drive and drove out to Joliet. It was decided not to bring Carlo along on this preparatory trip, since they might be stopped if a black man was seen in their company. Some discussion ensued about Carlo's traveling in the trunk, but caution won out in the matter. Tim, who was an excellent cook, prepared some sandwiches for the occasion, consisting of homemade bread, bean sprouts, garlic butter, and raw Bermuda onions. These proved purifying to their systems, if not altogether satisfying. The travel time and notable landmarks were noted by Professor Kunkel in her "Metaphysical Journal," which consisted of revolutionary meditations written on water-soluble paper. If they were arrested, she could erase the evidence with a simple glass of water.

The most daring part of their research involved Tim's going into the building on the pretext of joining the army. The draft board, it turned out, shared offices with the army recruiter, so while Tim bullshitted Sergeant Cannon, he could check out the location of files. Meanwhile, Professor Kunkel, using only the perspective of imagination, drew an aerial map of that part of the city, at about the height a pigeon might fly. There was no need for such a map, but it did look attractive in the journal.

Research concluded, the group returned to Chicago. Tim calculated his gas mileage, round-trip, at nearly twenty-four miles per gallon, which satisfied all concerned. They had reservations about the use of fossil fuels, but the ends seemed to justify the means, and the automobile did offer certain advantages over ten-speed bikes or the train. Carlo proved persuasive about the need for the car ("You stupid honkies can walk, but I'm sure enough gonna ride"), and soon his street experience and forceful advice became crucial to the group.

On the night of the raid, everyone wore dark clothes and checked their watches again. Carlo was to sit up front with Tim, so it wouldn't appear they were on a double date. Society's prejudices in such matters were shocking, they agreed, but for the time being they would capitulate. Arriving in Joliet, they quickly accomplished the deed, loading the car with manila folders, smearing the thick, unsatisfactory ketchup, and nailing Trotsky's shoes to the floor. There was some concern about the noise of hammering, but Elizabeth concluded through a mathematical formula that, given the grades of steel of both hammer and nails and the distance of the nearest dwelling, there was no real basis for concern.

They climbed back into the car and headed back toward I-55 when Tim did something that cost them dearly. He missed the turn onto the access ramp and did a U-turn in the middle of the road. Out of the darkness, blooming like a poisonous flower, came the lights of the Illinois State Police, who'd been waiting for speeders. They pulled over the green Dodge Dart, approached it cautiously with drawn guns and flashlights, and immediately saw the heap of manila folders stamped "Property of the U.S. Government" that occupied the backseat. All four offenders were cramped into the front seat, and Professor Kunkel, attempting to eat the pages of her journal, was perched on Carlo's lap. The officers knew what case they had before they even checked. What's more, the FBI tail showed up a minute later in a Holsum bread truck.

Tim had been an informant all along. It was part of his semester project in political science, so he really couldn't be blamed for the U-turn after all. This was pretty disappointing news to Elizabeth, since she'd been Tim's lover for the last six months, but she forgave him when the federal district attorney offered a plea-bargaining deal. If she would tell the government about the workings of the FU before Tim went underground, they would release her into Tim's custody, but only into his. This was one of Tim's demands from the beginning, and the DA was an honorable man. After some tears and scenes, she joined him in Sausalito, California, where with the government's money he was setting up a French restaurant. In his own mind, Tim was committed to the revolution, but he now believed it could only be accomplished through the use of diet. If people ate well, he reasoned, their inner being would be uplifted. It was much the same logic that led the Académie Française to constantly purify the language, reducing the vocabulary to such basic and stringent terms that it was finally democratizing. Since vulgar idioms and dialects couldn't creep in and challenge the dominant idiom, users of the mother tongue would feel they shared the same goals and aspirations. They were not rich or poor. They were a language group. Tim's theory was that food is democratic because everybody eats. Food, like art, would ultimately make us better people.

Elizabeth said the surrealists held beliefs of this kind. It had something to do with the nutritional value of strangeness. Factory workers and owners could be thrust together in the name of beauty, but that beauty had to be violent, like a revolution. It had to be the strong beauty of a dream, since as sleepers we are equal. Tim said he preferred a good sauce to a good nightmare, but he sensed Elizabeth was on to something, and with shared idealism they opened The Sliced Parrot. The fare consisted of surrealist cuisine such as Agneau d'André Breton and Fingers of Veal à la Isidore Ducasse. Tim had found a way to sculpt veal into the shape of a hand, on a bed of hearts of palm. The latter was arranged to resemble an octave on the piano. The medallions of lamb were topped with halves of boiled egg, to give the impression of two blind eyes. This was symbolic, said Elizabeth, of the blindness of society, as well as of the dreaming prophet, the inner person.

Professor Kunkel and Carlo hadn't fared so well. It was suggested by the FBI to Eleanor Kunkel that Carlo was the chief instigator in their little chapter of the Union for a Free Union. He had a record of arrests back to the age of eleven, and it was documented that he'd organized for the Blackstone Rangers. Wasn't it true, Professor Kunkel, that Carlo Emmanuel Bledsoe Jones was the author of the Cyclops tracts? Had he not organized the other members of the group through drugs, sex, and insidious forms of intimidation learned in prison? Had she seen these pictures, taken with a telescopic lens on infrared film through the bedroom window, of Carlo Jones and herself? An anagrammatic study of Carlo's name kept including BLEED SO, regardless of other variants. What was the significance of this, and what had it to do with her own metaphysical journal?

To her credit, Eleanor Kunkel refused to cooperate. That is why, after a period of solitary confinement, she was herding sheep on a mountain in Spain. She'd naturally lost her position at the university and her academic career was ruined, but there were compensations. The lanolin in the wool was good for her skin, and she'd developed an interest in the mountain waters of her region. She kept flasks of the clear liquid on shelves in her room, along with extensive notes about its taste, color, weight, and texture. Carlo, who received her letters, had no idea what was meant by the "texture" of water, nor did he understand how certain water "could only be dirtied by sunlight." But since the last of these letters was received some time ago, her whereabouts and state of mind were no longer certain. Edgar planned to look her up the next time he was in Europe, but his approach would have to be disguised, he said, in case any of the shepherds or sheep turned out to be CIA.

Everyone felt bad about Professor Kunkel, but no one had taken the rap the way Carlo had. In fact, no one could have taken it as Carlo was able. He knew his way around prison, so the first day he worked a piece of metal loose from his bed frame and filed it into a shiv on the concrete floor of the cell. After wrapping the handle with binding tape stolen from the prison library, he had all the protection he needed. Young men like himself were "chicken" to the older prisoners, meaning they were sexually attractive. While Carlo had done some male hustling when he was sixteen or so around Surf and Broadway, he was not about to become the chicken of some fat biker from Calumet City. He used the shiv on two occasions, he said, and when word got around the cornholers left him alone. Besides, he'd made an arrangement with his cellmate, and they were considered "married." The older inmates often had "wives" of their own, and they respected these betrothals.

Carlo said his cellmate was a young white guy who had refused the draft. His name was Albert, and he spent all his time reading books. They got along pretty well, and Carlo protected him as well as he could. Albert had been given a sentence of six years, a period of time equal to his "military obligation," according to the judge. When one of the other prisoners tried to hassle Albert, who was thin and pale, Carlo sculpted the attacker's face into something new and strange. When Carlo last heard from him, Albert had over four years left to serve, but things would be all right with him. Before he was released, Carlo had seen to it that Albert was protected by a huge black guy named Boner, who'd been in the Blackstone Rangers. It meant, of course, that Albert would be Boner's chicken, but it was better than some other options.

It was getting late. Everyone was tired from the grass and conversation. Rose and Carlo went into the kitchen to get some food together, and Edgar announced his new plans. He wanted to organize the sausage workers at a local factory, and he wanted to knock over another draft board. He hoped we would help in these projects, but if we didn't want to get involved, that was all right, too. Then we had a dinner of heavily spiced spaghetti that was prepared by Carlo and Rose's fresh spinach and garbanzo bean salad; our heads were full of outrageous plans and inventions. We knew there was little chance of our acting on them, but it made us feel important to be in the company of real revolutionaries.

The main thing, said Carlo, leaning over the dinner table and meeting each of our eyes, which of us is the spy? Who is the son of a bitch who's going to sell out the others in exchange for a lobster farm or a piece of fine pussy? We swallowed our food more slowly after that, and in between bites, we looked at each other glancingly, with a hint of suspicion. Even if nothing happened, who indeed was the Judas?

12

■　　■　　■　　■　　■　　■

I met Martin Baum when Romona walked down the hall of Orthopedics with him in tow. He wore a tan manager's smock, and looked suave and old-fashioned, like Rudy Vallee. His black hair had a spectacular rolling curl, and his clothes and shoes were expensive. Romona said Martin would be taking over Ed's position on the eleventh and twelfth floors. Dr. Rocks and Normal Cane had wanted Ed's head because of the missing equipment during the carotid blow, but she'd managed to get him transferred to other units. There was also a problem, she said, with missing drugs. Since so many people had access to the drugs, it was difficult to determine who the culprit was, but suspicion pointed to Ed Grabowski.

"That's ridiculous," I said. "Ed doesn't take drugs. All he cares about is corpses."

"I know that, and you know it," she said, "but Norm

Cane and the boys from Security have their own ideas. They're going to be snooping around, so watch your step."

Romona's warning was given from the heart. All of us took home some extra drugs now and then, especially those left over when a patient was discharged. They were supposed to be sent back for credit, but usually they would gather for a couple of days at the back of the unit before anyone got around to doing so. Meanwhile, they were open game, and nurses, doctors, clerks, and everyone else helped themselves. Usually it was sleeping pills, and Romona filched them, too.

"How do you like the job so far?" I asked Martin.

"It seems very interesting," he said, barely disguising his boredom.

Romona wanted me to break Martin in, so she left and I walked him around. I showed him where the supplies were kept, both medical and clerical, where the linen cart was supposed to go, and how to hide from work in the office if you'd had enough for the day. The idea was to bring a good book and close the office door. If anybody wanted you, they could use the paging system.

One of the first things to do on the evening shift was to check the dinner trays. It was mostly a courtesy, like the maître d' going from table to table, but now and then a patient would have a real complaint. One day, for example, the fresh fruit was an apple, and a patient had his Macintosh delivered with a bite taken out of it. He said it didn't inspire much confidence in the rest of his food. Our job was to agree with such patients.

We hit the sixth floor first. It was the first time he'd been in a patient's room, and he entered with cautious reverence, almost tiptoeing through the door. One of the first things you learn when you work in a hospital, I told him, is to forget the patients are sick. After all, they don't want to be reminded of it, and there's no real privacy anyway. Just open the door, stroll in, and take care of your business. This is what I did, sailing through all of Six South without any problems, but he still stayed shyly behind me.

On Six North, there was a private room, 695, occupied by Mr. Prentice. He was a Parkinson's patient, and his wife was always there. She was a pain in the neck, because something was always wrong with the food. She was lying in wait when we entered the room.

"You call this food?" she screamed, jabbing her finger at the tray.

"What's the problem this evening?" I said politely.

"Feel these mashed potatoes," she said.

"You want me to feel the mashed potatoes?"

"Come on, they won't bite," she said, and before I knew it, she grabbed my hand and thrust them into a cold, meager pile next to the Salisbury steak.

"They're cold, all right," I said, looking around for a paper towel.

"You're damned right they're cold. What are you going to do about it?"

"I'll get you some warm ones," I promised. "How are you today, Mr. Prentice?"

He nodded with his whole body, the way Parkinson's patients do. It meant that he was fine, and I patted him on the shoulder. His incessant shaking had rattled the sheets off of him, and his knees were bent and trembling. Martin withdrew toward the door.

"Come here, Martin," I said. "Feel these mashed potatoes."

"Do I have to?" he asked.

"Part of the job," I said.

He put a reluctant finger to the top of a curd and instantly withdrew it.

"They're cold, all right," he said to Mrs. Prentice.

"We're paying eighty dollars a day for this room," she said, "and we want warm mashed potatoes."

"I understand," he said.

"You do something about it, young man."

"Yes, ma'am," I said. "We will," and Martin and I left the room.

We ordered the mashed potatoes, and I got a call from Pediatrics.

It was Mrs. O'Hara, the head nurse, a very disagreeable character. She was feared by the nurses under her, and by everyone else, for that matter, but her way of instilling that fear was indirect. She would leave a small blue "drug card" on a patient's Kardex, with a harsh note for the nurse to discover herself. The nurses called her the "Kardex Commandant" and other names that were not so polite.

Without telling me what the problem was, she insisted that I come down to the unit. When we got there, O'Hara was nowhere in sight. The invisible dictator who worked the day shift had finally gone off duty at seven P.M., but she'd left a note for me about the "immediate" need for more pillows on the unit.

"Look at this," I said to Estelle, the unit's only nursing assistant, "O'Hara wants more pillows."

"You better get 'em," she said, cutting her throat with a finger and smiling.

I grabbed Martin by the sleeve of the coat, walked him down the hall, threw open a closet door, and turned on the light. There, in its glory, was a shining mountain of fresh pillows without their cases. The whole large closet was filled with them. It was O'Hara's main obsession. Before I started getting them for her, she sent Estelle out on raids to other units. As a result, there was always a shortage elsewhere in the hospital. I had begun to steal them back, one at a time, but it was like taking hubcaps from under the gaze of a junkyard dog. Estelle was devoted to O'Hara, and she watched the unit with a constant eye. In order to get them by her, I'd create subterfuges, like turning on the call light in one of the kids' rooms.

The irony was that there were only five or six kids on the unit at any given time. That meant seven or eight pillows for each patient. Most sick kids went to Children's Hospital, so O'Hara's urgency was of the lifeboat variety. She feared the unit was going to be closed altogether.

We went back to the station.

"Estelle," I said, "I'm not getting any more pillows. The closet is full of them."

"I'm gonna tell O'Hara," she said.

"Fine."

A little kid named Nicky whizzed by us, holding his arms out and making airplane noises. Then he flew back our way and pounded into Martin, slamming his fists into Martin's leg and making ack-ack sounds like a machine gun. Estelle pulled him off and walked him back to his room.

"What's the matter with him?" asked Martin.

"Hyperactive. They give them uppers to slow them down."

"I would think the opposite," he said.

"It's like with cats. For some reason you speed them up to slow them down." I knew a nurse at Metropolitan who gave tranquilizers to her nervous cat, and they made it even worse. It spent the night circling the walls at eye level, like cars at Daytona.

Nancy, the beautiful nurse on the evening shift, came out of a room looking distraught. She had plastic gloves on both hands and a stethoscope around her neck. "Where's Estelle?" she said.

"What's wrong?"

"We've got an expiration," she said. "It's Charles."

Charles was an ethereal little boy of about five who had leukemia. They'd been keeping him going for two or three weeks with blood transfusions, IVs, and all the rest.

"I'm going to need some help," she said.

We entered the room, and there was Charles, voluptuously dead, in a bed with chrome bars to keep him from crawling out. The disease had yellowed his skin, giving it a soft glow, and his lips were purple. Scattered around the bed were various toys he'd been given, and next to his face, stained with blood, was a teddy bear. Even though I'd become hardened to these scenes of death, I felt like I'd been punched in the stomach.

"Oh, God," said Martin, looking like he was going to faint.

"Why don't you find Romona?" I said. "I'll take care of this."

He was extremely grateful and left the room. Estelle entered, looking put-upon as usual, and Nancy and she began to straighten up. They put all the toys into a plastic bag for the parents to take home later, but there was disagreement about the teddy bear. Nancy thought we should throw it out, while Estelle insisted the parents would want it. It was decided that Estelle would try to wash it clean, but if that failed they would toss it down the garbage chute. I ordered the death pack and they washed the body, laying it out on clean sheets and propping the head with two pillows. Estelle had wet his hair and combed it nicely. It looked like a kid's on the first day of school.

Half an hour later, the doctor came in with the parents. Everyone knew that Charles wouldn't live long, so an order had been placed on the chart not to call a Dr. Blue. The parents wanted him to die with some peace. Nancy was in the room when it happened; the death was mercifully quick.

The doctor went into the room first, then he called the parents in. They were a nice-looking couple in their thirties, and they handled it well until it was time to leave. Then the mother collapsed in grief and had to be helped into the lobby.

Charles's body was so light I took it to the morgue myself, lifting it up in my arms and placing it softly onto the cart and later the morgue slab. For some reason warmth seemed to come from the body, and the shroud smelled sweet, more like clean laundry than death. The family said we could keep all the toys, so it didn't matter that Estelle, unable to wash the bear clean, had dropped it down the chute.

I got down to dinner late. Romona, Martin, Ed, and Barbara had finished eating, but they were hanging around as usual, having more cups of coffee.

"Sorry about the business with Cane," I said to Ed, sitting next to him.

"That's all right," he said glumly, "I'll make a comeback," but I could tell he was pissed that Martin had taken his place. He kept looking across the table like he might throw something at him.

Barbara was telling a story about Radiology earlier that evening. She had taken a patient to get an X ray, and while she was waiting for him, a midget wearing a hospital gown walked into the area and sat down across from her. He was about the size of a three-year-old, and his legs dangled far above the floor. Barbara felt him looking at her while she read a magazine, and pretty soon he hopped down and walked over to her.

"How ya doin'?" he asked.

"Oh, fine," she said. "How are you?"

"Do you mind if I sit here?" he said, patting the chair beside her.

She said she knew what was coming next, but what could she do? He scrambled into the chair beside her and looked at her with intense devotion. The ring on his finger had a Playboy emblem, a black rabbit on gold.

"I'm not very good at small talk," he said, looking very serious.

"Me, either."

"You're supposed to laugh at that," he said.

"It was a dumb joke," she said, "I bet you use it on all the girls."

"That's true," he said, sitting up straight and cracking his knuckles. "Look," he continued, "let's cut through the fog. I'm attracted to you, and I'd like to take you out. What do you say?"

"I'm pretty busy."

"We can go over to Rush Street. There's a great bar there called Jay's."

"I know Jay's," she said, "I just can't find the time."

"You don't want to go out with me because I'm small, right?" His voice was both belligerent and hurt.

"It's not that at all, really," she said, crossing her long legs in the other direction.

"Honest?"

"Cross my heart," she said, crossing her heart and feeling stupid.

"I believe you," he said, putting his hand on her leg, high on the thigh.

"You never stop, do you?" Barbara said, standing up and glaring down at him.

"You can't blame a guy for trying," he said, shrugging his shoulders.

Romona thought the story was hugely funny, and so did Ed. I didn't feel so hot myself. I kept thinking of Charles lying so perfectly in his freshly made bed, and the absurdity of Barbara's story didn't charm me at all. Apparently I was scowling, because Romona said, "Hey, Jim, what's the matter with you?"

"Oh, nothing," I said, rousing from my introspection.

"You look like hell," said Romona.

"The world is dark," Martin said.

Everyone turned and looked at him.

"What do you mean?" Romona asked.

"It's why I chose the evening shift," he said through a small mouth, "because the world is so dark."

"I like the nights, too," Romona said. "It's hard to get up in the morning."

"I don't think that's what he means," Barbara said.

Martin had been doodling on his paper napkin with a pen. All available space was filled with tortured, swirling lines. A figure half cobra, half vulva dominated the center, then he flipped the napkin over and started on the other side.

The rest of the shift was relatively uneventful. Martin and I sat in my office most of the night, waiting for one of our Pagemasters to go off. We had to leave only a few times, to check the snack trays around ten o'clock, and to get some coat hangers for a patient with a private room on one of his floors. It was a woman of about forty-five who was in for a face lift, and she sat on the bed with one leg up, wearing silk shorty pajamas that showed off her figure. She cocked her eye at Martin, trying to be seductive. He seemed puzzled.

Back at the office, I told him her behavior could be explained. People get nervous when they're admitted to a hospital. They think they're going to die, and their craziness comes out. My theory seemed to interest him, because he became animated. He said people were always crazy. The world was dark with craziness. In fact, the bizarre was the rule, because of human will. It was will that held the world together, not good or evil. No matter what we did to limit our desires, even the attempt was another form of will. Saints and hermits are better than us because at least they try not to be willful, but of course they are crazy too. He'd been so quiet all evening, but now he was masterful as he launched into his topic, leaning back in his chair like a college professor lost in his lecture. Schopenhauer had a lot to teach us, he said. His spiritual pessimism was restorative, because nothingness is basically good.

"You think too much," I said.

"Maybe you're too dull to understand."

"Look, Martin, you'd better relax. There are things happening here that will tear your head off if you don't watch out. Schopenhauer isn't going to do you any good at all."

We talked better after that. I said I thought that by not going to Vietnam, I would have no contact with death, but every day I carried bodies to the morgue. Sometimes on the el I felt I was choking to death. The other day a drunk woman stood between two moving cars and took off her bra. The train rocketed into the tunnel and she nearly fell, but she caught herself, her broad face smeared against the window. Once a rock flew against the el car window where I was sitting and shattered the glass in a weblike pattern. There were people out there who wanted to do me harm, even though they didn't know me.

"What you are feeling is perfectly normal," he said. "I have these feelings myself, but I understand their origin. You are anxious because the world reveals its intentions, but if the world is will, it is also capable of change, provided your will is stronger."

I said the subway was the main problem with western civilization. Last month a woman threw herself onto the el tracks at the Chicago Avenue station. The train ran over her, but it only cut off her arm, which the doctors sewed back on. She was all healed up and back playing bridge with her friends. They said the hand on her severed arm was still clutching her large white purse when they found it on the tracks.

Martin said that my darkness was my sense of the absurd. I thought everything was significant in life, which made me into an absurdist. A sense of the absurd and sentimentality were essentially the same thing, he insisted.

"But you believe in nothingness," I said. "Isn't that sentimental?"

"Maybe you're right," he said, looking depressed. "Maybe we're the same." He gave the impression the comparison had lowered him in station.

Martin was weird, all right, but at least with the patients he kept it to himself. Now and then one of us would find him sitting alone in his office with the lights turned off, but at least he didn't spread his pessimistic philosophy while checking the dinner trays. A number of the nursing assistants liked him, and he also got along with the nursing supervisors, which was important. They'd gotten George Simas, the day manager on the seventh floor, fired over the size of a wastebasket.

A couple of months later Martin didn't show up for work. It wasn't like him to be even five minutes late. Romona called his number but there was no answer, and that night at dinner we speculated on what might have happened to him. Barbara said maybe he was too shy for such a job, where you had to meet people and all. Romona said maybe the pay wasn't enough, what with all those nice clothes he wore, and Ed was convinced Martin couldn't handle the pressure on the twelfth floor.

The next night he didn't show either. This time Barbara called his number, and there was still no answer. We all had an image of his apartment, which was on Sheridan Road, facing the lake. He'd had us over one evening, and everyone had gotten quite drunk.

After two days, Barbara got really worried about Martin. It wasn't like him not to call, even if he was quitting. She called the management of his building and asked them to check the room. After a few minutes, the doorman came back to the phone sounding very irritated. It was against the rules, he said, for him to check on one of the tenants, but just between the two of them, he thought he heard music inside the apartment. Barbara then checked all the major hospitals, and there was no Martin Baum to be found.

"I think we should check the morgue," Romona said.

Ed liked that right away, and Barbara agreed. At midnight, after work, we got into a Yellow cab and drove over to the city morgue. It was located near City Hospital, in a black neighborhood near the expressway, and the driver gave us a second look when I gave him the destination.

"You wanna go where?" he said.

"The morgue," I said. "We want to check if our friend is there."

"Oh," he said, and headed toward Lower Wacker, an underground street which gets you there fast, past Billy Goat Tavern and Tribune Tower, where gleaming white trucks were being loaded with the morning edition. We glided along the Chicago River, following the curving street at fairly high speeds, then we burst from underground onto the expressway. As the lights of other traffic flooded into the car, I noticed that Ed was wearing sunglasses. It was a fairly warm

April evening for Chicago, and he had a window open so the wind blew in his face. Romona's hair was pulled tight in a bun, which made her look tough and mannish, and Barbara sat between them, thin and nervous. I was in front with the driver.

"How come the sunglasses, Ed?"

"Car lights," he said.

"The legend continues," I said.

At Ashland the driver got off the Eisenhower and turned back onto Harrison. Near the hospital, he turned down a side street in front of a building that was old and dark. There was a single light above the door, and one of the two doors was open, so you could see inside.

"Can you wait for us?" I asked the driver.

"No, thanks," he said, "I got fares to catch." Each of us chipped in a dollar, and he was on his way.

The attendant was a black man in his thirties who didn't have a uniform. He had on a rust-and-tan striped shirt and wore glasses. There was an open book on the counter that looked like an accounting text. He must have been a student working the midnight shift.

"What can I do for you?" he asked.

"We're looking for a friend who may be here," Barbara said. "We haven't heard from him for several days."

"You think he might have been run over or something?"

"That's right," she said. "Maybe he was run over."

She turned and looked at us. Maybe it had happened that way. Or he had been mugged.

Barbara gave the attendant the name of Martin Baum and he checked the records for the last two weeks. There was no one by that name, but they had several bodies that were unidentified. We were free to look at them.

We walked down a flight of wide stairs and through a couple of doors. Now we were in the morgue itself, a long gallery that was surprisingly well lighted. The old wood trim, the table in the middle of the room, and even the design of the ceiling lights gave the impression of grace. It wasn't cold and depressing like the small one at Metropolitan; it reminded me of a library basement—old, a little musty, but not scary.

They didn't have books on the slabs, however. We looked at the bodies of two white men, and neither was Martin. They were derelicts—old and puffy, with partial growths of beard. The attendant said he had one more possibility, and asked us to follow him almost to the end of the gallery. There he pulled out another slab, and we gasped when we saw the body. It was a younger white man whose throat had been cut. The head was tilted back, so the wound opened like a mouth, and the mouth itself was stuffed with gauze. Barbara turned away in shock when she saw him, and even Romona seemed shaken.

Ed had removed his sunglasses at the front door. Now that our business was done, he asked a few professional questions of the attendant, like how many bodies they could accommodate, who did the autopsies, and what they did with the bodies after they were done. The attendant hadn't heard of Princetti's, the funeral home Ed stood to inherit, but he accepted his business card and slipped it into his pocket. Romona was strangely silent, but once we were back upstairs she came to life again.

"Let's all go to Janie's," she said. "We're gonna need a drink after this."

We called a cab, which, to our surprise, came right away. It was the same driver as before, and he asked us how it had gone. The voluble Ed told him all about it, sitting in front with his sunglasses on. The three of us sat in the back, glad to be gliding down the expressway into the heart of the city. We asked the driver not to take Lower Wacker back, for the sake of our spirits, and I put my arm around Barbara, to Romona's motherly pleasure. Soon we were inside Janie's sitting at the bar. Roark was nowhere in sight, but Tony served us countless drinks. No one was singing tonight, and the place was nearly empty.

It wasn't until Barbara and I got to her place that she told me about her and Martin. They had been dating, she said, and she thought I should know about it.

"You mean you've been sleeping with him?" I asked.

"Well . . . ," she said shyly, looking down at her fingers.

"I don't believe you've slept with him."

"Why not? Why shouldn't I?"

"To tell you the truth, I don't think Martin's slept with anybody. He's just too weird somehow."

"Holder," she said after pause, "I like you a lot, but the truth is, Martin and I have slept together. He's very sweet, really."

My ego went down like a dynamited building. Each brick of this building had a weight and a dust of its own.

"I don't know what to say, Barbara." I walked around in a circle like I'd dropped something near my feet, then I faced her again. "Why are you telling me this?"

"Because what if he's dead? What if it's my fault?"

"You think he committed suicide? If he has, it's Schopenhauer's fault, not yours. Anyway, I don't know why I'm consoling you. I'm the one who should be upset."

"What if I told you we slept together but never had sex?" she said.

"I'd say you both were crazy."

We touched each other at the same time, and the result should have been on film. We stripped off our clothes while standing and left a trail of them down the hall to the bedroom. In bed, we kissed and twisted and clawed, as if we wanted to hurt and heal at the same time. But for what our lovemaking lacked in mental health, it made up in gymnastics.

"Too bad we can't tell our grandchildren about this," I said when we were done.

"You can tell yours," she said. She got up on her elbow and touched my mouth with a finger. Pretty soon we fell asleep.

At four in the morning, I woke up with a start, put on my clothes, and sneaked out of Barbara's apartment. There seemed no point to leaving a note, and I felt better sleeping in my own bed, in the small room next to the kitchen.

A week later we got the news that Martin was dead. He'd taken several containers of pills with Metropolitan Hospital labels. The police lieutenant told Gary Janush that he'd apparently taken whatever he had on hand: Valium, codeine #3, Seconal, Tuinal, and a bottle of aspirin. The body had been lying on the bed the whole time, and it wasn't in very good shape. Martin's roommate, a salesman for a printing company, had been out of town for a week and a half, and found the body when he returned. The radio was tuned to WLS, the top 40 station, and it was playing loud. The neighbors had complained about the loud rock music, but the management failed to look very far into the matter. All around Martin's bed, hundreds of books lay open, and he was fully dressed, as if for a dinner party. A high-powered telescope, fixed on a tripod, was focused on a window in the building across the street, and in a closet one of the detectives found a cache of pistols. There was no suicide note.

The funeral was in his hometown of Mickle, Illinois, about three hours south of Chicago. Mickle was mostly a farming community with a downtown consisting of a hardware store, a small bank, and a couple of service stations. It was one of those quiet places where you're aware of the trees, and the grass looks extra green, but while a few of the old buildings were nice, most of the new were ugly, made of green fiber glass and whatever else was cheap. The IGA was made of concrete blocks, and a few muddy trucks and cars were parked in front of it. One of the town's distinctions, I'd read in the Chicago papers, was being the site of one of the earliest nuclear plants in Illinois. It was just outside town, on the Mickle River, and there were reports of a high leukemia incidence downriver, especially among children.

Barbara and I got a ride to the funeral from Gary Janush himself. He wore his best blue suit and looked shaken by

Martin's death, even now, three days after the news. We didn't say much on the way downstate. Barbara was in a quiet mood and had dark circles under her eyes. She'd taken up smoking again, and would light up every few miles. There was some small talk about work, and we gossiped about Romona, Ed, and others on the evening shift. We didn't see Janush that much. He always went home as soon as he could, to spend time with his family. His son, he said, was in a Pop Warner league, learning not to cry when he was tackled.

At the edge of Mickle, we stopped for a bite to eat at a place called The Country Kitchen. There were gingham curtains in the windows, but the food was industrial strength. Barbara had a hamburger, which is usually pretty safe, and I had fried chicken, which was rubbery and tasteless. Janush seemed to like his chicken-fried steak. He ate with the fork in his left hand, the knife in his right.

"European style," he said, holding up his utensils.

"Don't drink the water," I said to Barbara as she held the glass to her mouth.

"Why not?"

"Oh, never mind," I said, not wanting to talk about leukemia on a day like this. She drank the water as if dying of thirst.

It had been overcast on the way down, but now the sun broke through. It gave everything a piercing brightness, reflecting off the cars outside, the silverware, and the windows, which hadn't been washed since the fall. It gave me a headache, and the waitress gave me two aspirin from a bottle she kept right in the pouch of her official Country Kitchen apron.

On the way to the funeral home, Janush mentioned Martin for the first time.

"We never suspected anything like this," he said. "He seemed like such an old-fashioned kid."

"Maybe too old-fashioned," I said.

"He used to talk about change," said Barbara as we passed an old Victorian home that doubled as a doctor's office. "He said if a person could only empty himself enough, he could stop things from changing. He talked about how sad it was that time kept moving in such a straight line, so that things would drop off the edge."

"I don't get it," said Janush.

"He said if things went in tighter circles, it would be more reassuring," she continued. "We would know who we were and where we were going."

"Sounds like somebody lost in the woods," Janush said. I had an image of the boss stalking through Canada with a rifle, looking for deer.

"The world is dark," I said.

"Huh?"

"Martin used to say how dark the world was. It was our own craziness that made it dark, but craziness also holds the world together."

"He's got that right," said Janush.

The funeral service was in another Victorian house downtown. The casket was laid out among lots of flowers, but it wasn't open, thank God. We sat in the second row on some creaky folding chairs with the funeral home's name stamped on them. Back when it was really someone's home, this room had probably been the parlor, where company was greeted on special occasions. It still had that little-used smell. In front of us was a podium with a light, and an antique organ was at the rear of the room. We were a little early, but after a while the room started to fill behind us. In came an extremely thin brunette in her twenties wearing a white coat and business suit, and Barbara tugged at my sleeve.

"That's Earline," she said, "his wife."

"I didn't know he had a wife," I said.

"They broke up. That's why he came to Chicago."

"No kidding."

"She's a real bitch. Her father runs a hardware store, and when he didn't want to work in it, she started dating other men. She would even have them over to their house, but first she would throw all his things in the closet. It was as if he didn't exist. She wouldn't even bother to put his things back, so he would have to straighten up the house after each of her affairs."

"Brazen hussy!" I said.

"What's going on?" asked Janush, leaning close.

I whispered the story again, and he sneaked a look at Earline over his shoulder. She looked at everyone there with undisguised contempt, or so it seemed to us.

A family that was unmistakably Martin's came in the door. The father and Martin's two brothers had the same hair, and the mother was dressed in black. She had Martin's chin and small, strict mouth. As soon as they entered, the funeral director signaled the organist, and she began to play a dirge very softly.

To our surprise, the music continued throughout much of the service, rippling and sobbing in the background. A Protestant minister with wonderful black hair got up and talked for a while about the Baum family and what they meant to Mickle. He said what a hardship it was for Lloyd and Florence, but what a strength their two remaining sons, Lloyd, Jr., and Tom, had been. It was a shame that what God had given, a human soul could take away, but we lived in strange times indeed. At this, a murmur of agreement went up through the crowd. He remembered when Martin was a paper boy and always did his job correctly. There was never any problem at all with Martin, as far as anyone knew. Many felt, quite frankly, that trouble began when he moved to the city and met people of indifferent character. It had brought him down. The world outside was full of sin. The world was a dangerous place, he said, pointing at a window that looked out over some white-frame houses, and it was getting crazier all the time. We must sacrifice our separate wills to the higher will of God. God was the light, but when he was angry he came as darkness, blotting out the soul of the unbeliever. Yea, verily, though I walk through the shadow of death, I shall fear no evil.

We all bowed our heads as he prayed for Martin, for Earline

and Martin, for Lloyd, Jr., and Earline, who were soon to be married, for Lloyd and Florence, and for the sick children at Gale Storm Middle School. Outside, the sky alternately darkened and brightened. The ground was a patchwork of light and shadow that worked like a flag.

The organ music got louder after the service was over, and everyone filed to the back. There we were introduced to the family. The father and younger brother Tom even stood the same way as Martin, a little too stiff in the back. The mother was very grateful that we had come and invited us out to the farm, but we had to get back to the city. I kept touching Barbara on the elbow, because I sensed her filling up with grief. We avoided talking to Lloyd, Jr., and Earline, who were standing on the porch, smoking cigarettes and talking to another young couple. At the cemetery, Janush joined the graveside ceremony beneath a blue tent. Barbara stayed in the car. I stood at the near edge of the service, barely able to hear what was said. After a while I started wandering around, reading the names on the stones and watching the April wind shake the budding branches of trees. There was a feeling of fullness in the air, a perfumed smell to the soft ground and new grass. The clouds moved with dreamlike speed. My feet were wet and muddy when I got back into the car, and I was dazzled with the physical presence of things, the shape of the blue tent, where a few people were sadly standing, the starkness of the trees, the smell of Barbara's hair.

"Sorry," I said.

"We were a lot alike, Martin and I," she said.

"Not like this, you're not."

"Maybe not," she said.

"You've never tried it, have you?"

"I've only thought about it, the way you'd think about going to Texas."

"I've never thought about it," I said, "I think I'm too young."

"It's the other way around. You think about it in your

teens, but later it seems sort of childish, like a way of getting attention."

"Actually," I said, "I used to have this fantasy in church of throwing myself from the balcony, flying over the crowd and landing splat in the aisle."

"I'd be too embarrassed. I couldn't stand to be found not looking perfect," she said, sitting up to look in the rearview mirror. "But my worst fear is getting killed on the street. There I would be, my dress over my ears and people looking at the color of my panties."

She shuddered and laughed at the same time. The ceremony was over, and Janush was walking toward us, sober as a deacon. He climbed into the car, sighed, and turned the key in the ignition. Nobody said anything until we got back on the highway, and then we had a wonderful time, telling stories and singing snippets of rock songs from the fifties. In no time at all we were back in Chicago.

13

■　　　■　　　■　　　■　　　■　　　■

Carlo thought Rose's habit of walking around in the nude was hilarious, but the obsession with locking the front door rubbed off on him, maybe because of Carlo's time in prison. When Rose would go into his lengthy inspections, Carlo would assist, standing outside on the stairwell landing, turning the knob, and shouting through the door. Edgar spent much of his time at a small typewriter, working on the political tracts he signed "Cyclops," but in the evening and on Saturday morning he'd be more sociable, watching TV with Rose and Randy. Since he'd become a revolutionary, Edgar said, he didn't have time for television. Moreover, it was the primary tool of capitalist education. When he watched Randy's favorite shows, he did so as a scholar, analyzing the plot and themes until the imperialist guilt of Krazy Kat and Bugs Bunny was revealed.

Randy differed in the matter of Bugs. Wasn't it true, as

the French surrealists believed, that Bugs Bunny was an anarchic hero of the Left? His outrageous behavior symbolized revolutionary youth, the mad and dispossessed, while Elmer Fudd was the bourgeois ideal of militarism (Fudd as hunter), imperialism (Fudd evicts Bugs from his home), and the leisure class (Fudd has no discernible job).

Edgar thought about that. While Randy had a point about Fudd, Bugs Bunny was also a landholder, in spite of the "underground" metaphor of his living conditions. And his frequent recognition of the audience, by winking or waving in its direction, was a formalist gesture characteristic of the most retrograde antisocialist and decadent phases of modern Russian literature. Bugs was "avant-garde" on the surface, but his embracement of the paying audience was no different from that of a butcher shaking a pork chop in a housewife's face.

Randy scowled and worked his hands together. He believed in the antiauthoritarian stance of cartoon characters, most of whom conspired with the youthful audience to subvert parental authority. If Bugs Bunny were co-opted by the status quo, then revolution would be in a sense impossible, opposition reduced to an adolescent gesture, to be outgrown as one entered adult society. Children understood better than their parents what it was to be free, and they must teach their anarchism to the Fudds of this world.

Edgar thought Randy was a revolutionary simpleton. Randy had to understand that the whole medium of television was empowered by capitalism. It was saturated with the values of that system and reiterated them. Weren't there commercials for toys and cereal between the cartoons? What about the violence? Even when Bugs kissed Fudd on the face, causing him to blush, he was performing a bourgeois act. Capitalist technology was designed as a hymn to itself, and that included movies and television.

"Not books?" I asked from the dining room.

"Certainly not," said Edgar, "because there the technology is so archaic the medium has entered the populist realm. It is roughly equivalent to speech, which is free. Virtually any-body can get his hands on a printing press."

"But the education that shapes that speech is not free," I said. "What school did you attend?"

"Princeton," he said.

"Rhineland College," I said, pointing at my chest.

"Never heard of it."

"There you go," I said.

"It proves nothing," Edgar replied.

We argued for a while about the relative value of our ed-ucations, and I asked Edgar how he made a living. The ques-tion caught him off guard and his eyes narrowed.

"I can't talk about that," he said.

"Because you get your money from home?" I asked.

"Certainly not!" he said. "At least not at the present time."

"Tell the man where you get your bread," Carlo said, looking at me with yellow eyes.

"I did get a certain amount from my trust fund," Edgar said, "but that is no longer necessary. Now I have my own income, earned through my own efforts." He seemed very proud of his abilities as a wage earner, yet I'd never seen him go to work.

"But what do you do exactly?" I asked.

Edgar looked around the room, and Carlo nodded OK, as if giving him permission to talk. "Actually," he said, "I go around the world cashing stolen traveler's checks. I get them from an associate who works hand in hand with the owner of the checks. The owner buys ten thousand dollars' worth in large denominations and gives them to my friend, then goes to American Express and claims they're missing. They give him replacements, but meanwhile I travel from London to Amsterdam to Paris, cashing the checks as quickly as I can. I go only to the largest banks, where the size of the checks will prove no problem."

"You got to work fast," said Carlo, "before the list gets around."

"They compile a list of missing checks," said Edgar, "so

all transactions must be complete within two days. Of course, the original owner gets a share, and my associate and I keep the rest."

"Aren't you afraid of getting caught?" asked Rose, in awe of Edgar's life of adventure.

"There is some risk involved," Edgar said coolly, "but the rewards are very good. There was a real problem on only one occasion."

"Dallas," said Carlo, laughing to himself.

"I was scheduled to receive the checks directly from the owner, whose name was Howdy Brown, but when he showed up, he was already being chased by the state police. He picked me up in front of a suburban motel and sped off in his blue Cadillac convertible at a hundred miles an hour. We were a few miles down the road, heading into the desert, when I heard the siren. It was pretty far behind us, but getting closer. None of this concerned Howdy Brown in the least. He was a big red-faced cowboy, and he made normal conversation about football and the weather before pulling the checks out of his jacket."

"Tell 'em about the baby," Carlo said, gesturing with a quart of beer.

"The craziest part was Howdy Brown's little boy," Edgar said. "He'd been sitting on the backseat the whole time, playing with some toys, but when the cops got nearer, Howdy thought he would have some fun. He yelled at the kid, whose name was Goober, to climb up in front with us. Goober had blond hair and couldn't have been more than two. He was still wearing a diaper. But he climbed over the back of the seat, which is difficult at that speed, and stood at the steering wheel. Howdy sat in the middle with his foot on the gas, and Goober held the wheel with both hands, jumping up and down with excitement. The wind blew into his face so hard, it made him look Chinese. He was an excellent driver. Most of the road was dead straight ahead; he kept it right in the middle, so we cut the white line right through the middle of the hood ornament. When a car came in the other direction, he'd ease the Cadillac over into the right lane without any problem. Evidently, he'd done this kind of driving before."

Carlo loved the story, even though he'd heard it many times. So did Randy, who'd forgotten his philosophical differences with Edgar. Rose seemed to regard Edgar as a celebrity.

"So what happened?" I said. "Did you get away from the cops?"

"It was a supercharged engine, according to Howdy. They were chasing him on a speeding violation. He let them pull up next to us, laughed at their reaction to the baby driver, and floored it. They didn't have a chance against us."

About this time we decided to go down to the Loop for a demonstration against the war. We hated the war, we especially hated the government, but most of all we hated LBJ showing his surgical scar to the nation on television. It was all right if your uncle did it, between the fourth and fifth beer, but the president wasn't allowed. It symbolized the crassness of our leadership, its essential mediocrity.

The demonstration was to take place on State Street, in the heart of the shopping district. Carlo and Edgar had something to do with it, indirectly, through the Union for a Free Union. Randy and Penelope were going with them, and Rose and I planned to meet them later. Around noon we climbed the subway stairs into warm sunlight. A large crowd looked on from the sidewalk, mostly office workers on their lunch breaks. A smaller group of about two hundred white college students sat in the middle of the street. They were relaxed and cheerful, as if on a senior-class picnic.

Rose had been smoking joints all morning in preparation for the event, but grass had begun to make me nervous, so I was laying off. He talked softly to himself in a rhythmic fashion, as he often did—a list of the states and their capitals in alphabetical order. He was up to South Dakota. I told him I'd always liked the sound of "Helena, Montana."

We had expected a stage and microphone, some minimal preparations, but there was nothing. The stage was the street itself. The idea was to stop traffic, and it had worked. Buses and cars were lined up to the south and north as far as you could see. Not too far from us, two buses were side by side with their doors open; the drivers leaned on their steering wheels, watching the demonstrators through the enormous windshields. They seemed in no hurry. The faces I saw through the windows were all black. Some looked restlessly down at the crowd, but most were reading or staring into space. The sky was a perfect blue, a shade you see only in Chicago, or maybe Oslo. Every blink of the eye was a perfectly developed picture. Rose looked straight in the air, and people around us looked up, too. A few people leaned from office buildings. A couple of pigeons struggled over the crowd, as if inconvenienced.

I saw Randy and Penelope sitting on the curb across the street. They had half entered the demonstration, like bathers testing the water. Carlo was not in evidence, but Edgar was at the rear of the crowd on the other side, taking photographs of the FBI with a small camera. Poorly disguised as students, they walked blatantly among the seated demonstrators, taking their photographs. The two agents in plain clothes pointed to each other, indicating a sector of students that had been missed. I wondered what kind of files they must have, to go to this kind of trouble.

The crowd began to stir as the agents moved through. One of them must have stepped on someone, because a young guy with brown hair and a denim jacket shoved the agent from a sitting position. The agent shoved him back, and suddenly the crowd began to writhe, like planarias around a particle of food. Some of the demonstrators stood, trying to calm things down, but it didn't work. The guy in the denim jacket, possibly a provocateur, leaped on the agent's back, and the whole street went up for grabs. The agent swung around in anger and threw him over his shoulder onto a group of women. One of them screamed and held her face; blood ran between her fingers. A few Chicago cops, who had been standing at the edge of the crowd trying not to call attention to themselves, waded into the street with clubs, knocking people aside. Most of the demonstrators jumped to their feet and danced away from the blows, but a few more stalwart types linked arms and stayed where they were. It was a classic nonviolent position to take, but the cops hadn't read Gandhi. They laid into the group with the ends of their sticks. People ran and screamed, and Edgar spun this way and that, recording fragments of chaos. The two bus drivers had closed their doors and dropped out of sight. Passengers were looking at the street with horror; one elderly black man screamed something that could not be heard.

Rose and I leaned against the building behind us, amazed at the swiftness of events and unable to run. A few squadrols pulled up on Monroe Street, and about fifty cops wearing riot gear marched around the corner, holding extra-long clubs ahead of them like flagpoles, one end braced on the stomach. The first row was especially impressive. They were tall and heavy, with faces like bulldogs'. By now the street was mostly deserted, but the sidewalk was swarming. The cops had dragged off many of the demonstrators and stuffed them into squadrols. The riot squad spread out to sweep the street, creating a rush of onlookers in our direction. Clinging to the building didn't work. Somebody knocked into me with tremendous force, and I fell into Rose. We went down on the sidewalk, pressed against each other. Somebody stepped on my back, then several people fell on us. Rose pushed me in the face with both hands, as if I was smothering him, and somehow I got to my feet and started running. It must have been in the wrong direction, because there was a stinging blur. I couldn't see and hear anymore. I was lying on the sidewalk in a pool of blood, dead to the world.

Mistakes get made at the hospital, no doubt about it. There's a test they give to find the site of a spinal injury. The doctor puts the patient on an X-ray table, injects a radiopaque dye into the spinal column, and tilts the table to make the dye run up or down. He watches the traveling dye bump along the column, and the beauty of medicine is never more clear. When the dye reaches the injury, it stops or spreads, and the doctor makes a note on the chart. On the day Dr. Wing performed the test on Johnny Matthews, a twelve-year-old quadriplegic who'd been struck by a stray bullet on New Year's Eve, things didn't go so well. The story was that the doctor forgot what he was doing and allowed the dye to flow all the way to the brain. This caused a respiratory arrest, and the boy died on the table. Wing covered his tracks by shading the history and progress notes. No one in the family was astute enough to sue, but the nurses knew what had happened. When Wing sat down with them in the employee dining room, they'd leave or sit in icy silence.

That's why, when I woke up on the neurological unit and Dr. Wing was looking into my eyes, I was a little concerned. His cold finger lifted an eyelid while he shined a light in there.

"I think he's awake," he said to the nurse. It was Eileen Bass, from the day shift.

There was an IV in my right arm, and the bed rail on the other side was up. There was also a tightness in my left arm that I realized was a restraint. This was quite a surprise, since they're usually only applied when the patient is out of his mind.

"Nagloo," I said.

The doctor stood back from the bed in an attitude of caution, but Eileen came close to look at me.

"Why, he's all right," she said. "He's trying to say something is all."

She lifted the small green oxygen mask from my face and rubbed the cheeks to get the red marks out. It must have been on for quite some time, because the skin felt numb.

"Are you all right, hon?" she said, giving me a pat.

"Fine," I said. "What happened?"

"We had to tie you down," she said. "You were pulling out the IV."

"I don't remember."

Wing took her place as she went to the other side and straightened the covers. "We put you on the intravenous basically for feeding. We didn't know how long you'd be out. We'll start you on a liquid diet at lunch and see how you tolerate it."

"Can you take off the restraint, please? It's hurting my arm."

"Are you sure you're feeling OK?" he said in a patronizing voice. "You didn't behave very well last night."

"I promise to behave."

"That's a good boy," he said, patting me on the head. He waved his hand, and Eileen started undoing the restraint.

"You've had a concussion," said Wing, pushing on the bridge of his glasses. "We're going to do some tests, but if everything works out, you can think about going home in a couple of days."

"What kind of tests?"

"Brain scan, skull X rays, and EEG."

"You think I've got a fracture?"

"We'll see."

He looked like he'd been on duty for a day and a half already. His clothes were wrinkled and his face sagged. Yawning broadly, he rubbed his hand through the thick black hair that was matted here and sticking out there.

"What time is it?" I asked.

"Nine in the morning," said Eileen, struggling with the final knot.

"So I've been here since yesterday afternoon?"

"That's right," said Wing, looking at his watch.

The nurse got the restraint undone, and I lifted the arm to get blood into it. The shoulder was a little sore.

Wing looked into my eyes again with the penlight, as if frowning at the back of a cave, then held up four fingers and asked me how many there were. Pulling down the sheet, he stuck a little pin into the soles of my feet to see if there was feeling. There was. Then he ran his fingernail the length of the sole, from heel to toe, to see which way the toes would curl. If they curled down, it meant you were OK, and if they curled back toward your face, you were brain damaged or something. I was not brain damaged, but I had a huge ache where the head met the spinal column. I pointed to where it hurt. Wing frowned.

"Not good?" I asked.

"Could be a subdural hematoma. Some people can walk around for a week with one, then they drop dead from it, just like that." He snapped his fingers with finality. "It's just like a time bomb, a walking time bomb."

"That's reassuring," I said.

"Usually it's a sign if one eye dilates more than the other."

"What should I do—carry a mirror?"

He was one of those guys who had worked so hard ever since med school, he couldn't tell if you were kidding.

"That wouldn't be very practical, would it?" he said.

"Subdurals can be tricky," said Eileen. "Remember Weinstein?"

"Before my time," Wing said.

"He was getting married, and when he went to step on the wineglass, he went down on the back of his head."

"I've read about that," said Wing.

"About his falling?" I asked.

"About stepping on the glass. It's supposed to consecrate the marriage."

"The poor guy's eyes looked like stoplights," Eileen said. "He went into a coma for six weeks, and his wife, Sheila, brought things from home for the bedside table. There was a picture of her in her wedding dress and one of his mother with her cocker spaniel. It could just break your heart."

"Did he die?" I asked.

"No," she said, brightening. "It was like a miracle, really. She sat beside the bed, holding his hand, and one day he just woke up."

"Don't tell me," Wing said, holding up his hand. "It was the power of love that saved him."

"Actually, it was the bread."

"Bread?" we said together.

"It wasn't just the pictures she brought. There was this loaf of bread."

"I see," said Wing, as if that was possible. After all, there were healing molds like penicillin. But how did she get him to eat it?

A tall kid in a white intern's jacket walked in the room. His blond hair fell over one eye; his pink hands were huge.

"Walters!" said Wing. "Just the man I wanted to see."

"Is this the patient?" said the intern, looking at Eileen, not me.

"Yes. I want you to take him to EEG, but first do a full work-up."

"OK," said Walters with no enthusiasm. He acted like he wanted to be outside playing basketball with his friends.

"Walters here is your doctor," Wing said. "I'm just supervising. If there are any problems, you let me know, hear?" Then, as if Walters weren't there, he said, "He looks young, but he's brilliant. Best scores on the state boards in thirty-seven years." With that he left the room, and Eileen went with him.

Walters didn't have much to say. As he did yet another work-up, he sighed a lot and looked out the window. He seemed to know what he was doing, which was exactly what Wing had done. If I wasn't mistaken, my toes curled the opposite direction this time, but he didn't say anything. He looked very sad and disconcerted.

"Is something wrong?"

"I was just thinking about home," he said.

"You miss your parents?"

"Yeah," he said.

"I guess you're on a pretty fast track."

"Pretty fast," he sighed. "Dad thinks it's not fast enough."

"You're not from Chicago, are you?"

"Elwood, Illinois. Downstate."

"Are you going back there to practice?"

"Got to. The chamber of commerce is paying my tuition."

"You have a contract with them?"

"I have to take up with Dr. Summers, who's about to retire, and stay in town for at least five years."

"Do you want to do that?"

"Oh, sure," he said morosely. He went to look for a cart to take me to EEG.

There was coughing on the other side of the curtain. I'd thought I was all alone.

"Hello?" I said.

"Hi!"

"I didn't realize I had a roommate."

"The name's Feller," he said, "Arnold Feller." His voice sounded muffled, as if it passed through two or three doors.

"Any relation to Bob?"

"Who's that?" he asked softly.

"Baseball player, one of the greats."

"I don't follow sports," he said.

"My name is Holder. Jim Holder."

"Pleased to meet you."

"I got hit on the head at a demonstration," I said.

"What were you demonstrating?" he asked with great labor.

I realized he thought I meant a Ronco vegetable slicer or something. "You sound like you're in pain," I said. "Maybe we should talk later."

"That's all right. I like to talk."

"Too bad I can't reach the curtain."

"Me neither," he said.

A suction pump engaged on his side, a little motor that sounded like someone's fingers tapping on a table. He must have had surgery, since the pump, called a Gumco, is used to drain a wound.

"I don't see a TV in the room," I complained.

"It's over here, up on the wall. I'm watching 'Captain Cartoon.' "

"I don't hear anything."

"With these shows you don't need sound," he said.

"The doctor says I might have a subdural."

There was no answer for a while. Then he said, "What did you say?"

"I might have a subdural," I said much louder, as if calling over a wall. "A bruise on my brain."

There was another long pause.

"It can knock you over anytime," I said, snapping my fingers. "Just like that."

It was my turn not to talk. I thought I could hear, very distantly, the frantic sounds of cartoon mice pounding each other with clubs. After a while, his suction pump went silent.

"You there?" he said.

"Yeah."

"Just checking."

Walters wheeled in a cart, but its pad was missing, which filled me with horror. Somebody must have recently used it to take a body to the morgue.

"There's no pad," I said. "It's got to have a pad."

"I had a hard time finding this one," he whined.

"Where did you get it?"

"Back by the elevators."

"Look in the stationery closet around the corner from there."

"Doggone it," he said, as if complaining to one of his parents.

We got off the elevator on the third floor and wheeled down a long hall, Walters's long head over me like a horse's. At the very end, there was a door that was painted red instead of stained and varnished. A plaque on it said, EEG and under that DEATH STUDIES.

"Wait a minute," I said, "what's Death Studies?"

"It's the same as EEG," he said, opening the door, "only we do it to see if you're dead."

Death Studies was a small windowless room, about the size of a Buick Electra. Walters could barely fit the cart inside. I had to stand in the hallway in my hospital gown, then climb back onto the cart once he'd wedged it in. Next to me was a large gray machine with dozens of lights and electrodes and a wide strip of gray paper under several dormant styluses. There was no technician, just a chair for Walters to sit on. It took quite a while to get me hooked up, since electrodes had to be placed all around my head.

As the machine jerked to a start, the styluses flipping like crab claws, I remembered one of the CO jobs I'd seen advertised. Every evening, at some university lab in New Jersey, they would hook you up to one of these machines. While you slept, the machine registered changes in your brain waves. They could tell if you were restless and if you were happy. They could tell if you were in a creative state and if you had a reptile mind. It was rumored to be hard duty, however. One CO reported that the loss of privacy he'd endured during sleep studies had made him nearly crazy. Something wasn't right about sleeping under the gaze of a technician marking things on a clipboard. He said he aged ten years in six weeks.

I had no such problems. For some reason I was very relaxed, like a puppy curled up with a ticking clock. All sorts of things came into my head: Vicki throwing the roses, a math grade I got in grade school, the weatherman on channel 5 pointing at a bolt of lightning on a fuzzy map. The last thing I heard Walters say was, "It says here you're asleep."

Apparently I was, because I had a dream. In it, Dr. Walters was a patient, but he was forty years old. There were worry marks around his eyes, and the skin on his face was gray and tight, typical of alcoholics. In paper slippers and a hospital gown, he followed me down the hall, one arm straight over his head, like a student wanting to ask a question. I wanted to avoid him, and we chased through the hallways for some time. The question he wanted to ask was simple enough, I sensed, but I didn't want to be bothered answering it. At one point, we stopped and listened to one of the residents in Ophthalmology sing a very beautiful song to two nurses. One of them gazed at him with great admiration, but the other was extremely agitated, scratching her arms with her fingernails until they were red with blood.

14

■ ■ ■ ■ ■ ■

When I got back to the room from Death Studies, where nothing unusual had been revealed—I was, for example, not dead—Arnold Feller was gone. The curtain was pulled back, revealing a bed so well made you could bounce an aspirin on it. Eileen Bass, who was still on duty, said an infection had developed in the incision and he'd been put in isolation. They didn't transfer him in a cart; they moved the whole bed.

"Why the whole bed?" I asked.

"He weighs only about five hundred pounds," she said. "Didn't you get a look at him?"

"No," I said. "What's he in for?"

"Pickwick's Syndrome—where you're so fat you can't breathe. They took out a section of his intestines so he can't digest his food; he's lost seventy-five pounds already."

I said I didn't know they did that sort of thing.

"He started gaining weight when his girl friend left him," she said, "and just couldn't stop."

"Oh, come on."

"You know what, though," she said, "Arnold's a wonderful man. You should talk to him some time. He understands things."

The Food Service aide came in with my lunch tray, and the nurse left. Lunch consisted of beef broth, red Jell-O, and tea, but I didn't feel very hungry. I watched two soap operas on what was left of Arnold's rental. All the characters looked alike to me. The men had square jaws and looked stupid, and the women were pretty in a mean sort of way. Then I watched some game shows, but in the middle of "Hollywood Squares" a skinny guy from TV Service came in and turned the set off with a key. He said if I wanted it back on, I had to pay three dollars a day. I instructed him to put it on the hospital bill, and he twisted the key again and left. The set came on. Charley Weaver's face filled the screen, his moustache twitching. I didn't catch what he said, but it must have been funny, because Rose Marie laughed a lot, showing her equine dentures.

In came Romona, Norm Cane, and Bolger of Personnel. They all had their professional manners on, so I knew it was trouble. I turned off the TV again.

"How are you feeling, son?" said Cane, putting an oily hand on my shoulder.

"Just great," I said. "Never been better."

"Sorry to hear of your 'accident,'" said Bolger.

There was a pause as they decided who should speak, and Romona went to the door and closed it.

"Norm here has some questions for you," she said, looking embarrassed.

"We understand you were involved in a demonstration," he said, arching his eyebrows at Bolger.

"That's right."

"What was the extent of your involvement?" Bolger asked, sounding a little like Joe Friday on "Dragnet."

"Let me see," I said. "I think I probably went crazy and killed a few policemen."

"This is no time for cynicism, young man," Cane said. I noticed how yellow his skin was next to his white shirt collar. It was either a Miami tan or a liver condition.

"When we hired you," Bolger said, "we had an explicit understanding that there would be no political activity. Isn't that right?"

"I have a right as a citizen," I said, "and the demonstration wasn't on hospital grounds."

"That's true," Romona said, standing at the foot of the bed. "What he does at home is his business, Norm."

"There are some serious issues at stake here, Romona. We can't have the hospital embarrassed. I think you should know," he said to me, "the police and others have been asking questions."

"About what?" I said.

"About your loyalty to this country. About whether you've broken your agreement with the draft board. If you have acted violently in any way . . ."

"For Pete's sake, Norm," said Romona.

"All I did was attend a demonstration," I said. "The crowd started running, and one of the cops must have hit me on the head. I wasn't even sitting in the street yet. I was on the sidewalk."

"We will not have the hospital brought into this," Bolger said. "If you're going to carry on this way, you're going to have to go elsewhere to do it."

"Fine," I said.

"We'll give you another chance, young man," Cane said, "because it's only fair. Besides, Mrs. Fisk has spoken up for you. Frankly, if it weren't for her . . ."

"That's enough, Norm," said Romona.

"One more thing," Bolger said. "There have been reports of missing drugs on the units, in quite substantial amounts. If we find that you have any involvement in their disappearance, you'll not only lose your job, you'll go to jail for it. Understand?" He pointed his finger at me like a small-town district attorney, and Cane and he left the room.

"Great."

"Don't worry about them," Romona said.

"Thanks for sticking up for me."

"Take care of yourself, Jim. I'll be in to see you now and then."

As she was leaving, she turned to say something else; then she thought better of it and went out the door.

Dinner was an improvement over lunch. It was the soft-food diet, things yellow and white, like macaroni and cheese and tapioca pudding. Some of it came in white Styrofoam, the taste of which got into the food.

Barbara opened the door. She wore a blue dress under her tan lab coat, and she looked great.

"How's the food?" she asked.

"Here, put your finger in this pudding. It's way too soft."

I grabbed her hand and tried to stick it into the food, but she was too strong.

"Some adventure you had, according to Romona."

"It wasn't nothin', ma'am."

"Cane is all cranked out of shape."

"I know. He was just in here."

"Ed thinks you've gone completely crazy, going to a demonstration."

"That's nice. How about climbing into bed with me?"

"Later," she said, but I knew she wouldn't. She was far too prim for that. It was one of the things that attracted us to each other, our essential primness.

Barbara was on duty and left to check the rest of the trays. After a while, Carlo, Penelope, Rose, and Randy came by to see me, but Carlo was dressed like an orderly and came in separately, as if being followed. Rose seemed fine. There wasn't a scratch on him, but he mumbled more than usual, and his fascination with a green plastic water pitcher on the bedside table was approaching a trance. It appeared that someone had stepped on Randy's face, because the curving imprint of a boot sole ran across his cheek. He said it was a footprint all right, but now Anna was jealous. She thought it meant he was fooling around. Penelope said she had managed to hobble into a doorway, and someone had pulled her inside the building. It was all very heroic and exciting, and she couldn't wait to tell her friends in Australia. She clasped her hands together under her chin and looked at the ceiling as she talked.

Carlo said he had caught the whole thing from the roof of a nearby building. He was stationed there with a camera to record police brutality, but he hadn't realized a long-distance lens was needed for that sort of thing. The shots from his Polaroid looked more like embroidered rugs than scenes of rioting police.

I told Carlo it was paranoid to dress up like an orderly.

It wasn't paranoia, he insisted; it was Edgar's old Nehru jacket. Didn't I know shit from Shinola?

Randy said some people had been snooping around the apartment. Tough-looking guys with flashlights kept knocking on the door, asking to read the gas and electric meters. They claimed they had to walk through the apartment to get to the meters, which were in the basement. This made him suspicious.

Carlo, who talked in whispers and kept checking the windows, said Edgar had disappeared. The last time they'd seen him, he was running down the street, holding the hand of a girl they'd never seen before. They jumped into her yellow Porsche and sped away. Carlo said he slept last night at the Starr Hotel on Madison Street, the flophouse where Richard Speck was found, because someone had turned the apartment upside down. He figured it was the cops or FBI.

"Wait a minute," I said. "How do you know the apartment wasn't broken into by thieves? Was anything missing?"

"The TV, the stereo, and all of the weed," he replied, scratching behind his ear. Randy and Penelope nodded, to affirm the truth of this.

"The FBI wouldn't want all that stuff," I said. "If they found grass, they'd have something on us, right?"

"That's for sure," Randy agreed.

"So why don't you just go home," I advised, "and report the break-in to the police? If they wanted to find you, they would have by now."

Penelope was still worried. "I could lose my visa over this," she said.

"I could lose my ass," said Carlo.

"Anna is willing to take us all in," said Randy, "under certain conditions."

"Ain't no way I'm submittin' to bondage," Carlo insisted. He explained that one evening, while visiting Anna with Randy, he woke up handcuffed to the kitchen sink. There were also teeth marks on the top of his feet.

Randy looked hurt by Carlo's refusal, but he didn't say anything.

"There was a new mailman today," Rose said, "and he asked funny questions."

"What kind of questions?"

"He asked if someone named Green lived with us, and when I said no, he asked for the names of everyone who lived in the apartment."

I told them to stop worrying. We hadn't done anything wrong, so they had no right to persecute us. Probably they were imagining the whole affair. This was the United States of America, and under the law we had certain protections.

They all looked at me like I'd sprung a leak.

"Well, maybe there's some reason for concern. But they can't put us in jail."

"They can put my ass in jail," said Carlo. "They do it all the time."

The evening nurse, Sarah Mudd, came into the room with a thermometer and clipboard. This startled Carlo and he leaped behind the door.

"Who are you?" she said, looking straight at him.

"I don't know," he said.

"He's a friend of mine," I said, "and he's on the run from the law."

"Oh," she said. "Well, visiting hours are over, so you're gonna have to leave." She threw a thumb at the door, meaning right now.

Carlo said maybe I was right. He wasn't going to sleep at the Starr Hotel anymore. If he had to hide out, it would be in the park or something. Randy said he was going over to Anna's now, but first he needed some pancake makeup to hide the bruises. The nurse busied herself filling the ice pitcher and taking my temperature, but I could tell she was amused by my visitors.

"OK, that's it," she said, shaking the thermometer, "everybody out!"

I said good-bye, and she showed them the door.

"Weird bunch of friends you have there," she said.

I told her they came with the apartment.

"Was that a footprint on your friend's face?" she asked.

I said it was.

"Looked like a size seven to me," she said.

"By the way," I asked, "where did they transfer Arnold? I never got a chance to say good-bye to him."

"He's in 901."

That was a room often used for infectious cases. There was always a special laundry cart outside the door with yellow isolation gowns, disposable paper masks, and rubber gloves. Every time you went into the room, even to change a light bulb, you had to wear these things. The patients in isolation were usually depressed because they were cut off from the world. People were afraid of them. You could see the anxiety in a visitor's eyes over the paper masks.

I asked if I could go up and see him.

"Not really," she said. "But I won't tell. Just don't let Wing or Walters see you."

She left and I found my clothes in the locker. The shirt was dirty and the knees of the pants were torn. I washed my face and straightened my hair as well as I could without a comb. In the mirror I saw a tall thin person with a headache, which was about what I'd expected. It felt funny to be standing after being in bed for a whole day. For some reason, I now walked like John Wayne, leading with one leg and dragging the other behind.

His room was near the Nine South nursing station, and all the paraphernalia was there. I put the yellow gown on backward, as you're supposed to, and tied it behind my back. The sleeves were too short and had white elastic around the wrists. This made getting the mask on a little more difficult, because of the bind in the arms, but I managed, tying the double strings behind my head and pinching the wire in a seam so it fit snugly over the nose. The rubber gloves were the final item. I pulled two of them from the box, and they went on easily because of the talcum powder they're dusted with at the factory.

Maxine Watson, a housekeeping aide, came by and said hello. I waved to her stiffly and muffled a reply through the mask. Then I tottered into the room like someone who'd recently landed on earth.

There was a screen beside the bed, so I couldn't see him yet, but I could hear the pump sucking away at the incision. Someone had sprayed Glade in the room to cover an unpleasant odor.

"Hello?" I said, as if calling into a stranger's home.

"Hello," came the clear, bell-like reply. It sounded stronger and more cheerful than the one I'd heard earlier that day.

"It's Jim Holder. I came upstairs to see you."

"Oh, yes. Come on in."

I stepped around the screen, and there he was, a white man in his thirties with a flattop haircut and very pale skin. From the neck up, he looked pretty normal, but at his shoulders an avalanche of flesh began. The protective bars were up on the sides of the bed, and his mass flowed around the chrome, nearly meeting on the other side. In order to cover him, the nurse had pinned two sheets together, but they still didn't do the job. A drainage tube ran like an umbilical cord into a pile of dressings in the middle of his stomach. On the bedside table was a portrait of the praying Christ, in rich bad taste, with drops of blood trickling down his forehead from the gruesome thorns. In front of the crucifixion scene, two small American flags were tied together with a piece of red ribbon.

"I hope you'll forgive my appearance," he said. "It's quite a mess I've gotten into here."

"I'm sure you'll be better soon," I said.

"The doctor says I'm losing weight, which is very good, I guess." He seemed a little sad, like a man who was moving away from his old body and hadn't seen the new one yet. "Perhaps they've told you about me."

"Well, a little bit."

"I don't mind really. People have been very kind. I know what they say, of course, about eating so much from a broken heart." There was a pause, and he said, "Have you ever had a broken heart, Jim Holder?"

"I don't know yet," I said, thinking about Vicki.

"You're young," he said, "and there's plenty of time. Everyone has one sooner or later."

It was one of the compelling things about him. Beneath his grotesque appearance was a stable, normal person. He made you feel at home because of it.

He glanced at the bedside table, where his snack tray, consisting of tea and a small cup of red Jell-O, remained untouched. "I'm sorry, by the way, there's nothing decent to offer you. There's not even a chair."

"That's all right," I said, "I'll stand."

A smelly laundry hamper was in the room, near the door. The air was thick with presences, odors, intimations, fears, and hints of other patients who'd thrived or perished there. I began to sway, and sweat came out on my brow.

"Are you all right?" he asked, looking very concerned.

"I'll be fine," I said, wiping my brow with a sleeve.

"What is it, exactly, you came for?" he said politely.

"I just thought I'd pay a visit." What could I say? I wasn't sure myself.

"I've gotten used to it," he said, trying to shift his weight in the bed and failing. "At the hotel—I'm night clerk, you see, at the Clark Hotel—people want to talk to me for hours. They think because I'm fat and ugly, I'll tell them the truth about things."

"You're not ugly," I lied.

"I'm not exactly handsome."

A nurse from the unit walked in, her isolation gear hastily donned. It looked like Cindy Betts, from the blond hair and dark eyebrows. She was very attractive, and I'd flirted with her a couple of times.

"Oh, hi, Holder," she said, clearly disappointed. "What are you doing here?"

"It's a long story," I said.

She emptied his catheter bag, but then she lingered at the foot of the bed, looking back and forth between Arnold and me.

"What is it, Cindy?" Arnold asked.

She said she had a problem. Dr. Rugero, the new resident in plastic surgery, had asked her out. He was cute, she said, and he had all the money in the world. The guy was a catch and a half, but there was only one problem—he was married.

"That's not a problem," said Arnold. "It's an advantage. If he's married, he already loves you more than his wife."

"But I want the money, too, Arnold," she said with great firmness.

"You should date him anyway," he said, "provided it makes you happy."

"You really think so?" she said.

"Sure. Do what you'll remember doing twenty years from now."

"Oh, good," she bubbled, but then she gave me a guilty glance. "You won't tell anyone about this, will you?"

I said I wouldn't.

"He's a wonderful person, Holder," she said, patting me on the shoulder. As she left, I saw what a tight little stride she had, like a chihuahua.

"You see," Arnold said. "I can solve all their problems. All I do is tell them what they want to hear."

"I've got some problems right now," I said, and told him about Cane's response to the demonstration. He was interested in learning about conscientious objectors, because he hadn't known they existed.

"The problem with you," Arnold said, "is that you're trying to be good and bad at the same time. It doesn't usually work out. The best thing is to go to jail. Then the good and bad will be clearer in your mind." As he spoke, he kept looking over at the bedside table, with its bleeding Jesus and American flags.

"You want me to go to jail?" I said through the paper mask. "I thought you only told people what they wanted to hear."

"That *is* what you want to hear, isn't it?" He looked at me squarely, and I couldn't tell if he was crazy, patriotic, or full of good advice.

"Maybe you're right," I said. "Are you doing what will make you happy twenty years from now?"

"I won't be alive in twenty years," he said.

I didn't know what to say.

"Do something for me, will you?" he asked, turning to look at the table. "Open that drawer for a minute."

I opened it, and there were several things inside: a turtle shell, an ashtray from the Badlands, a 1963 calendar from the Mort Coal Company with an airbrushed photograph of President Kennedy, a small silver whistle, and a plaster of paris bust of Beethoven such as children receive for taking music lessons.

"This is quite a collection, Arnold."

"That's nothing. You should see my room at the hotel."

"What do you want?" I asked.

"Give me the ashtray," he said, waving an arm that looked like a tidal wave.

I pulled the ashtray from the drawer and Beethoven fell over, chipping off his nose. I quickly shut the drawer again, so Arnold wouldn't see.

He balanced the ashtray on his stomach and pulled a pack of Camels from under the sheet. Deftly, he lit a cigarette and blew a perfect ring of smoke toward the ceiling. "I've got some thinking to do," he said and turned on the television by touching the remote control. "Laugh-In" came onto the screen, and Arnold smiled broadly as Ruth Buzzi, as the prim old lady, smacked Arte Johnson, the dirty old man, with her umbrella.

The yellow gown made me sweaty and dizzy, and I needed some fresh air. "It's been nice talking to you," I said, edging toward the door, but he was too absorbed in the show to answer. As I took off the gown and threw it into the laundry hamper, I turned and looked at the painting, which had ultraviolet undertones and glowed on the bedside stand.

A couple of days later Dr. Wing signed me out of the hospital. He came into the room in a hurry and started to shoo me out.

"Go, go, you're fine," he said. "I've got to get busy here. We need this bed for a myasthenia gravis that's coming in this afternoon." Myasthenia is a deadly disease in which the patient loses control of all his muscles. Usually it occurs in middle-aged men, and after a while they lose the strength even to open their eyes. Finally, they're too weak to breathe. But the disease couldn't have gone too far, if the patient wasn't in Intensive Care. At the last stage, they had to put you on a respirator. If you lasted out the episode, which many people did, you would be all right until the next occurrence.

I thanked Dr. Wing for his care.

"Yeah, yeah," he said, "get out of here, will you?"

This was the sort of bedside manner I liked. Don't give me sympathy; just show me the road. I put on my clothes as fast as I could.

In the visitors' lounge by the front elevator, a scholarly-looking man and his wife sat on the couch, an overnight bag beside them. She held his limp hand. I figured he was my replacement. I wanted to go over and say something comforting, but couldn't bring myself to do it. That was the sort of cheap theatrics Normal Cane went in for, feeding on the family's grief until the balance of sympathy changed and they felt sorry for him. I threw a prayer at the ceiling that the poor man wouldn't die in my bed.

The elevator finally arrived. It was smaller than the ones in back, and bad music played softly through speakers in the ceiling.

On the sixth floor, the doors opened, and Robert Sage stepped on, wearing the kind of clothes Edd "Kookie" Byrnes wore on "77 Sunset Strip." He looked hip and out-of-date in one gesture. The scars from his lobotomy were still visible, but his hair was much longer. I said hello, but he didn't recognize me. He must have returned to visit his old nurses, because he'd been out of the hospital for months. Sure enough, when he turned around, there was a sign taped on his back: "My name is Robert Sage. Please return me to Six South." Around the margins were signatures of nurses and aides on the unit.

I got off the elevator on the first floor and walked into the Gothic lobby, but Robert Sage stayed where he was. I watched as some people got on and did a predictable second take at their skeletal companion. Then I headed out the door. It was a beautiful day. I walked down the street sideways, the same way I'd walked since the accident. One leg seemed always to strive ahead, and the other to drag behind, as if they weren't legs but political leanings. When I got to State Street, my limp allowed me to observe myself in store windows without turning my head. I'd asked Wing if the subdural caused this behavior; he said it was just sore muscles from falling on the sidewalk.

As I headed back to the apartment, it occurred to me that Metropolitan was now my family—Barbara, Romona, Ed, and even patients like Robert Sage. I knew the place like a home, its frailties and secrets. I knew, for instance, that in the seventh-floor broom closet Mr. Flanagan's leg leaned against the wall next to the garbage chute. It was a full prosthesis, meaning from the knee down, and a black shoe was tied to the foot. His wife hadn't wanted to take it home with her when I appeared with the other belongings. In fact, she broke into tears. Not having it available would create problems for the undertaker, Ed said, but that was her business. There seemed no other place to put it, so it remained there, like an old umbrella in a hall closet. It became part of what was familiar. I could go there now and see how shiny and well made it was, and if I felt like it, I could toss it down the garbage chute. The first day I returned to work, that is exactly what I did, because it was mine to do.

15

■ ■ ■ ■ ■ ■ ■

I'd just finished checking the dinner trays on the seventh floor when news came that Jack Triplett had died on Six North. The nurse had turned his Stryker frame over, and his mouth was hanging open. One of the roommates said he'd been talking just a few minutes before about wanting to be a sports reporter. This had long been one of his goals. He thought he could dictate his stories and reports into a tape recorder and that the newspaper would pay a team of attendants to carry him around. His knowledge of baseball statistics was good, especially the White Sox, but he was barely literate, and it never seemed likely his dream would come true. He'd gotten the idea, he said, from a television report about a blind baseball announcer who would reenact the game from Braille notes and box scores.

We were deeply affected by Jack's death. He was such a lively character, in some ways the spirit of the unit. Now that spirit was nothing but a bunch of bones and teeth to be wrapped up for the morgue. Yolanda, the LPN who'd been Jack's lover, was in such bad shape that Dr. Simmons, the resident, injected her with Valium. Even then, you could hear her moans through the closed door of the break room. Emory Ashworth came down from Orthopedics to fill in for her. He rushed here and there, not getting much done, and adding to the feeling of helplessness. His usual campiness and humor were gone. He seemed about twelve years old. For an instant, I imagined my own corpse lying in bed, looking bucktoothed and stupid. I could feel millions of microbes crawling over my skin, incessantly eating each other. Everything in the world is constantly being buried by a fine layer of dust; it even falls on your eyeballs as you lie in bed after sex.

A couple of paraplegics sat in wheelchairs near the nursing station, smoking cigarettes and talking quietly, and one of the nurses yelled at them to do their smoking in the visitors' lounge. Then she apologized to them. It was a death of enough magnitude that the nursing supervisors came down to express their sympathy to the nurses.

While Jack was special, any death on the spinal cord unit was significant. The patients were so helpless. Their absolute dependence on the nurses and aides was heartbreaking, and made the relationships very strong. When one of these men died, the nurses felt they had failed terribly. If only the kidney infections and bedsores had been caught sooner. If only they had changed the dressings better, and gone to mass more often when they were children.

It was always harder to take the body to the morgue and collect the valuables when I knew the person. Standing next to his body, listing the pairs of socks and searching for the second shoe, I half expected Jack to sit up and talk to me. There weren't many valuables, just a lot of junk from the gift shop like car magazines, cigarettes, and packages of Twinkies. Nevertheless, everything had to be listed and released to the family.

The paper bag containing the belongings was at the back of the unit when Jack's father showed up. He wore a brown Shell gasoline uniform with "Rowdy" stitched on the jacket, and his hair, a sleek salt-and-pepper, belonged on a movie star. If his teeth hadn't been missing, he'd have looked like a business executive or U.S. senator.

The problem was, he was drunk. When I took him to the room to view the body, he claimed it wasn't Jack lying there. It had to be somebody else, he said, because Jack didn't look like that the last time he saw him. Jack looked awful thin, and look how his cheeks were sunk. Before the nurse and I could stop him, he touched the face of the corpse, working expressions into it with his fingers. In one drunken blur, he made Jack smile, frown, and doubt. Then he stepped back from the corpse. It might be Jack after all, he said, acting truly surprised. Incensed, the nurse steered him out of the room. When I offered the list of valuables for his signature, he scrawled something illegible, holding the pen as if he were trying to drill it into the desk.

"Shack was a good boy," he gurgled. "Isha damn shame."

"We're very sorry, Mr. Triplett," I said. "Everybody liked Jack a lot."

"You better believe it," he said, jabbing a finger into my chest. "Shack was the besh they ever wash."

"There's a gun to claim from the cashier," I said, "if you haven't picked it up already."

"Thash right," he said, putting an arm around my shoulder and swaying silently back and forth. He was either nodding off or dreaming of better times in Tennessee, when the kids ran around in the yard, among old refrigerators and the remains of a dozen cars. Now he probably lived on Wilson Avenue, where many poor whites resided. He would take the bus home with Jack's Twinkies and cigarettes, but he was so drunk, he'd probably leave them on the bus. They'd ride around the city until somebody found them and took them home.

I steered him down to the lobby, where the cashier was,

and asked for the envelope containing the gun. It made a bulky package. The cashier looked at us skeptically, as if he could sense what was in the package. I took Mr. Triplett around the corner by Outpatient Accounting, opened the envelope, and handed him the weapon. As I did so, the bullets, which had been removed for safety, spilled onto the tile floor. Since we were still in partial sight of the lobby, where people were coming and going, I dropped down in haste and started to gather them up. Rowdy Triplett swayed above me, holding the gun as if he'd staggered out of a gunfight.

"Git 'em," he said. "Git them critters."

I hurriedly shoved the shells into his jacket pocket.

"Don't put those in the gun until you get home," I said. He appeared to understand, because his head shook up and down.

I worked the gun loose from his hand and tried to find a place for it. The Shell uniform was tight-fitting. Anywhere I put the weapon, it would make a bulge, and he might get arrested. I decided to put it in the bag containing the valuables. The gun might drop through the bottom onto the sidewalk, but that would be his problem. Then I guided him out the front door and headed him in the direction of State Street. His good-bye handshake was sober and tough, but the rest of his body waved like a flag. He gave me a "Thanks, pardner" and was on his way, weaving through the minimal sidewalk traffic.

Emory and the other aides had Jack wrapped up and ready to go when I returned. They had even put the body onto the cart and closed all the doors in the hall. It wasn't that necessary—everybody knew he was dead, because news like that soaks through the walls, especially on a unit where patients know each other mainly by rumor.

It was pathetic to see Honest John moping around the unit. While Jack had been in the hospital for months, getting worse and worse, Honest John had been in and out several times. When his family went on vacation, they got the doctor to sign him into the hospital, like putting a dog in a kennel. He knew they were dumping him, but he didn't mind. He liked the camaraderie of Six North and preferred being there to living at home.

Emory volunteered to help me take the body to the morgue, but when we got Jack into the hall, Honest John wheeled around the corner with authority. He pulled up next to us, and while the humming elevator threw its lights into the hall, Honest John said farewell. Dressed in GI camouflage, with combat boots on his shriveled feet, he touched the body with one hand and put his head down as if praying, crying, or thinking very hard. The elevator operator, who was a grouchy SOB, turned to look at the wall. Under other conditions, he would have told us to hurry the fuck up.

When Honest John was done, he saluted us and headed briskly back toward the station, a look of grim death on his face. Two days later he was released, and I never saw him again. I don't know if he died, moved away, or spent the rest of his life at the VA Hospital, where most of the veterans went. Louie Bottoms, the roommate Jack thought was trying to kill him, had died months ago. Wilson, the other roommate, married one of the nursing assistants and moved to San Diego. The story came back that he had started a tool-rental business and was making tons of money.

When we put Jack's body down on the slab, I could feel the difference from a normal corpse. He seemed more like a collection of parts than a whole body, and weighed very little for such a big man. It made me think of high school dances, how some girls seem made of air when you hold them. On the elevator back to the floor, Emory cried and wiped his eyes with a hankie.

Later that night, I was hanging around Orthopedics, talking with the clerk, Mary Patterson, when Dr. Storck went by, guided down the hall by his resident and the intern on call. He was a brilliant surgeon, capable of rebuilding whole hands from a few stray bones and muscles, but he couldn't find his patients' rooms if his life depended on it. A staff member always walked with him, to make sure he didn't walk into a wall or fall down an elevator shaft. He also never remembered a patient's name, but he knew sinew and bone as a sculptor knows granite.

Mary said the nine-year-old girl in room 711, Storck's destination, had arrived from Iran the night before. The daughter of a wealthy oil minister, she'd lost her finger in an accident, and Storck was going to build her a new one from bone and muscle in her calf. After a period of stiffness and puffiness, it would look and work like a normal finger, unless you looked very close. It would take all day to put the finger together, because the doctor was so meticulous.

Years ago Storck had invented the total hip replacement. This operation was usually performed on older people whose bone structure was weakened by osteoporosis, resulting in a serious hip fracture. Grandmother doesn't fall down and break her hip; the hip snaps first, causing the fall. Storck would install brand-new hip sockets of plastic and some wonderful new metal, and the patient could think of taking up tennis again.

One morning, however, he absentmindedly put a hip on backward. No one noticed until the next day, when the chief orthopedic resident took students and interns on rounds. When they pulled back the covers, Mrs. Smith's legs were splayed out sideways, like she wanted to walk both east and west. It was embarrassing for Storck when the case went before the review board, but he was too well respected for anything to come of the hearing. Meanwhile, the patient was taken back into surgery, where things were put right. Now Storck wanted to help little girls pick up pennies, and he was brilliant at it.

A couple of days after Jack Triplett died, Patsy, a nurse in Intensive Care, called up sounding frantic, which was unusual. She was cool and tough, as one had to be in ICU. There had been a shooting, she said, please come right away.

I raced down two flights of stairs and burst onto the unit. Not ten feet away, a middle-aged man stood at the Five South nursing station, a large pistol on the desk beside him. Dr. Raphael, the cardiology resident, was with him.

"Holder," said Dr. Raphael, "I'd like you to meet Mr. Emmanuel."

We shook hands and his was surprisingly warm. He had thinning black hair and worry lines on his forehead, and looked a little like Johnny Carson.

"How do you do?" he said politely.

"There has been an unfortunate incident," said Dr. Raphael. "Mr. Emmanuel's mother, as you know, has been very ill in ICU."

I did know. She'd been admitted for the excision of a mole, but suffered a heart attack during surgery and had been comatose for weeks. It was as if she had fallen into an atmosphere, a climate, of illness.

"What's the problem?" I said, glancing at the gun.

"Mr. Emmanuel has killed his mother," Dr. Raphael said.

"I've only done as she asked," Emmanuel said. "She always said she wouldn't live like a vegetable."

"I understand," said Raphael, "but there was a small chance of recovery."

"No chance," said Emmanuel. "There was no chance." He shook his head left and right like a confident child, and then he started to cry in a very repressed way, with tight little sobs.

Dr. Raphael put his arm around Emmanuel for a second, then withdrew it, unsure of what to do. Was he supposed to comfort the man who'd killed his patient? With the family's permission, he had the right to "pull the plug" on the patient, so he was a little peeved that the son had not come to him first.

"I'm afraid we'll have to call the police," Raphael said. "You understand, don't you?"

"Yes, I understand. I fully expected it," Emmanuel said. He looked down the hall toward the room where his mother lay. Nurses passed back and forth, trying to calm down the three other cardiac patients in the room. Economy required that many beds in ICU, but the practice was self-defeating. When one person went into arrest, it would set off dangerous patterns in the other patients' EKGs. You could sit at the desk in the middle of the room, where the central monitor was located, and watch the panic set in. The nurses were used to this, so when an arrest occurred, they would hand out tranquilizers to the other patients. One hotshot administrator had the idea of putting carpet on the floors of ICU, in order to maintain quiet. Then it was discovered that the static created by nurses walking back and forth would set off all four monitors at once, scaring the patients half to death.

I called Security from the unit phone, and within a couple of minutes half the force was there, standing around in their blue uniforms. Most of them were in their fifties and overweight, but one was a younger man named Connor who wanted to become a Chicago cop in the worst way. We called him "Cowboy" because of the way he swaggered around the hospital, one hand playing around his holster. Connor grabbed Mr. Emmanuel by the arm and attempted to put him in handcuffs. This was too much for Dr. Raphael, who shoved Connor in the chest, knocking him against the wall.

"Leave him alone!" he yelled, loud enough that the nurses down the hall stopped what they were doing. I thought Connor was going to fight back, but he dusted himself off and walked over to the other officers, who turned their backs on him. They were embarrassed by the guy. A few days later, he pulled his gun on a visitor who was smoking in an elevator. The hospital fired him and took the weapons from all the other officers.

Raphael and I stayed with Mr. Emmanuel in a fifth-floor office until the Chicago cops arrived. He was very quiet at first, but then he began to talk about his mother. She had been an inspiration to him, he said, because she'd raised him and two brothers without the help of his father, who'd run away when he was five. Years ago, he tracked down his father in a small mining town in northern Michigan, where he was in the hospital with Huntington's chorea.

"When I entered his room," he said, "he was eating dinner. A spoon was strapped to his hand, and now and then he managed to bring a small amount to his mouth. Most of the time his arm would explode against his will, and food would fly in all directions."

"Did your father recognize you?" Raphael asked.

"No, how could he? I was only five when he left. I told him I was a volunteer and helped him eat. The next day I drove back to Chicago, and he never did know who I was. A few weeks later, he died from the disease."

"That's terrible," I said.

There was a knock on the door, and two policemen entered. One of the officers put the gun into a plastic bag, and detectives stayed around most of the evening, asking questions of Patsy and the others. The nurses said he would visit every night and stand quietly beside the bed, watching the machine breathe for his mother. Sometimes he would bring candy and flowers for the nurses, and they thought he was the perfect son. Tonight, he had shown how perfect he was, drawing the .38 out of his clothing and putting a single bullet in her chest. It was a famous case, much discussed in the media that summer. A surprising number of people came out in favor of mercy killing, including some noted theologians. Meanwhile, the police discovered a firing range in the basement of the home Emmanuel shared with his mother. He had practiced his shooting there so he wouldn't miss at point-blank range.

Before he was taken away, Emmanuel asked Raphael to honor his mother's request that her eyes be donated. Sure enough, there was a permission form at the back of the chart— she had willed away her eyes. The nursing supervisor was in a tizzy because it was a coroner's case, and she wasn't sure they would allow it. To settle the issue, I called the coroner's office, and a guy who sounded more like a Mafia hit man than a doctor said hell yes we could take out the eyes, she wasn't shot in the face, was she? We should stop calling with these fucking infantile questions.

The Ophthalmology resident on call came to the unit right away, since eyes will spoil if not removed within an hour of death. Under his arm was a Styrofoam container the size of a shoebox. A red label on top of it said EYE BANK in large letters, with the address on LaSalle Street below. The resident asked if I wanted to watch the removal, but I waited outside the room, nervously pacing. Fifteen minutes later, he emerged with the box, handing it over with a smile. Holding it gingerly, I hurried down to the street and hailed a cab. The driver, a handsome black man named Gabriel Swan, didn't refuse the fare, but he didn't want the box up front with him, either. I placed it on the backseat, and he headed away, closely watching the object through his rearview mirror.

Romona was sorry she'd missed all the excitement, but she'd been busy dealing with Normal Cane and Desiree Hawkins, a station clerk on the eleventh floor. Everyone knew that drugs had been missing in massive amounts, but they couldn't figure out where they were going. One theory was that someone on the unit was ordering drugs that weren't required for the patients' care and selling them on the street. Now it looked like Desiree, a large white woman with broad teeth and a tough manner, had done just that. Romona said Desiree had been hospitalized with a drug overdose that night. Needle marks were found on her arms, and, of all places, on her vagina. Barbara shuddered when Romona reported this last detail.

"You mean she actually shot it into her, her . . . ?" she asked, unable to say the word.

"That's right," Romona said, her red lipstick looking especially lopsided. "She thought no one would look there."

"Ick!" Barbara said.

"So it was Desiree all along," Ed exclaimed. He admired Cane's style, but having accusations aimed at him hadn't been pleasant. I felt relieved, too.

"Let's go up to see her," Ed suggested, and after break we did. Desiree was in a private room on the tenth floor, perhaps to keep her away from other patients. Cane had suggested guards outside her door, but the nursing supervisor said forget it.

The room was dim when Ed and I entered. Head back on the pillow, she appeared to be asleep. The television was on, and its blue light played over the bed. It gave her face a psychedelic look.

"Desiree," said Ed. "Are you awake?"

She turned her head slowly toward us, and I realized she was still drugged. When she saw us, her smile broadened like a highway.

"Well, I'll be a son of a bitch," she said, "come in, you two."

"Thought we'd come and see how you're doing," Ed said.

"I'm doing just fine, and the sight of you two makes me horny." She turned sideways in bed and leered at us. Desiree often said things like that, and a couple of interns had taken her up on it. There had been some stories about bed use in empty rooms.

"Come closer," she teased, but when we did, she reached out with a quick hand, cupped Ed's balls, and gave them a jiggle. The undertaker blushed so hard I thought his ears would blink off and on.

"Hey!" he said. "Let go."

"Haven't felt something like this in three days," she said. "Feels good."

"Maybe I should leave," I suggested.

"Stay where you are," she said. "You're next!" But she wasn't serious. Desiree did a lot of things for show, and it was especially funny because Ed had been her supervisor. Here she had been stealing the drugs, selling them on the street for heroin, and Ed was getting the blame. Now she had the nerve to grab him by the balls, and he couldn't even get mad at her.

What was it about Desiree's obscene behavior that made me philosophical? On one hand, she was completely vulgar. While on duty, she would step into the back room at every opportunity for a cigarette and a drink from her purse, and

orders would pile up on the desk. More than one nurse had
asked to be transferred because of her, but somehow she
always managed to land on her broad feet, no matter how
serious the infraction. Maybe it was the purity of her vul-
garity that charmed us, and finally even the nursing supervisors were persuaded. Desiree was an institution. She was
a breath of rich summer in a bad alley, but if anybody knew
who she was, it was Desiree Hawkins. In a time of anxiety
and identity crisis, when every other person you passed on
State Street was a psychiatrist, that was worth a lot. That's
why, when she placed her hand on Ed's crotch, I thought,
This is a philosophical issue. This has to do with identity,
being and nonbeing, and the will to power. Someday she
would drive over a Hollywood cliff in a Cadillac, eyes dilated
like skies. Meanwhile, there was something almost normal
about her manic behavior, since we both permitted and expected it.

Desiree was telling us what the bastard Cane had said to
her, when her eyes went back in her head. Only the white
parts flickered below, like night lights on a bumpy road. She
threw her head back on the pillow, arched her back as if in
orgasm, and made low choking noises in her throat. Ed and
I looked at each other oddly, dumbly, for what seemed like
seventy-five years before we realized what had happened. A
padded tongue depressor was taped to the wall near the bed.
These were present when the patient had a history of grand
mal seizures.

We leaped into chaotic action. Ed grabbed the tongue depressor and made a poor effort at getting it into her mouth.
Desiree thrashed and bucked.

I found myself in the hall calling for a nurse. I must have
yelled pretty loud, because everyone at the station looked up
in alarm, and in no time at all Gwyneth McCarthy, the charge
nurse, was in the room shoving Ed out of the way. No arrest
was called, but the intern, Tim Pagel, and resident, Dr. Bernstein, got there fast. Bernstein told us to pull the bed away
from the wall and to surround it. This way, we could restrain

Desiree from hurting herself on the bed rails, which were already up. Bernstein stationed himself at the head of the bed, where he manipulated the tongue depressor and gave orders. I took charge of one of her powerful legs and Ed took the other, while the intern and Gwyn handled the arms. She was unbelievably strong. We were tossed around like sailors in a storm. Ed took a kick in the chest and bounced off the wall, but gamely he came back for more.

On Bernstein's orders, the aides brought pillows, which we used to line the sides and head of the bed. Then a nurse entered the room with some Valium in a syringe. The resident shot it into her hip with difficulty. The first ten milligrams didn't do any good at all. After five minutes, Bernstein gave her another ten, then another. Those didn't help either, so he gave her even more. The resident was beside himself, and Pagel was no use. This was his first week on the job, and he looked scared.

Bernstein was complaining of the blood on his fingers when Allen Kranz, the hospital's single hippie resident, came in the door. Desiree wasn't his case, but he'd been walking down the hall and seen the commotion. He had long curly hair that was held with a rubber band in back, a mystical medallion of some kind around his neck, and a ring on every finger.

He held out his arms in a gesture that looked vaguely prophetic and said with great command, "Stop what you are doing! Stop it right now!"

"What's the meaning of this, Kranz?" said Bernstein.

"You're making a mistake. Take your hands off her and she'll be all right."

"Look at this blood," Bernstein said. "If we don't hold her down, she'll bite off her tongue."

"Take the Zen approach," Kranz said calmly, taking the tongue depressor out of Bernstein's hand. "Everyone loosen your grip until you're barely touching her, like fog on a beach."

He held out a hand to illustrate what he meant, and Gwyn McCarthy turned to me and mouthed the words "fog on a beach." Everyone thought Kranz was a little strange because of the way he dressed, but he was also incredibly smart, so we did as he said. To our amazement, the less we pressed down on Desiree, the less she resisted. Almost immediately, she began to subside into less serious seizures. Kranz didn't bother with the tongue depressor. He placed his hands lightly on each side of her face and stared contentedly out of the window, as if he were thinking of going sailing.

Soon Desiree was almost normal. Bernstein left the room, shaking his head. Ed, whose attitude toward hippies was somewhere to the right of Mussolini, had gained real respect for Kranz. What he loved was the spectacle. It was like sitting in mass on Sunday morning, hearing tales of the saints, the grand and theatrical miracles.

It turned out that Desiree had overdosed on purpose. Luckily, just before she fell asleep from the alcohol and heroin, she'd made a call to a staff psychiatrist. Dr. Grabart, an undesirable man with an ill-fitting wig, was known to sleep with his women patients. He had apparently had an affair with Desiree, and she called to tell him what a jerk he was. It was the middle of the night, and more in irritation than in a spirit of mercy, he called the police. When Desiree didn't answer the bell, the landlady let them in. Desiree was sprawled on the couch, bottles of pills from Metropolitan spread around her, and an empty syringe clutched in her hand. The pills were reported to hospital authorities, and after her recovery she was quietly fired. We all felt sorry for her. There was a little good-bye party with coffee in Styrofoam cups, and a cake one of the aides had made. A few weeks later Desiree showed up on the unit in an Easter ensemble from the fifties. Everything was white, from the skirt and jacket to the pillbox hat with attached veil. It was her way of telling us things were working out for her, but the nylons were torn in back, her fingernails were dirty, and the lipstick was smeared.

Not long after that, she did commit suicide. The coroner found that she had eaten a peanut-butter-and-rat-poison sandwich. This would have killed her within five minutes, but to make sure, she covered her face with a clear plastic bag, tied it shut with a long piece of string, and attached both ends of the strings to her wrists. When she fell unconscious, the weight of her arms pulled the bag even tighter around her face. When the police discovered the body days later, her face was black beneath the plastic, like that of an African god.

16

∎　∎　∎　∎　∎　∎

I hadn't seen my parents in quite some time, even though
they lived only 150 miles away. Weeks would often go by
before I opened their letters, and sometimes I didn't open
them at all. Now, because of events at the hospital, I wanted
to lie down on their couch in the sunny living room and fall
asleep while a Big Ten basketball game was being played on
the black-and-white television. I wanted to eat some of my
mother's chicken and dumplings, then sit with my father on
the porch, watching cars pass on Route 31 in the distance. It
would be a nice change of pace from lugging corpses.

Rose had a theory about why I never got in touch with
them. He said it was guilt. I really wanted to be in Vietnam
getting killed like all the rest. Not contacting my parents was
a way of dying.

"When's the last time you talked to your parents?" I asked.

"Last year sometime."

"Maybe you think you ought to be dead in some rice field."

"The difference is, I'm no CO, man. If I was a CO, I'd want to be dead in a rice field."

"Fuck you, Rose. You're a fake."

"What do you mean, a fake?" he said, fingering his long black hair, which he always kept nice with Prell and conditioner.

"You're a fake hippie. You do all the right things like writing poems and casting your cock in plaster, but you don't really believe in anything."

"That's not true. I believe in the Hobbit, the Rolling Stones, and Richard Brautigan."

"Well, that just goes to prove it," I said. "That's all fake shit. If you were for real, you'd have said J. D. Salinger."

"You're fucked up," he said with a smile, and gave me a fake karate chop to the stomach.

We decided to be friends, and I had the day off, so Rose dusted off some mescaline he'd been saving for a rainy day. It reminded me of a blood-brother ceremony—you know it's going to hurt, but at least you're doing it together. I had one acid trip to my credit, but it hadn't gone well. My legs seemed to lose all their feeling, and I scooted around the apartment on my backside, while Rose and Penelope tried to talk me down. Another time I snorted some angel dust, a horse tranquilizer, and felt I'd been absorbed into the wall I was leaning against. The cells of my body were as loose as smoke, mingling with the atomic particles of wallpaper.

It was a nice day, so Rose and I headed for Lincoln Park. Families were touring the zoo, and a young working-class couple was fishing in the lagoon. A couple of hippies were throwing a yellow Frisbee for their dog to catch, but it was clumsy. Suddenly they flung it hard in our direction, and I knew I was high when the plastic disk struck me between the eyes. I'd forgotten to put up my hand to catch it. Rose missed the whole thing. He continued walking, gawking at the park as if it were television, a smile slapped onto his face. It reminded me of the time we were stopped by a cop while smoking a huge joint and he popped it into his mouth. When

I got back to the car from getting my ticket, his teeth were green from eating it.

At Lonnie's, an outdoor restaurant on Clark Street, we ordered a hamburger and beer, but after a couple of bites I made the mistake of looking at it—a quarter pound of flesh on a sesame-seed bun. Its purple pinkness astonished me; it was as if I'd taken a bite from the side of a cow. When Rose heard this, he put down his hamburger, took a pen from the pocket of his jeans, and began to write all over the paper tablecloth. I could read some of the magnified script as it orbited toward my plate—it was all about the animal nature of man, man the killer and eater.

I liked Rose, but things were changing around the old dump. Edgar was somewhere in Europe, and Carlo had come up with a new scam. He'd been awarded a lectureship in the Art of Social Change by New Left College. He now wore a full-blown Afro, beads, and a dashiki, and had moved to the college's suburban campus, where he was quite a hit. New Left had only one department, which they called Revolutionary Arts, and you could get credit for life experience. For instance, if you went to church as a kid and challenged the Sunday-school teacher, you could get four hours' credit in the Spirituality Today class. Nobody attended class, of course, because that was too uptight. Tuition was required, but otherwise you could do what you wanted. Carlo said the Revolutionary Arts Department was cochaired by all college faculty and that decisions had to be unanimous. That was no problem, since everybody thought the same way. Decisions just came to them, like the weather. The faculty agreed with Rousseau that education should be nonspecific. Nothing should be learned by rote, and facts themselves were unimportant. What mattered was the development of a personal stance or attitude in the world. The dean of the college, Marlin Winesap, was impressed with Carlo's anarchic personality, and he wanted that communicated to the students. It didn't matter that Carlo had no degree, not even from high school. His prison experience was training enough. As for the hierarchy implied in the existence of a dean, Winesap said his position existed, like good government, only to do away with itself. The happiest moment in his life, he told Carlo, would come when the students and faculty dragged him from his air-conditioned office with sauna and wet bar and set fire to the administration building. Unfortunately, he said, shaking his great mane of white hair, the level of education at the college was not yet that advanced. The problem was how to instruct the students without using corrective teaching methods. It was wrong, perhaps evil, to ask them to revise their behavior. One could not revise his breathing or the way he walked across the room. That came spontaneously from the soul. Where could they get students with enough fire?

"I couldn't believe that shit," said Carlo. "Ol' Winesap got down on his hands and knees and crawled around the office like a fuckin' dog. He said the world was turning to stone, fuckin' stone, man, because there was too much logic."

I asked him how much he got paid at New Left College.

"It's on commission," he said. "Twenty percent of new tuitions we bring in. Plus all the white pussy a youngblood needs."

It was obvious that Carlo liked his new position, but the suburbs began to change him. We saw him less and less. The last time he came around, he was wearing his academic dashiki and had two white transvestites on his arm. They were going out for pizza, they said, and wondered if we'd like to go along. No, thanks, I stammered, but Randy went with them. He reported later that the transvestites, who wore blue denim miniskirts and platform shoes, were commodities brokers from Winnetka. In spite of their conservative politics, he'd found them intellectually stimulating. I guessed that Carlo had learned to deal with the drag thing in prison, and Randy confirmed it. That evening Carlo had confessed to doing some male hustling when he was sixteen years old. One night he was picked up in a limousine by a guy who drove him to a cemetery and asked Carlo to make love on his former lover's grave. The fee was two hundred dollars, but he refused it.

The situation was too weird, since the chauffeur was the man's current lover, and would be watching from the driver's seat, headlights blazing. Randy and I shook our heads at each other. We felt Carlo had made the correct decision.

Randy said he and Carlo had decided nothing was innate in the way people dressed. If a man wanted to wear kilts or negligees down the street, that was his business. In fact, the fashion statement was, in a real sense, the final statement of the revolution. When everyone felt free enough to risk the ridiculous, society would be truly free, not before.

"Did you sleep with them?" I asked.

"Sure," he said proudly. He winked and went into another room.

It made me feel better about Randy. He had always been so self-conscious and anxious, which made him the perfect victim, and here he was, the seducer and flirt. If this could happen after being beaten up by your girl friend, world peace was possible.

It was the Fourth of July, and I had trouble getting to work because of all the traffic on Lake Shore Drive where the annual Air Show was going on. Sitting on bleachers, the family audience watched their country's war machines fly over Lake Michigan. As I sat in the middle of a traffic jam, ten minutes late for work, an enormous jet flew in at high speed, braked in the air, and floated over the harbor like an ancient reptile. The exhaust from its ventral jet made the water concave in an area the size of a baseball diamond. Its power was disgusting and frightening. Then the Blue Angels streaked out of the horizon, the four planes peeling off from the center. The picture they painted in jet exhaust was that of a flower. The crowd sighed and clapped at the beauty of it all.

That night nobody died at the hospital, but a black nursing aide named Ida came to work beaten up. One eye was nearly closed and the cornea of the other was red with blood. She looked like she needed to be hospitalized.

"What happened?" I asked Linda Ruh, the nurse on Six North.

"Ida was raped last night on her way home from work," she said as she put the six o'clock med tray together.

"She looks terrible," I said. "Why is she at work?"

"She called in sick," Linda said, "but Graven wouldn't let her take the day off. She said if she didn't show up, she was fired."

Malvinia Graven was probably the most feared nursing supervisor. She was of the old school and gave no slack. When she came onto a unit, everyone sat up straight and tried to look busy.

"It isn't fair," I said. "She was really raped?"

"He pulled her behind an elementary school," Linda said, "and stuck a gun in her mouth."

I went into the supply room, where Ida was collecting towels for the bedbaths she had to give.

"Hi, Holder," she said.

"I heard what happened," I said. "I'm sorry."

"That bitch Graven is gonna get it someday," she said with surprising heat. She was usually very mild-mannered and one of the best aides in the hospital. I knew she couldn't afford to lose the job, because she had three small children and no husband. She could have made more money on welfare than on an aide's salary, but she was too proud to accept it. At that moment, I hated Graven, the United States Air Force, apple pie, hamburgers, and the sky over Montana. Life had never seemed more outrageous.

"Maybe Graven will fall down a laundry chute and die," I said, but as soon as I said it, Ida's face told me to shut up and turn around. There was Malvinia Graven, clipboard in hand, regarding me with cold fury. She didn't say anything, but I knew I was in for some serious trouble. Blue veins stood up on the backs of her hands, and her gray eyes quivered.

Around ten o'clock that night, Barbara, Ed, and I took the elevator to the seventeenth floor, where there was an exercise deck and solarium for ambulatory patients. It was rarely used, but now and then you'd see some sturdy soul out there, struggling in the wind. There was something about the place that communicated sadness. In one corner of the solarium, old hospital furniture and equipment was stacked in disarray. Behind the heap, where you would least expect an office, a door opened and a small man in a rumpled suit walked rapidly toward the elevator, holding a sheaf of rumpled papers. This Kafkaesque figure was David Timor, whose job was making out employee schedules. That was all he did, high above the city, in a room with no windows. All evening he filled out grids with names and dates, in two-week segments. You could request a certain schedule, but it was finally David Timor's decision, filling in an O for a day off with impeccable penmanship. According to Romona, who had told us of his existence, he never mixed with any of the other employees. As far as I knew, this was the first time any regular employees had seen him. The moment was eerie and giddy, as if we'd come across an obscure salamander that was only rumored to exist. We couldn't help laughing because of the way he carried himself, like a common little god. When he saw us, he scuttled into a stairwell and was gone.

Seeing him reminded me that a patient was rumored to live on the eighteenth floor. His name was Harms and he had been there for years—wealthy, eccentric, and chronically ill. After he donated a few million dollars to the hospital, they converted a storeroom into a penthouse, where private nurses tended him around the clock. In fact, his was the *only* room on the eighteenth floor. One floor below, in the fenced-in exercise area, we could see the lights of his room, mysterious and yellow. Nobody ever saw Harms except for nurses and doctors, and I often wondered if he wasn't a myth, like the phantom of the opera. Timor was his gnomic assistant, and Malvinia Graven, with her Medusan disposition and transparent teeth, was the agent of change, the one who went forth from this high place.

Our plan was to watch the fireworks display over Oak Street Beach, some of which had already started. You could hear dull thuds and explosive static. After a while, the show grew in intensity, and the near sky filled with light. The deck on which we stood was brightly lit for a moment, then shivered into darkness. It was like the flares in Vietnam, I imagined, but no enemy soldiers flickered along the horizon. Barbara put her arm around me when Ed wasn't looking, but she nervously dropped it after a while. The fireworks didn't please her very much and she wanted to go back inside. Ed was having a wonderful time. He'd noticed other fireworks displays all over the city and ran from one parapet to another, pointing at them. One was on the West Side, perhaps in Garfield Park. Another was on the South Side, in Comiskey Park, where the White Sox had just finished a game. Two displays of lesser intensity could be seen farther out, perhaps in the suburbs. You couldn't hear them, but they gave you a sense of fireworks going off all over the country at that moment, in the small towns and fading cities, in ball parks and broken-down drive-in theaters. You could imagine the faces of people gazing up at the fire, but they weren't the confident faces of a Norman Rockwell drawing. They were tense with history, because they knew someone fighting in Vietnam, and the fireworks made his peril real to them.

Barbara asked me to come home with her that night, and when I gave an excuse she looked hurt. I couldn't tell her that Gary Janush had called from his home with news about Malvinia Graven. She'd called repeatedly, asking for my resignation. He said he'd try to protect me, but his own job was in jeopardy, and Normal Cane had already spoken of me with suspicion. If my involvement in the demonstration and the insult to Graven were put together, I didn't stand a chance. That was too bad, he said, because I had only two months to go. At any rate, there would be a meeting tomorrow to decide my fate, and I wasn't invited.

The apartment on Halsted was desolate and dreary. When I turned on the kitchen light, cockroaches exploded out of the sink and headed for every crack and crevice. Nobody else appeared to be at home. All the bedroom doors were open except for Penelope's. I knocked on it, and when there was no answer, I entered. The room was extremely small. There was space enough for the bed and a small nightstand, but there wasn't even a closet. A small pile of her sad-looking clothes occupied one corner. They were dark and musty, and, standing near them, I could smell camphor, wool, lonesomeness, and weekends. There was also the unexpected smell of men's cologne. I thought it was probably Edgar's, then I was sure it was Edgar's, and to my shock I felt a stirring in my groin. Olfactory voyeurism? Penelope and Edgar? It didn't seem possible.

My face in Penelope's small antique mirror was a shock. It was known to me, but it was new. It seemed to belong to someone of vast inexperience, or even to a person who had never *had* an experience. There was intelligence in the eyes, but, on the whole, this was the icon of a face, the drawing of a face, faceness. I pushed the rubbery features with my fingers, as Rowdy Triplett had done to his dead son.

Exhausted, I lay down on the bed, which was far too short for me and narrow, nearly, as a bench. The ceiling looked very distant, as if drifting out of reach. During the day, light came into the room feebly, colored by years of dirt on the glass. It was as if the light withdrew at the very moment it entered. For all I knew, someone from the government was watching me even now, taking notes and smiling. It was the smile of that invisible agent that crossed my mind as I drifted off to sleep, arms and legs askew. Not even the drowned, floating underwater, ever slept so soundly.

I awoke at four in the morning, staggered down the hall, and peeked into my own bedroom. Penelope wasn't there. An emptiness filled the apartment that was change itself. None of us were the same as yesterday, and we would be even more different tomorrow. I wanted this change to stop. I wanted leaves to stop falling, and meat to stop rotting. The rivers could all stop flowing, as far as I was concerned. We needed a little stability here.

A cigarette glowed in the dark of the front room. It was

probably Randy scrunched down on the couch, having intense and dark thoughts. Instead, it was Penelope and Randy, sharing his cigarette. They were also entirely naked.

"Hello," said Penelope crisply and brightly. "Did we have a good sleep?"

"I should be asking you that question," I said.

"It's the bed," she said, stroking Randy's chest with one hand. "It puts one into a virtual coma."

I studied their bodies. In spite of her limp, Penelope had no signs of a crippling injury, and she was better put together than I had thought. In fact, she looked a lot better naked than she did dressed. In the nude, she had the confidence of a professional model. It was I who felt ill at ease, slumped in a canvas chair, shaking the sleep out of my head. Randy gave me a look that mixed snideness and pity. Disengaging himself from Penelope's arms, he leaned forward, his round face illuminated by the available light from the hall.

"Want a cigarette?" he asked.

"No, thanks," I said glumly.

"What's the matter, Jim?" asked Penelope with concern.

"Oh, nothing. I was just thinking about things at work. About things in general."

"You should take a break from that place," Randy said. "It's not good to be around death so much."

"Maybe you're right. Every time I take a body to the morgue, I think, This will be me someday. Somebody will wrap me in cloth, load me onto a cart, and drop me onto a cold slab. They won't know who I was or what I thought about life. It won't matter; I'll just be dead."

Wind came through the window behind Penelope, the slightly chill wind of early morning. She shivered and reached for her purple top, which was on the floor beside her. It immediately made her smaller and mousier. As Penelope retreated into a more timid persona, Randy also seemed less confident. His eyes made an anxious accounting of the room, and he puffed nervously on the cigarette.

"I don't know how you can stand that job," said Penelope. "It would drive me absolutely into an asylum."

"The job is all right, actually," I said. "The people are nice, and you more or less get used to the bodies. There are exceptions, of course. The other day, when we pulled back the curtains, the corpse was sitting up in bed. My friend Ed and I jumped back about six feet."

Randy was interested in the story. He liked all my morbid stories about the hospital, because they fit into his superhero conception of the world.

"How can a corpse sit up?" Penelope asked.

"It was actually a little old lady with a humpback that made her appear to be sitting," I said. "It wasn't only her position that was scary; it was also her height. She was only four feet tall."

"Like Isis," said Randy, more or less to himself, "a tiny Isis embalmed in Memphis." Lost in thought, he tapped cigarette ashes onto the coffee table.

A shudder ran through Penelope and she began to look around on the floor for another article of clothing. She slipped a man's blue sock onto her right foot, but made no attempt to find its mate.

"The body was so light," I said, "you could reach over with one hand, pick it up like a satchel, and lift it onto the cart. It couldn't have weighed over fifty pounds."

"Is that what you did?" asked Randy.

"Actually, I picked it up with both hands, gripping the sheet from above, swung it around . . ."

"Like a derrick," said Randy.

". . . and lowered it onto the cart. But the body still looked like it was sitting up. We had to push the head down in order to get the slab back in the wall. Ed said it was like shoving a kid downhill on a sled."

"Disgusting," said Penelope.

"Once we had a body that dripped blood all over our pants and shoes," I said, remembering how Ed and I had to change into surgical trousers for the rest of the shift.

"Stop right there!" said Penelope, pointing at me with one of her shoes.

I stopped by Gary Janush's office before the evening shift started the next day. As soon as I entered, he rose and came to the door. The news wasn't good. Graven and Cane had indeed gotten together. They wanted me fired and insisted a letter go to the draft board, notifying them of my behavior. He walked me down the hall, where we could talk without the secretary hearing. We stopped in front of room 785. Inside, a teenaged girl in a body cast looked at us quizzically, as if we were discussing her.

"I made the best deal I could," Gary said, "but my own position isn't the best. Graven wants to get rid of the management program altogether."

"I understand," I said.

"We worked something out with Bolger," he said, looking down the hall at an open window. "We can keep the management program for one more year if you agree to leave."

"Leave!" I whispered loudly. "You want me to leave? I didn't do anything, Gary."

"Don't make so much noise," he said, looking fearfully at the nursing station. "The fact is, Holder, I had to make a deal. If I let you go now, I can save twenty-five other jobs. It's like bleeding. You've got to stop the bleeding or the patient dies."

"That's just great," I said. "Thanks for your help, Gary."

"I busted my ass for you, Jim," he said, offering his hand, which I let freeze in the air.

"No," I said, "I busted my ass for *you!*" I must have spoken loudly, because everyone at the station was staring at us.

"Look," he said with surprising heat. "You must have fucked up or things would never have gone this far. I tried for you, I really did. . . ." His voice trailed off. He stopped looking at me directly. He said I had until the end of the week. Meanwhile, they were sending notice of my termination to the draft board. Cane had insisted on it.

Janush turned and walked back to his office, but I knew it was no use to follow him. I stood in the hall feeling like a tunnel had opened beneath my feet. The girl in the body cast motioned to me. "Hey, you," she said, "how about some service around here?"

"What's the problem?" I said.

"The service here is shit," she said. "Why don't you do something about it?"

"You shouldn't talk like that. Your mother wouldn't like it," I said, leaving the room.

That evening I worked the shift as usual. Most of the time I sat in the office waiting for the Pagemaster to go off. At ten-thirty, however, everybody gathered in room 725, where some patients were watching a "Tonight Show" rerun. It was the one in which Tiny Tim, who sang "Tiptoe Through the Tulips" and whose humor depended in part on his ugliness, was getting married to Miss Vicki. The ceremony, which had been funny the first time, seemed more solemn. Johnny Carson, as best man, acted as if he were attending a real wedding. It reminded me of another evening when some of us gathered to watch Neil Armstrong step on the moon. Most people thought it was a great moment, but I stood at the back, completely bored with the idiot astronauts. The nuptials of Tiny Tim at least had the charm of a fairy tale. We knew the marriage had been a shill created by agents, and the artifice relaxed us. Armstrong probably had his lines written for him by a NASA publicist, even though his adventure was for real. "A giant step for mankind, my ass," I had said to no one in particular, whereupon everyone in the room, the patients, visitors, private nurses, aunts, nephews, parents, children, and spiders on the wall had turned and glared at me with intense patriotic fervor.

The American Friends Service Committee, I discovered the next morning, was located on LaSalle Street, in an old building near the Midwest Commodities Exchange. Rumpled brokers stood on the street, their pockets bulging with pieces of paper, smoking cigarettes and talking conspiratorially. I'd heard they traded in things like plywood, gold, and pork bellies—anything that had a price subject to fluctuation. If they had bought some wheat and disaster struck the crop, sending prices sky-high, they were enormous winners. In a sense, they were betting against nature, against some principle of fertility itself. I had heard that even farmers had begun to protect themselves by buying futures, betting, in effect, that their own crops would fail. It was a far cry from the image of agriculture I possessed from attending the Church of Peace, where the pastor prayed for rain in times of drought, for sunshine when the fields were too moist to support the weight of a cornpicker.

The Merkel Building, where the Friends had their office, was on the verge of being condemned. Nothing was rented, and the old elevator, with its open grating, revealed one empty dentist's office after another on the way to the fourth floor. The operator, who was very old, wore the uniform of a security service, but his black holster was empty, as if someone had stolen his weapon and he didn't know it yet.

The Service Committee was at the end of the hall. The office consisted of two large rooms with old desks and a few antiwar posters on the wall, including the famous one of a Chicago cop leaning on his motorcycle and giving the photographer the finger. Another had a large photo of a gas mask, superimposed with an excerpt from Shakespeare that began, "What a piece of work is a man! how noble in reason!"

Two counselors were on duty, young men with white shirts, black vests, and wireless granny glasses. As I watched them counsel the men ahead of me, I realized they were twins of some kind. There was a basic resemblance, but one was puffier in the face and looked like he'd been in a motorcycle accident. While I waited, I looked through a black ring binder that was on the table. It was a list of available CO jobs, and it wasn't in very good shape. Pages had been torn out, and much of what was left didn't look current. There was a job as a milk tester and collector of bull semen in Delaware. There was another working as a laboratory animal in New Jersey. You let them inject you with drugs, and they hooked you up to a machine that measured the resulting spasms. There was another working in a home for children who liked to set fires, or so I gathered from the garbled description the home's administrator had provided. That was about it.

"We don't recommend any of those," said the thinner twin, who sat down across from me. He reminded me of Strelnikov, the heartthrob Communist youth in *Dr. Zhivago*.

"Why not?"

"We keep those around for the CO types who want to cooperate with the system," he said, straddling the folding chair and twisting an old copy of *The Chicago Seed* in his hands. "Our thrust is to defeat the war machine altogether. We do that by recommending resistance."

"You mean you tell all these guys to go to Canada?"

"Or to jail," he said calmly. "In fact, jail is the higher form of resistance ethically. Judges put the sentence at an average of twenty-six months."

I looked around the room. Most of the previous clients had left, but one guy in secondhand fatigues and blue jeans was reading a pamphlet called *Doing Time*.

"Name's Rudy," said the counselor, extending his hand.

"Jim," I said.

"That's my brother Carl," he said proudly, indicating the other counselor. "He just got out of Leavenworth—thirty-six straight months!"

"That's great," I said.

"Yeah, Carl's the best," he said, and the brother looked in our direction. A thick red scar ran across Carl's neck and into his hair behind the ear. His lower lip looked like it had been sewn back together.

"Are you identical twins?" I asked.

"We used to be," said Rudy, looking down at the backs

of his hands. It was clear that Carl's injuries had occurred in prison, but I didn't have the nerve to ask what had happened.

"What about you?" I asked. "Have you been in jail, too?"

"I was convicted the same time as Carl," he said a little sadly, "but my lawyer's appeals have slowed everything down. To tell the truth, I'd like to have it over by now."

I explained my case to him, and he studied the floor for a minute. "I'm afraid we can't be of much help," he said, "unless you want to go the resistance route. Then we can provide legal services. Our priorities, frankly, are as follows: jail, going underground, and Canada. Most of the COs just figure things out for themselves." He said "COs" with a hint of sarcasm, as if it were ethically akin to selling used cars.

"I don't get it," I said, my face getting red. "You act like being a CO is the same as serving in the army."

He shrugged his shoulders and said nothing.

"COs do a lot of good," I said. "They help people in hospitals and things like that. They also aren't in Vietnam, killing a lot of innocent people . . . killing anyone for that matter." But my indignation was hollow, because I'd already begun to wonder if Rudy wasn't right.

A guy wearing a lumber jacket and work boots entered the office with his girl friend, who wore an India-print dress and long earrings. He had a batch of papers in his hands. They both looked worried.

"Gotta go now," Rudy said, rising. "Good luck to you." He walked over to the couple, and an earnest conversation began. It was obvious that the kid had been drafted, and I could see Canada all over his girl friend's face.

I was lost in thought when Carl tapped me on the shoulder. This close, his scars were frightening, but his eyes and voice were gentle. "Consider prison," he said. "It's what you can do for your country." I left the office with that advice in mind, feeling as if I were buried in my own flesh. The chatter of brokers on LaSalle Street brushed by like so much fuzz.

17

■   ■   ■   ■   ■   ■

My father had given me some old luggage, but I couldn't find it anywhere. All my clothing fit into two pillowcases and a cardboard box, but there wouldn't be room for the books. From the stack along a bedroom wall, I chose *Rabbit, Run* by John Updike, *The Great Gatsby,* and a weird book on Victorian sexual practices by David Brain, a captain in the Salvation Army. There was a picture of him, overweight and chinless, on the back of the wrinkled, sun-bleached book. It had been left behind by a previous tenant, and I thought someday I would read it for the charming oddity of its prose— a text full of typos, blots, blurs, and goofs.

It was eight in the morning, and the day was beautiful. Sunlight cut deeply into the apartment and found me standing at my bedroom door. I'd slept only briefly, wearing the clothes I'd come home in. That sweet odor of gasoline and flowers was me. I went to the bathroom, stripped off my clothes, stepped into the shower, and turned it on full-blast.

After dressing in some fresh jeans and a white dress shirt, like someone getting his senior-class picture, I went to the refrigerator. There was nothing in it but an empty milk carton, a dozen bright apples, and two tired-looking potatoes that had slowly grown eyes. I took two apples and stuffed them into one of the pillowcases.

I made a smooth exit without any awkward good-byes. Randy and Penelope were probably in one of their bedrooms, sleeping off their astonishment at having paired off. Wherever Rose was, he was probably dreaming about doors.

At the bottom of the front stairs, Gus and Larry, the giant neighbors, were in warm-up outfits that said "Temple University" across the front. Gus was wearing roller skates and making surprisingly graceful figure eights on the sidewalk. Larry was jogging in place.

"Leaving town?" said Larry jerkily.

"Yeah."

"Anyplace special, like Aruba?"

"Just home," I said, "to see my parents."

"See you later," said Gus, executing a brilliant backward leap and turn on his skates. He landed so softly, you could barely hear the skates click on the sidewalk. All of his great height seemed to unwind and regather during the maneuver.

"So long!" I said, but they were already moving away.

I drove to the Metropolitan, parked the car in front, and left the keys inside. If somebody stole it, I wouldn't go anywhere. If it was waiting when I returned, the fates had decided.

The Hospital was bright and busy. Patients were being wheeled off to tests and surgery. Volunteers and candy stripers walked here and there, carrying out the useless tasks to which they were fairly accustomed, their very inefficiency a sign that somebody cared.

Janush's secretary was in the office, but he wasn't, which both pleased and disappointed me. On the one hand, I wanted to get even with him, as Harvey Kolwitz had done when Gary fired him a few months ago. In anger, Harvey had swept everything off Gary's desk, including the prized pictures of his family. On the other hand, I didn't want the aggravation of seeing him again. The secretary was on the phone with a friend, so I pointed to my paycheck, which was on the desk in front of her. All the paychecks were there, since that was the routine every other Friday. I picked it up and waved good-bye with it as I headed back down the hall. Neither of us spoke a word. In the elevator, I opened the envelope and there was a letter of termination inside, signed by Bolger. Having no use for the letter, I handed it to a kid from Pediatrics who was being wheeled down for an X ray or test. He gave me a smile and tucked it into the Mickey Mouse coloring book he had on his lap. He would draw on it later. The other people in the car—an intern, a dietitian, and the transportation aide—smiled mechanically and looked up at the floor numbers blinking over their heads.

The car was where I had left it, keys in the ignition. I started the engine and steered dreamily to the Hancock Building, which soared to a point overhead. The doorman at the side entrance on Delaware Street didn't challenge my parking there, even though the 1963 Chevy Nova had rust spots around the door and gave off blue smoke. In fact, he held the door for me, and I entered the lobby regally.

The Lake Shore National Bank was on the second floor. I cashed the paycheck, which amounted to $230. Then I wrote a check for the balance of the account: $189.10. The teller had to check with the manager, but after a while she handed me the cash with a look of commiseration, as if she wanted to go somewhere, too.

The doorman opened the car door, which squeaked on its hinges. I offered him a dollar from the bank envelope I'd stuffed my money into, but inexplicably he refused it, tipping his hat and smiling. It was so nice of him, I waved good-bye as I made an illegal U-turn in the direction of Lake Shore Drive. All the lights were timed in my favor. Soon I was a part of the high-speed traffic flowing out of the city as if fleeing a storm or god. All around me, people had two hands locked on the wheel, their eyes straight ahead, intent on where they were going rather than on where they had been.

The car wasn't prepared for any kind of trip. It was hardly ready to go around the block. A blue pigtail of smoke trailed behind, and the engine could be heard roaring through a hole in the floor, which was covered with a cheap rubber mat. Even with the pedal floored, the engine compression was so bad that the car could only do fifty miles an hour. It was all my fault. I'd never learned the least rudiments of car care. You were supposed to change the oil every few thousand miles, but I couldn't imagine going to all the bother. As a result, I'd gone through a few used cars in pretty quick succession, as if they were designed to be thrown away. The old Chevy Nova was about to go under, too. When I got to the Interstate, I removed the rubber mat covering the hole in the floor and watched the road fly under my feet. This was a lot of fun on a country road when no traffic was coming. The idea was to straddle the middle of the road so the white line flashed across your vision like a blinking light.

It took about three and a half hours to get to Malta, Indiana, the "Circus City." My parents lived about six miles on the other side of town. Malta used to be the winter headquarters for the Barnum & Bailey Circus, among others, because the railway lines crossed there. The town was filled with retired circus people: jugglers, clowns, roustabouts, and acrobats. Every summer they had their own little circus to remember the glory days, but mostly it was the local people who showed up, in spite of the chamber of commerce's ambitions for tourism. About a mile from my parents' home in the country, you could often see the heads of giraffes and elephants sticking from the windows of a barn near the highway, but today the doors and windows were all sealed and the gate across the entrance road looked rusty. Had they died from a mysterious fever, or had the owners given up the location? Malta itself had looked small and empty, as if people were sneaking out of town in the middle of the night.

My mother, Elizabeth, was in the yard poking at the ground with a stick when I pulled up. She seemed not to recognize me at first, squinting and staring. She always was slow to acknowledge people anyway, as if she were thinking about something else.

"Hi, Mom!" I shouted as the car got close enough.

"Oh, Jim," she said, squinting with confusion. "What are you doing here?"

"This is where I live, remember? What are you doing with that stick?"

"Testing the ground," she said, "to see if anything will grow here." She always had an enormous garden, from which we were fed from July until the first frost. Over the years it had gotten so large that it surrounded the white frame house almost entirely, except for a shady part near the outside cellar door where nothing would grow. As with most country homes, no one entered through the front door. Even the Bible salesmen came to the kitchen door in back.

I got out of the car and gave her a kiss on the cheek.

"Where's Dad?"

"He's in the house," she said, pointing with her stick, even though it was only a few feet away. For a moment, I thought I saw my father's dark round face at the window, like a figure in a gothic novel. He preferred the indoors, where he sat reading mystery novels and religious literature. It was my mother who seemed more comfortable outside, in spite of a pale complexion that caused her to burn easily.

"You go on inside," she said, returning to her agriculture, "I'll be along in a minute." As I carried my belongings to the door, I watched her poking at the ground with great concentration. She had always been the pioneer woman, and the developing age of suburban ease was foreign to her character. One day she opened a kitchen cabinet and a mouse, made frantic by its discovery, leaped out at her. She batted it down with one hand, watched it scramble along the counter and fall into a wastebasket. Then she calmly bent down and smashed the animal with her hands, the only available weapons. At nine years of age, I was more impressed than you could possibly imagine.

My father sat in the living room, reading a detective story with oversized print. He looked up the way someone looks up in a library, with a pleasant, abstracted smile on his face. He was half in the book and half out of it.

"Oh, hello, Jim," he said, as if I'd just come back from an errand. "I saw you come up the drive through the window there. Why didn't you tell us you were coming?"

"I left on the spur of the moment," I said.

"You're not in any kind of trouble, I hope." His face clouded over.

"No trouble. I haven't been home in a while, and it seemed a good time to come."

"Well, we're glad to see you," he said, glancing at his book as if I'd already left.

I sat at the center of the sofa, the cardboard box and pillowcases at my feet.

"What you got there?" he asked.

"Oh, just some clothes."

"Why don't you use that nice Samsonite luggage we got from Mother?"

"This seemed easier," I said.

His eyeglasses flashed window light in my eyes. Mother was his mother, Earnestine Summers Holder, and she had a room upstairs. She was eighty-two years old, but she'd nearly lost her vision from a fall and her speech was impaired by a stroke. She had been visiting some relatives in Georgia, and one night they were sitting on the back porch, eavesdropping on the neighbors. Leaning to hear better, she'd lost the edge of the chair and landed hard. The jolt had shaken loose pieces of her retina. Because they were opaque, she could see only a small part of anything, like an unfinished jigsaw puzzle.

"How's the car running?" he asked, looking up from *Mission to Madrid*.

"Oh, great. Just great."

"Thought I saw some smoke coming out of its tail."

"Needs a tune-up, that's all."

"If you take care of a car, it will take care of you. Dad used to say that. You getting good gas mileage?"

"Oh, sure," I said, but I was thinking how funny the conversation was. I'd been at country get-togethers where nothing was discussed but gas mileage.

"You should say hello to Mother," he said. "Before dinner."

"I will."

We sat in silence then. My body felt heavy, my eyes weighted down; my feet were sinking through the floor. I leaned over, put my head on the couch, and entered a deep, profound, and useful sleep. This was what I always did when I came home for a visit. When I woke up, my father was shaking my shoulder gently and the dinner table was set. My belongings were gone, except for the two apples, which were on the coffee table. In my drowsiness, I looked twice at them, confused. I knew instantly that my mother had washed and ironed my clothes, what there was of them.

We went into dinner and ate mostly in silence, as usual. Every now and then, Dad would say something like "The weather today was really something" without having a real point. He felt something had to be said in order to make the meal pleasant. The only thing mother said was "Richard, don't eat so fast," because she wanted him to lose weight. I said nothing at all. In this way, we finished our meal of pot roast and mashed potatoes, which was the best I'd ever eaten.

After the dishes were done, we went back into the front room and turned on the TV. By now it was getting dark outside, but they didn't turn on a lamp in order to save on electricity. We sat bathed in the blue-and-violet light of "Bowling for Dollars," their favorite show. They were never more animated than when this show was on, and the host,

Sammy Speaks, delighted them. The format was pretty simple. Sammy would briefly interview people, then they would
try to get two strikes in a row. If they were successful, they
got the money that had built up in the pot, which was now
at $350. If they got one strike and a spare, they got a Ping-
Pong paddle or something. Sammy always asked guests the
same question, "What do you like to eat?" They acted like
it was a tough question and screwed up their faces in intense
concentration. Yes, that's right, it's coming to me now—I
like spaghetti, or steak, or fried chicken! Everyone in the
studio audience would laugh warmly and sympathetically,
because they liked those dishes too. I felt an overwhelming
affection for my parents as they enjoyed their television show.

"Bowling for Dollars" was over, and since no one had
won the big pot, it went up to four hundred dollars. Then
the evening news came on, and Walter Cronkite announced
in his avuncular fashion, laden with tragedy and importance,
that a major bombing raid had been carried out in Cambodia,
as ordered by President Richard Nixon. Many of the enemy
had no doubt lost their lives, but what was the cost in terms
of foreign policy? The NATO allies were in disagreement.
How far would the U.S. go to turn the tide of the war? It
was announced that momentarily the president would speak
from the Oval Office, explaining his decision.

Nixon appeared, his entire being neurotic, like a failed high
school principal. He seemed always on the verge of crying
or breaking something on his desk. Whenever he was on the
air, I had to check the air above him for wires, since his erratic
head and arm movements suggested puppetry.

I thought back to Lyndon Johnson's announcement, in the
spring of 1968, that he would not seek reelection. Those of
us who watched the speech on television in the student union
were nearly dizzy with glee and amazement, and we leaped
around, hugging each other. But the war dragged on anyway,
and Terry Grubbs went and got killed in it.

Earlier in the war, Walter Cronkite had gone on the air
with similar gravity in his voice. Some Viet Cong comman-

dos on a suicide mission had invaded the U.S. embassy compound in Saigon and destroyed much of the facility before they were killed. The last commando had been tracked down in the hallways of the compound by an assistant undersecretary of something or other, who'd been handed a pistol through a broken window. The small bodies of the dead commandos, wearing civilian clothes, were laid out in a neat row on the perfectly groomed grass of the embassy. Soldiers and bureaucrats stood around in their crew cuts and tans looking worried, as if the frail bodies might leap to their feet and start fighting again. The tone of Cronkite's voice expressed what everyone already knew, that this war was going to be different. Everybody was going to get hurt this time. The war was outside the door right now, breathing the night air of Indiana.

While Nixon talked, my father's face screwed up with emotion. As a member of the Church of Peace, he despised Nixon's policies, but his respect for the office itself drove him nearly to tears. It was too much. I excused myself, went out to the car, and drove fifteen miles through the summer darkness to Tin Cup, the small town where Terry Grubbs's family lived. Along the way I passed through Need, an unincorporated village consisting of a mom-and-pop store with a gas pump in front. I imagined other towns on the road with names like Pride, Avarice, and Kindness.

I found the Grubbs' house easily enough, since there were only eight houses in the whole town. Besides, the windows were ablaze with light, in contrast with the dimness of the surrounding properties. Slashes of light fell onto the ground, as if from a spaceship. There were no curtains. You could see everything inside very clearly, as if lighted for a theatrical performance. I had turned off the lights of the car when I rounded the corner, so I sat in darkness, the engine noisily idling, watching Mr. and Mrs. Grubbs stand in the living room. He wore dark green work clothes and held a can of beer in his right hand. She wore a bright green apron and what looked like a wig, the color of orangutan fur. She also held a frying pan at waist level, as if she'd just left the stove. Neither moved an inch.

I felt a little guilty watching them, if they *were* the Grubbs and not wax models. They were absorbed in something I couldn't see, perhaps the Nixon speech on television. It was also possible they'd gone catatonic, but then Russell Grubbs was always crazy. On Halloween he would lie on his yard under a blanket, wearing commando gear and waiting for kids to soap his windows. If some poor kid so much as stepped on the property, he was on his feet like a demon, chasing him with a club. As a result, people went out of their way to vandalize whatever he had, lobbing paint balloons from passing cars. His high-speed pickup truck, with rifle rack and CB antenna, was parked in the yard, facing the road and looking lethal.

The longer I watched, the creepier I felt, as if I'd entered Russell Grubbs's state of mind. He was reduced to a statue of himself in his living room, and I had become the paranoid watcher. My gaze careened along the side of the house like a spotlight, licking the paint, teetering along the edge of a window, making the spidery figure of a bullet hole in the pane of glass framing Russell Grubbs's skull. What if he turned and saw me? In my immobility, I was prey. It was as if we had entered a dome of blue light, American icons in fixed positions.

I eased the car past the neighboring houses and out of town. As soon as I thought Terry's father couldn't see, I turned the lights back on and followed the river road, which curved under trees in full summer leaf. Every now and then I would look in the rearview mirror to see if his truck was following, but the only lights were those from farms.

The Calvary Holiness Chapel was an old brick country church the Pentecostal Holiness congregation had bought from some failed Presbyterians. They'd removed the stained-glass windows and put in plain glass, since decoration was next to sin. Every Sunday morning and Wednesday night, they rolled on the floor, shook tambourines, and spoke in tongues of fire, but they wanted an austere building in which to practice these things. They had also inherited the Presbyterian dead, who were interred in the cemetery on the rise behind the church. I figured this was where Terry would be, if he was anywhere in the world.

I drove the car through the gravel parking lot and up the hill into the cemetery as far as I could go without knocking down a stone. Then I put the lights on high beam and started walking toward the far end of the cemetery, where the new graves were probably located. The car lights made my shadow enormous against the hill, so that walking became a grotesque kind of dance. My shadow's head disappeared into the darkness above the cemetery.

Terry's grave had to be the one with the small American flag provided by the local American Legion. I knelt by the stone, which was small and flat to the ground, and ran my hand over the lettering. Memories shivered through me. I thought of Terry the night he threw the steering wheel hard with one hand, like he wanted to send us into the trees. The car went into a controlled wobble from one side of the road to the other, and an oncoming car pulled onto the shoulder, the driver's eyes as big as tires. Another time, Terry grabbed the steering wheel while I was driving, forcing the car off the road and across someone's lawn. He was so strong I couldn't fight him off, and he laughed like crazy. I saw him climb to the top of a small country bridge and step casually off, his huge body an absurdity in midair, landing in the deepest part of creek water.

Someone had left flowers in a glass tube beside the neighboring grave, which was that of a little child. A teddy bear leaned against the stone, but it wasn't yet weathered, as if someone had left it there that afternoon. I pulled the glass tube out of the ground and transferred it to Terry's grave. Then I stepped back and stood for a while in respectful silence. The wind came up and jerked the little American flag on his grave to momentary attention. It was all very peaceful and sad, but everything was also made strange by the car lights.

Even the grass was menacing and larger than life. I shuddered because I imagined Terry lying in his casket, mouth open like a lady's purse.

It was enough. I started walking back down the hill. I had no prayers to offer, and there was nothing I could do to bring him back. The lights of the car dimmed as the engine turned over, and I thought for a the moment that it wouldn't start. It growled weakly and finally roared, and I backed quickly across the lot, spinning gravel in my haste. The car lights flashed on the church windows as I bumped and swerved onto the highway. I threw the car into forward gear and nearly floored the pedal. The old Nova swooned down the road. All the way home, it was Terry this and Terry that, tears streaking down my face.

My parents were in bed when I got home. I watched Johnny Carson for a while, but his humor seemed pretty lame. He kept winking at the audience to get their sympathy, and it worked. The lamer he was, the more they liked him, as if the whole point of entertainment was to show your vulnerability.

I turned off the TV and went to bed. My room was the last one on the right, across from my grandmother's. When I got to the door, I could see her lying sadly in bed, and a wave of guilt went over me. I'd forgotten to say hello to her earlier, and Dad had probably told her I was home.

The night light was on. Her bed was in the corner. As I got closer, she startled me by turning her milky blue eyes in my direction. She had been awake all along, listening to the house, its aches and movements. I kissed her cool cheek and held her bony hand with its slim, crooked fingers. She couldn't talk anymore, due to the stroke, and she could only see me in pieces, but she was aware of everything. She knew how I was feeling just by holding my hand. There was irony in that, because much of what I thought and said was offensive to her. She was a dyed-in-the-wool conservative. My parents had never told her I was a conscientious objector, because she thought the war was good, in spite of the church's position.

Tonight, however, there were none of these differences. I held her hand, and pictures of things ran through my body. I saw old photographs of her and Grandfather, after whom I was named, standing in front of their ancient farmhouse, constructed of fieldstone. I saw him lying dead on the shady, slanting lawn of the same home a few years later, having died in his forties while working on the farm. It was only a few minutes after his death. His face was gray and his cheeks were strangely sunken for so young a man.

I kissed Grandmother good night again and went to bed in my old room with its high school memorabilia and musty country smell. Someone had left the window open to air out the room, and the cool breeze felt good. I lay on sheets so fresh they were scratchy, listening to dogs bark on neighboring farms. The extended arm of an old trophy, about to loft its basketball, could be seen in outline against the window.

18

. . . . . .

Breakfast was grits and eggs. We ate in silence for a while. Then my mother said Vicki had sent a nice photo of her little boy.

"What do you mean, little boy?" I asked.

"We wrote you about it," she said.

"I didn't even know she was married."

"Oh, yes," Dad said. "We wrote you about that, too. That happened not long after you started working at the hospital. Who was it she married, Lizzie?"

"The name was Miller, I think."

"That would be Tom Miller," I said, feeling my throat constrict. He'd been Vicki's boyfriend in high school. He'd attended Beloit College, where he was president of the local Campus Crusade for Christ.

"That was the name, I think," said my mother, looking

at my dad. He looked at me with sympathy, holding his knife and fork in his fists like a little kid.

"We shouldn't have told Jim about that," he said with gentle conviction. "Vicki was his sweetheart."

"They don't call it that anymore, Dad."

"What do they call it then?"

"I hate to tell you," I said.

"Main squeeze," said my mother. "That's what I saw on television."

"That's in bad taste," he said, forking some eggs into his mouth.

"That's what I thought," she said, shaking her head from side to side. "It makes love sound like adultery."

"There's a tooth in my egg," he said, reaching into his mouth. Sure enough, he extracted a small piece of his own tooth.

"You better see a dentist," Mother said.

"I haven't seen a dentist in eight years," he said proudly, "not since I bought these shoes." He lifted one of his shoes to where we could see it, beyond the edge of the table. It was the black tie pair I'd worn in junior high school. They'd gone out of style, and he'd adopted them.

"Snazzy," I said.

"Haven't even had to resole them," he declared. "Had to replace the laces, though." He put the tooth, which was jagged and yellow, carefully at the edge of his plate.

"Be careful you don't eat that, Richard," said my mother, scowling at the table.

"Imagine that," he said, "a person eating his own teeth— that's age for you." He laughed at his own joke. Then he tested the other teeth with a finger to see if they were about to collapse.

I finished breakfast and looked out of the window. It was a beautiful day and there was nothing to do. I went to the closet in my parents' room, which smelled of lavender, moth-balls, and talcum powder, and pushed aside the three suits

Dad had inherited from a friend of his, a train engineer who had worn them only on Sundays for about thirty years. Dad hadn't bought his own clothes, except maybe for underwear and socks, for years. He waited for hand-me-downs from the dead, and he had no squeamish self-consciousness about the symbolism. I secretly admired him for these practical economies. Sometimes when water was running from a tap, I would nearly panic at the sight of it.

The .22 rifle was still standing in the rear corner of the closet. I picked it up by the barrel, found an old box of shells on the shelf, and went into the yard. There was a slope near the barn I could fire into. I grabbed a couple of empty soup cans from the garage and walked across the field. It was recently plowed and soft, and my feet sank into the carpet of it.

It made me think of a local man named Barnhart, who had been out walking on his property one day and found a canvas bag of money that had fallen from the sky. There had been a skyjacking attempt, but the criminal had lost his grip in parachuting. The newspaper said he'd landed three miles away and hitchhiked all the way to Michigan City before the police picked him up. He was a high school teacher from Nebraska, and it was his first crime. All his neighbors were frankly shocked. He had not only been a good citizen; he was also afraid of heights.

Barnhart carried the money back to his living room and spilled it onto the floor. He and his wife sat beside it in their easy chairs, thinking and praying about what to do. The next morning, in spite of the debts he had on the farm, he turned it all in to the Malta sheriff. There wasn't a dime of reward, and within a year his marriage of forty years broke up, one of his children got divorced, and another was arrested for holding up a grocery store. Barnhart walked back to the spot where he'd found the money and shot himself in the mouth with a starter's pistol. There was no bullet, but the wad of air from the shot pressed into his brain, and he fell down dead. The starter's pistol had been in a kitchen drawer for years, next to a measuring tape, refrigerator bulbs, and a wide assortment of broken tools. It had been his son's, from the days when he coached the local track team. It took three days, they said, to find the body.

The thought of Adam Barnhart was strong in my mind because I used to help him bale hay when I was about thirteen. He had thick red hair and a square jaw. I was scared to death of him because he looked like he'd just stepped from a fire. He would work you in a hot barn until you nearly passed out. Then, to give you a rest, he would make you turn over bales in the field, to shake the dew out of them.

I set the cans on the slope, walked about twenty steps away, and loaded the single-shot rifle with a .22 long. It took me five shots to put a hole in the one on the right, but I was firing and reloading as fast as I could. Each time I pulled the bolt, the small brass shell would fly out of its housing and land at my feet. Pretty soon the ground around me was littered with shells. The box of cartridges was nearly empty. I had three left, so I went down on one knee in a rifleman's position, steadied the gun, and squeezed off a round, like soldiers did on television. The shot made a small, hollow sound and the can on the left tipped backward at an angle. I did the same to the can on the right but missed. Then I stood, loaded the final shell, aimed a high-arching shot in the direction of town, and pulled the trigger. Since a .22 long travels only a mile or so, there was no danger. The bullet would come down harmlessly in a field. It was something Terry used to do for the hell of it, and in this way I honored him.

I walked back up the hill, opened the trunk of the car, and tossed the gun inside, where it looked like a toy. That was where it remained when I left the next day.

It wasn't too hard to find where Tom and Vicki Miller lived. Tom was always a very organized person, so you could count on finding him. According to Vicki, he'd made a brilliant

discovery in economics when he was in college. It had something to do with the fact that the more you earned, the more
you tended to spend. It sounded obvious enough to me, but
he had the statistics to back it up, and the professors and
foundations were certainly impressed. He'd been promised
an excellent job, Vicki had once said, at a Milwaukee bro-
kerage house. It took about five hours to get to Wisconsin,
bypassing Chicago on the tollway.

The phone book said they lived on Atlantis Circle. The
guy at the gas station said that was in a new development
out by the mall. He said the word *mall* with exaggerated
pride, and I looked at his face to see if he was kidding.

Atlantis Circle was situated in Oceanic Estates, which used
to be a cornfield. They'd put in a few trees, but they were
so scrawny it looked like somebody drew them with a pencil.
There was a man-made lake at the center of the development
to give a nautical flavor. A few ducks stood on the bulldozed
banks of the lake, staring at the homely water.

Taking the winding access road, I passed the entrance to
Pacific Shores, a part of the development where the houses
were smaller and had only a single window at the center of
each. This was the low-rent district. A mangled tricycle was
inexplicably located, with sculptural perfection, near the entrance sign. Under the words *Pacific Shores,* a winking red-
mouthed dolphin was depicted.

Next was La Mer Charmante. The French name revealed
the higher station of this community. There were three or
four designs to the houses, instead of one as in Pacific Shores.
The sign contained a tasteful, near-abstract drawing of waves,
and a green arrow with a small tennis racket next to it pointed
down the road.

Atlantis Circle was the best of the lot. The houses were
mostly classic white-frame structures of varying design that
were blown up to epic proportions. They would have looked
charming in a New England setting, tucked behind some
pines, but here the cottage effect made one uneasy, as if the

structure concealed a munitions plant instead of a well-to-do young family.

The Millers lived at 207. A huge lawn separated the house and the lake. There was no car in the drive, and all three garage doors were closed, so you couldn't tell if anyone was home. A lamp could be seen in the window, but it wasn't on. An American eagle emblem decorated the lintel, and the doorbell, which gave off pale light, was situated at the center of a marble Liberty Bell.

The white door hushed open: there was Vicki, standing partly in the dark. On her arm was an overwhelmed, suspicious infant about a year old, eyes red from crying. Vicki was pretty but looked a little worn. When she saw who it was, a look of vast irritation came over her face.

"This had to happen sooner or later," she said, holding open the storm door. "Come on in."

"Where's Tom?" I said, in what I hoped was a neutral tone.

"He's at the office," she said, disappearing through a doorway with the baby. "Make yourself at home."

I sat in a chair with a red, white, and blue diamond pattern. A few rooms away, Vicki could be heard talking to the child with reasonable moderation, as if it were an adult. "You must go to sleep now," she said. "Mother has many things to do at this time. It is ten in the morning. Now is the time for napping, and later is the time for recreation."

I couldn't believe my ears. She never used to talk that way, as if she were reading from a script. It then occurred to me that she *was* reading from a script, a child-development book of some kind.

Vicki came back down the hall and leaned against the wall, dragging on the cigarette and looking a little Lauren Bacallish, with Lucy and Desi undertones. "What do you want?" she said, squinting at me through hair and smoke.

"Just happened to be in the neighborhood," I replied.

"Well, if you want to go to bed, you can forget it," she said. I held up my hands as if she were holding a weapon.

"That was quite a speech you gave the baby," I said. "Where did you get it, Dr. Spock?"

"Tom wrote that out. He says we have to deal with Michael on a contractual basis. We make these agreements, then we live up to them."

"Does the kid have a lawyer?" I asked. "You have to watch out for the fine print these days."

"You're a riot," she said, pretending to gag on her finger. This gesture had always endeared her to me. She had a way of mixing crudeness and refinement that made her seem smart and sexy.

She went over to the shiny blue couch and sat clinging to one of the arms. Her long red hair dropped over her eye again, and she brushed it back with a hand full of expensive jewelry.

"Married life seems to suit you," I observed.

"It's all right," she said. "How about you? Got any girl friends?"

I held up ten fingers twice, and there was silence, like the Simon and Garfunkel song, "Dangling Conversation," she liked so much.

"Michael was conceived after the marriage," she volunteered.

"That's nice. I was worried."

"I thought you might think it was yours," she said coyly.

"Mine?"

"I just thought you might think that."

"Well, I don't think that," I said with childish sarcasm. There was meanness in the room. If it didn't vanish, we would soon be making love.

"This is a nice house," I said, trying to change the subject.

"It's only temporary," she said, collapsing back on the couch. "Tom got another promotion at work, and we're moving into a larger place."

"What did he do, come up with another theory?"

"Something like that. He figured out that as people get older, they tend to save more money. It makes a big difference in the way you sell bonds, so they gave him a raise and a bonus. He's a vice-president now, in charge of futuristics."

"Sounds impressive. What is it?"

"You know, the future. Like who's going to die when, and who's going to be born in what year."

"Then he's God," I offered. "You married God."

"They have a computer list on just about everybody in the country. We could go down there right now and look us up," she said with pride.

"You're saying Tom can tell me when I'm going to die?"

"Give or take three months," she said.

"Have you checked on your own life expectancy?" I asked.

"Tom has checked on all of us," she said matter-of-factly, "but he won't tell me what it is."

"That's manly of him," I said.

"Always good to plan ahead," she said, jabbing the air with a new cigarette. She lighted it with a coffee-table ornament that looked like a sea gull. Its head snapped back on a hinge, revealing the lighter.

"How about Michael? Has he checked on that, too?"

"Sure, why not?"

"So he knows when Michael is going to die?"

"Give or take three months," she said.

"That's amazing," I said.

"Listen," she said with sudden enthusiasm, "you want to watch some television? There's 'Love, American Style' and 'The Price is Right.'" Her eyes searched the top of her head, as if mentally flipping through *TV Guide*.

"No, thanks," I said.

"How are things at the hospital?" she asked.

"Oh, great," I said, "just great."

"I don't like the smell of hospitals," she said.

"You get used to it after a while."

"Not me," she insisted, "I don't even like to drive by them."

"I'm sorry the way it worked out, Vicki."

Her hand shook as she put the cigarette to her mouth. "Don't talk about that, Holder. That was then. We were different."

"I guess so."

"What did you really come for?" she asked.

"I probably wanted to see if you were doing better without me."

"And . . . ?"

"It looks like you are," I said.

Little Michael appeared at the end of the hallway, holding a teddy bear and a water pistol that looked like a German luger. He had apparently climbed out of the crib. He stared at us with curiosity while sucking on the end of the barrel.

"For God's sake," said Vicki. "Don't you ever sleep?"

"I've got to be going now." I stood up and moved toward the door.

"It's been real," she said, walking with me.

"Right."

"Oh, you know what?" she said as I stepped out the door into the recently remodeled sunlight of Atlantis Circle.

"What?"

"Tom did look you up on the computer."

"And you can't wait to tell me, right?"

"Put it this way," she said. "It's not what you were hoping for, but it's not all that bad, either." She winked at me and tossed her hair, one hand on her hip like Annie Oakley. It was something she used to do when we dated, and a twinge of regret went through me. I wanted to go back and kiss her good-bye, but I was frozen in my tracks. Desire and inertia were sliding into each other like two bodies of water.

"Thanks for the information," I said, opening the door of the car and waving good-bye. Michael appeared beside his mother, still holding the bear and water pistol. He looked sternly in my direction and followed me with his eyes as I backed down the drive.

The money was still in the glove compartment. I stopped by the front sign of Oceanic Estates, took it out of the envelope, and counted it again. Mostly tens and twenties, it impressed me with its bulk. I pulled out a ten and put it into my shirt pocket.

About twenty miles down Route 94, headed south, I pulled into a Sinclair station with a busted-up statue of Dino the Dinosaur standing outside. A mean-looking attendant with a thin black beard came over to the window. He wore the official green-and-white uniform, with a Dino patch over his pocket that said "Killer." The uniform was incredibly dirty, and his hands were darker and shinier than dirt ever was.

"What do *you* want?" he said, as if he knew me.

"Do you have a phone here?" I asked.

"In there," he replied, gesturing toward the station.

I got out of the car and he followed me into the building. The phone was next to a calendar from the Ridgid Tool Company. The Ridgid Tool girl was sitting in a chair with a wrench between her legs.

"You got change for a ten?" I asked, handing him the bill from my pocket. "For the phone."

"Wait a minute," he said, and disappeared with the money through a door to the service area. "D-i-v-o-r-c-e" by Tammy Wynette ended on the dirty white radio and "Okie from Muskogee," the Merle Haggard number, began. A minute later, he returned with a fat man whose hair was the color of dust.

"Whatchu want this money for?" he asked, snapping the bill and holding it up to the fluorescent light.

"Have to make some long-distance calls," I said.

"Where to?"

"That's my business," I said firmly.

"OK, Steve," he said, handing the bill to Killer. "Give him the money."

Killer looked disappointed but gave me the change, after counting it twice at the register. There was a five-dollar bill and the rest in quarters and dimes.

The phone rang eight times. Barbara answered.

"Guess who?"

"You jerk," she replied. "Where've you been?"

"Parts unknown."

"You made us all crazy," she said. "We thought maybe you were dead or something. Your nutty roommates didn't know where you were, so we checked the morgue again."

"I'm in Wisconsin," I said. "It's only like a morgue."

"Guess what?" she said with professional interest. "We saw a body that looked a lot like you, only it was bald."

"I'm glad you could share this with me."

"Ed thought for a minute it was you, because of the nose and lips." She laughed nervously at this, then she said, "Romona cried, if you can believe it."

I did believe it.

"When are you coming back?" Barbara asked.

"I guess I won't be," I said.

"Why not? You have only a few weeks to go."

"Didn't you hear? Janush fired me because of Cane and Graven."

"People have been asking about you," she said, as if she hadn't heard what I said. I could hear scratching, as if she were combing her hair near the phone.

"What do you mean, people?"

"People from the administration. Bolger and Cane came by a couple of times, asking questions about your roommates and how you lived. Janush said there was a man from the FBI or something, wearing a gray suit, and he had this folder on you."

"FBI!" I nearly screamed. "Why the FBI?" Killer heard this and grinned malevolently as he leaned against the wall.

"Cane said they had your college grades and asked if anyone knew what 'Peace Studies' meant."

"I got a B in that," I said. "I had problems with conflict resolution theory."

"It's a course, you mean?"

"Sure, you read Tolstoy and things like that."

"That was some weird college. The FBI said they thought it was some sort of Communist place, where they gave you credit for not fighting."

"It's a pacifist college, Barbara. You know, religious."

"Cane said you were probably a member of a Communist drug ring. You planned to steal morphine and sell it to crazed hippies."

"That's ridiculous. Does the FBI think that?"

"Not really," she said. "They just think you're AWOL. There was some talk of issuing a warrant."

"I've only been gone a couple of days."

"You know what I think?" she said. "I think you should come back right now and settle things. Then they'll just forget about it."

"It doesn't matter," I said. "Anyway, I'm not coming back."

"Where are you going?" she asked.

"Who knows?" I said. "It's a big country."

"But . . ." Her voice was in confusion.

"Love you," I said.

"You stupid idiot!" she shouted, but it was muffled as I hung up the phone.

Killer eyed me all the way out of the station. I got into the car, swung it around toward the highway and started driving. Either direction would do, I figured, but west seemed a good way to go, under clouds shaped like Viking ships and cowboy hats, crisply outlined on this beautiful day. West would take me places I hadn't thought of going. My head was incredibly clear. My body felt so light, I thought my molecules would scatter, like towns on a map.

Route 94 rolled smoothly under my feet. It was easy to blur my eyes a little and imagine the road moving instead of the car. It was a frictionless ribbon that transferred me from one state of mind to another. When I was a kid driving with my parents to church, there was always a stretch of road where the morning sunlight would project the car's shadow against an elevated bank of grass. I could see the outlines of both the car and its occupants—father, mother, and child. As the car moved higher and lower on the rolling road, the shadow would change its shape and size, like a flag. I would always wave my hand, to interfere with this magic and to confirm it.

Route 94 led to I-80, and by six o'clock that evening I was already west of East Moline, eating a sandwich and having a cup of coffee at one of those off-ramp gas stations. The coffee helped, and I did the Nova's limit into Iowa. The Mississippi River was astonishingly wide, as if an entire city might float down it. As night came on, semitrailers swept around me, their many lights shining. To pass the time, I listened to the radio, especially the wonderfully corny country stations. "Tiger by the Tail" by Buck Owens played every twenty minutes on one station, and as it dimmed I picked up another that carried a replay, from the previous winter, of an important local high school basketball game. It sounded like it was being played inside a shoebox, but I could follow most of the action, and I was sorry when this station also faded—I'd started to favor the Redfield Indians over the Panora Huskers. As the announcer's voice became obscured behind static, it seemed to pass into history, drifting through summer and time. In high school and college, I'd been on the basketball teams, but the war had made that kind of competition seem unimportant. Nevertheless, the blare of the timer's horn, announcing the end of a quarter or the substitution of a player, made me shiver with painful nostalgia. I imagined a raw-boned farm boy with a blond flattop haircut going up for a jump shot. The ball rose into the lights and descended toward the rim, as his father, tanned below the hat line, rose to his feet in expectation.

My legs were stiff from driving, and I had a headache from listening to the dull drone of the engine through the floorboard. But I kept on driving, until I was sleepily leaning at a forty-five-degree angle, both hands on the wheel. The car drifted onto the shoulder, and the rush of dirt and gravel suddenly woke me up. I took the next exit. Half a mile down the road, there was an abandoned farmhouse that had turned gray in years of weather. I pulled the car around back, where it couldn't be seen from the road. It was hard to sleep at first.

I was too tall, so I opened the car door to make room for my legs. Sounds seemed to come from the house, as if the families that had lived there were gathering to admonish me. At six A.M., I woke up with dew all over my feet and sat up quickly, as if someone were watching me. It was nothing, but my nerves were jumping as I started the car, which turned over poorly in the morning dampness. Pulling out of the yard, I saw a blur of white in a window of the house that might have been a face; but it was only a flap of ruined wallpaper.

Back on I-80, I kept looking in the rearview mirror, as if I were being followed, even when the road was empty. Scenes from old crime movies like *White Heat* kept appearing in my head—an endless stream of police cars racing from a garage, grim cops at the wheel. The lips of the dispatcher clearly pronounced "Nebraska" as I fled in the wake of my own fantasy. All the anxiety of the last few days—and the enormity of what I was doing—flooded over me. Laboring toward Grand Island and Cheyenne, I was lost in America, and even the landscape of the plains was foreign. The sky and trees met at awkward angles. Space was dizzy with its own size. I was homesick for the Midwest, with its thick woods and barns leaning toward each other. Here I was the missing piece in every puzzle. There were thousands of places, invisible from the highway, where I didn't belong. The highway itself was the only safe place, since travelers at least shared the idea of a destination. Not that I knew mine. I was free to go in any direction, but the possibility of pure aimlessness panicked me, and I kept the car pointed straight ahead.

The Nova had never had an oil change, at least by me, and it ran more sluggishly than ever. It had so little power, I might have been driving on Saturn. I had to nearly floor the pedal to keep the needle at 50 mph. In Canada, I imagined, a Chevy Sting Ray was tooling from Moose Jaw to Swift Current at a comfortable 100 miles an hour, and the driver had a French surname. It was a country where no one drove north, since few roads ever led there. They went east and west, like cracks in ice. But Canada wasn't a direction for me, and the scenery passed so slowly, I might have snatched it off some wall. It seemed I was spreading in every direction rather than traveling forward.

I daydreamed fretfully. Wearing a cap and gown, I was standing again on the lawn of the college, in a line of two hundred other graduates. The sun was bright, the grass vivid. I was amazed. It had never sunk in that I would actually leave college someday, that in roughly two hours I wouldn't be allowed to stay. After the ceremony, Vicki held my arm while my father took our picture, aiming the camera, as he always had, mainly at our feet. His photos came out strangely, with people cropped out of the shot or standing with missing heads. But this one turned out well. Beaming confusion and satisfaction, Vicki and I looked very much in love, while all around us the future teachers and insurance agents of America were posing for their parents. She stayed at our house near Malta that night, and we sneaked out to the car, making love in the front seat. The moon reflected off the Nova's hood. Vicki was beautiful and wild, straddling my lap and arching her back. We were already passing through each other, and didn't know it yet. In the morning, my mother discovered us sleeping in the same bed and backed out of the room without saying a word, then or later.

Crossing an overpass for a local road named simply "X," I thought of Romona telling off Cane every day of her life; saw her on the roller board, winking at GIs just home from World War II. Then I remembered the gangster's wife, scheduled for surgery, who stood outside her room, petting the poodle the hospital let her keep, while a half-dozen hoods stood around nonchalantly. I remembered Ed's "new" car, a 1959 Chevy Impala with fuzzy dice, plastic Jesus, and naked-lady deodorant strips. One night, after drinking a bunch of old-fashioneds at a bar, he'd driven me down Lake Shore Drive at five miles an hour, exactly his kind of crazy. I remembered piles of linen, empty rooms, and Barbara pulling my mouth toward hers. I was dancing again in a black neighborhood, where one of the station clerks lived. Her husband played jazz so loud it could have held back dam water, and he walked around with joints on a plate instead of hors d'oeuvres, singing "What a Swell Party This Is." I told him they looked like shrouded corpses, and he squinted at my eyes, as if there were someone else inside. I was going to miss all of them. Already they were in sepia-tone, slowly disappearing.

In Winnemucca, Nevada, I bought four brand-new tires because Buddy, an attendant at the Fli-Hi station, said I wouldn't make it across the desert without them. It cost $160 for the steel radials, the only kind Buddy stocked. I paid from the envelope. While he changed the tires, I had a Kayo soda, the chalky taste of which lingered to the California border. The state trooper at the agricultural check point, between Verdi and Truckee, asked to look in the trunk for out-of-state fruits and vegetables and found the .22 rifle. I'd forgotten it was there, or I would have thrown it out before Reno. My name and address were taken, a phone call was made, and the trooper gave me a Mount Rushmore look, but that was all. I was so relieved that three miles down the road I pulled over and, both shaking hands on the barrel, flung the rifle over the highway embankment and into a gulley of pines.

I'd never been to California. The steep tree-covered hills surprised me: they looked so perfect, like an entrance to paradise. It was here that I would live underground or be arrested—whatever fate had in store—but real life was in Indiana, as removed as the contents of a time capsule. My mother would go on tending her garden, and when frost seized the plants each fall, she would fold into herself, private almost to the loss of speech. My grandmother would lie in her bed, so sensitive she could feel the light on her skin. Day after day, she would ask my father "Where's Jim?" and listen for some hint in his voice, but he couldn't tell her. Maybe he wouldn't even know. When she died, I would probably be in prison.

It was evening by the time I pulled off I-80 at Berkeley,

taking University Avenue up the hill to Shattuck. On the corner was an apartment hotel with a metal security door that belonged in San Quentin. A number of street people stood near it, smoking and looking dangerous. Something about their outcast stance made me uneasy, a mood that was confirmed when a dazed young man ran down the street backward, circling the intersection and stopping traffic in all four directions. Down the street, a homeless hippie couple were camped out in front of Crocker Bank, their belongings in a shopping cart. They had wrapped themselves together in a brown blanket too warm for the weather. She was smiling out at the street. He was shaking his head with eyes closed, as if singing.

In first gear, the car made it to the top of the Berkeley hills, from which I could see the lights of ships and bridges out on the bay. I imagined that the freighters leaving for the Pacific were carrying rifles and grenades painted a dull green. When they arrived in Vietnam, tanks of green metal would be unloaded, floating on motor oil and American optimism through the jungle. Inside one, a twenty-year-old sergeant was fumbling with headgear that made him look like a praying mantis. His tank was headed for an ambush, and soon he would be on fire, writhing inside the metal housing like the smoke he was becoming. I thought of Terry lying on the ground in pieces, his head twisted sideways like a crazy pillow. Now Terry was at home, and I was somewhere else.

I fell alseep in the front seat, on a quiet residential street. At five in the morning, I woke up more wrinkled and dirty than I'd ever been. The car's windows were covered with my breath, and I wiped the inside of the windshield with my sleeve. When the car wouldn't start, I put it in neutral and pushed on the doorjamb with my shoulder until the weary Nova lumbered downhill. I leaped in, swerved left onto a major downhill street, and popped the clutch with the ignition on. It worked, but an hour or so later, in the town of Stinson Beach, north of San Francisco on Highway 1, the car died altogether. It was where I planned to go, but not where

I planned to be stranded. I pushed the old heap into the parking lot at the beach and squared it up in a parking space. For good measure, I left the keys dangling from the driver's door, where anyone could see them. If someone wanted the car, that was fine with me. All my belongings could be carried, and I concentrated my attention to that end, slogging in heavy sand to the beach. I carefully arranged my things on the dry part of the beach near the tide line and buried the envelope where I could find it later. Looking at the mist-covered hills leading back to San Francisco, I took off my clothing, including the underwear. Even though it was July, the ripest part of summer, the breeze from the water was chilly, so I moved quickly into even more frigid water. At first it took away my breath. Seaweed clung to my arms; but then the swimming got easier. I extended my arms toward an invisible point to the west, and I felt stronger and cleaner, stroke by stroke, a breath at a time.

ABOUT THE AUTHOR

■   ■   ■

PAUL HOOVER is a widely published poet whose work has appeared in the anthologies *Up Late: American Poetry Since 1970* and *Ecstatic Occasions, Expedient Forms,* among others. He is the author of four books of poetry, the most recent of which, *Idea,* won the 1987 Carl Sandburg Award. He has also received an NEA Fellowship and the GE Foundation Award for Younger Writers. Poet-in-residence at Columbia College and editor of the literary magazine *New American Writing,* he lives in Chicago with his wife, Maxine Chernoff, and their three children.

VINTAGE
CONTEMPORARIES

VINTAGE
CONTEMPORARIES

___	**Soft Water** by Robert Olmstead	$6.95	394-75752-1
___	**Family Resemblances** by Lowry Pei	$6.95	394-75528-6
___	**Norwood** by Charles Portis	$5.95	394-72931-5
___	**Clea & Zeus Divorce** by Emily Prager	$6.95	394-75591-X
___	**A Visit From the Footbinder** by Emily Prager	$6.95	394-75592-8
___	**Mohawk** by Richard Russo	$6.95	394-74409-8
___	**Anywhere But Here** by Mona Simpson	$6.95	394-75559-6
___	**Carnival for the Gods** by Gladys Swan	$6.95	394-74330-X
___	**Myra Breckinridge and Myron** by Gore Vidal	$8.95	394-75444-1
___	**The Car Thief** by Theodore Weesner	$6.95	394-74097-1
___	**Breaking and Entering** by Joy Williams	$6.95	394-75773-4
___	**Taking Care** by Joy Williams	$5.95	394-72912-9

On sale at bookstores everywhere, but if otherwise unavailable, may be ordered from us. You can use this coupon, or phone (800) 638-6460.

Please send me the Vintage Contemporaries books I have checked on the reverse. I am enclosing $_____ (add $1.00 per copy to cover postage and handling). Send check or money order—no cash or CODs, please. Prices are subject to change without notice.

NAME _____

ADDRESS _____

CITY _____ STATE _____ ZIP _____

Send coupons to:
RANDOM HOUSE, INC., 400 Hahn Road, Westminster, MD 21157
ATTN: ORDER ENTRY DEPARTMENT
Allow at least 4 weeks for delivery.

· 005   38